NOT WORTH YOUR TEARS

SARAH DELANY

Paperback ISBN: 978-0-6488144-4-3

Cover Design by: Michael Pati Fuiava
Editing and Proofreading by: Rebecca Andrews

Sometimes in life you need to be your own superhero.

Table of Contents

Preface

The characters in this book pushed their way to the forefront of my mind, demanding their story be told. The main male character may have you shaking your head at times but please give him a chance. I'm hoping you will love him as much as I do.

If you would like to read trigger warnings then please read below if you have no triggers then please continue and enjoy.

This book contains scenes of domestic violence and a scene of attempted sexual abuse. If that is a trigger for you then please consider whether this book is right for you.

Chapter One

Sully

"Come on Logan. Everyone is here," I plead with my best friend over the phone. Hanging out on the back porch with a few of the guys from the football team, I bring the red plastic cup to my lips and skull the contents.

"I wish I could but I'm stuck at this family dinner. You know these things tend to drag out all night," he explains. I throw the cup in one of the black plastic bags someone has dumped outside for rubbish. It must be their way to get a jump on the cleaning because this house is going to be a mess tomorrow. I'm glad it's not my responsibility.

"Fine. I'll have to celebrate the end of the school year without you," I tell him.

"Sorry Sully. We'll go for a skate tomorrow before you leave. I gotta go."

Releasing a breath, I say, "Bye," before my phone is shoved into my jeans pocket and forgotten for the remainder of the night.

"Here Sully, get this into you," Tanner says, as he hands me another red cup which I swallow in one big gulp. Cheers erupt around me. School is out for the year so everyone can drink as much alcohol as they want even though I'm pretty sure everyone here is underage. Tanner sits next to me as he recounts his best moments of the football season this year. I accept drinks as they are handed to me, not caring how much alcohol passes my lips.

More people make their way into the yard and the noise outside increases. Logan usually comes to the parties with me and we end up by ourselves somewhere we can drink and laugh the night away. You would think large crowds would be easier for me by now but they set off something inside which I struggle to cope with.

Logan and I aren't typical jocks as we don't play sports unless you count skateboarding. We are a pair of lone wolves who are always together and skate whenever and wherever we can. It's been like this since we met at the beginning of high school and we realised neither of us fit in with the cool crowd. We paved our own way, making friends with everyone but still set apart from them.

Excusing myself from Tanner, I search for the bathroom. After a long wait in the neverending queue, I relieve myself and stumble along the pristine hallway filled with photo frames. Perfect family pictures with big smiles for all the world to see. I continue to stumble down the hallway, find a door which piques my interest and decide to turn the knob. There's no one on the neatly made bed so I enter the dark room, close the door behind me and slide until my butt hits the ground.

I breathe deeply in and out and try to calm myself while the dark room embraces me. It's a nice contrast to the pounding music and noisy crowd outside. The sounds are muted in this bedroom, a reprieve for my overwhelmed mind.

The soft sound of a girl's voice breaks the tranquil atmosphere and I slam against the door with a fright.

"Are you alright? Sorry, I didn't mean to scare you. You came in and didn't turn the light on. I didn't want to interrupt you when it was obvious you needed a minute to yourself."

"Why are you sitting in the dark?" I ask, deflecting away from this stranger who saw me in a moment of weakness.

"I needed to get away from the party for a minute. I've never been to a party before. Are they always like this?"

"Yeah, pretty much. This one is a bit larger because school's out for the summer but all parties are the same. Lots of alcohol, noise and big crowds." All I can make out is the silhouette of the stranger, it's too dark to see any of her features. I breathe in deeply again to calm myself and catch a hint of apple. The new scent comes from her and it makes me curious to find out whether it's her perfume or her shampoo.

"Do you mind if we sit in the dark together for a while?" she asks, as she shuffles beside me.

"Sure," I tell her, and rest my forehead on my bent knees in a comfortable position. "Are you not from around here?"

"No, I moved here a few days ago to live with my mum. My cousin Lolly thought it would be a good idea to drag me here tonight. She was making out with some guy so I found a quiet place to hang out while I wait for her text and tell me she's ready to go home."

I rack my brain and try to think of a Lolly in our year at school but nothing comes to mind. It's a name you wouldn't forget easily so she must be from another school.

"I'm Reed by the way," unsure why I offer her my first name. Nobody calls me Reed, not even the teachers at school. Everyone knows me as Sully.

"Nice to meet you. I'm Willow." Hmm, what a pretty name.

"How come you were looking for a dark room to sit in?"

"I don't particularly like crowds," and I don't like small talk, I add in my head. Strangers are usually avoided if I can help it or if possible I make a quick getaway but find myself wondering about this mysterious girl so stay seated. She's hiding out in a dark room like myself when she could be outside partying, colour me intrigued.

"I don't like roses," she blurts.

"What?"

"Oh you confessed something so I thought I'd do the same." Her response makes me chuckle.

"Roses huh? What's so bad about them?"

"I find them so unoriginal. Everyone gives girls roses. How can they be so special?"

"What would make you feel special?" I ask, as my voice drops an octave.

"Something that took some thought or effort," she pauses before she excitedly adds, "Like a hand picked sunflower or a bouquet of wildflowers."

3

"How would you know it was handpicked? You can buy those from a flower shop too, you know."

"Obviously it would have dirt on the stem where they yanked them from the ground," she states, like it was an obvious answer. Laughter explodes out of me and causes my shoulders to shake.

"What if they wiped off the dirt before they gave it to you? How would you be able to tell the difference?"

"The dirt would be there because if I was so special, they'd pick the flowers and be too excited to give them to me; they'd completely forget about wiping the dirt off." This girl's quirky reply makes me laugh harder.

"Girls like dirty flowers then? Dirty flowers are the way to their hearts?" I query, trying my best not to laugh even more.

"No, they want proof you care and to know you think about them as much as they think about you. It isn't about the dirty flowers at all, it's about the effort and thought you put in to do something to make her smile," she softly says.

"Buying you roses isn't enough effort?"

"Anyone can buy roses and I know they say it's the thought that counts but I personally want a guy who takes an extra bit of effort to make it special for me."

"You do know sunflowers can grow to be pretty tall. What if he picked you a whole bouquet of sunflowers and they were taller than you?"

"I'd have to marry him."

"You're kidding. Something as simple as a bouquet of sunflowers would make you want to marry someone?"

"You don't get it. One day I hope you do and you go out of your way to do something thoughtful to make the girl of your dreams smile," she sighs at the thought.

"I'll keep it in mind. I take it you haven't found this dream guy yet?" I ask.

"No, not yet. It seems they don't exist," she says, making me laugh again which is a rare occurrence for me especially because of a stranger.

"It might be because you're looking in the wrong places."

"Yeah, I don't think hiding out in dark rooms at parties is helping me meet new people either."

"Hey. You met me, didn't you?"

"True but imagine if we were in a relationship. We'd go to parties and hang out in the dark," she says.

"There's nothing wrong with the dark," my voice drops lower, and she inhales sharply.

Clearing her throat she says, "So Reed, do you make a habit of sitting in dark rooms?"

I lean my head against the back of the door, close my eyes and inhale before answering, "Do you ever for a minute wish you were invisible?"

Her light laugh drifts over me, "No I'd probably wish for the opposite. I feel invisible all the time."

"It could have something to do with you hiding out in dark rooms," I tease, making her laugh louder. What a lovely laugh she has.

"Well I didn't claim to be smart," she declares, and I laugh along with her. "Why do you want to be invisible?" she presses.

"Like I said before, I'm not good with crowds." My open honesty surprises myself, not even Logan knows some of my quirks.

Her silence hangs heavy in the room for a minute before her hand slides over mine on the carpet and she intertwines our fingers. My heavy breaths fill the room because I don't know what is happening. Her touch spreads warmth through my chest and I find myself squeezing her hand.

"Don't worry Reed. Your secret is safe with me," she whispers, and my heart settles in my chest.

"Do you have any other secrets you want to divulge?" I ask, clinging to the sweet but peculiar stranger's hand.

"I hated having to move here, away from the only home I've known but now I'm thinking it might not be so bad," her soft voice says, as she squeezes my hand gently.

"Yeah, this town might not be so bad after all." My lips pull into a smile she can't see. The vibration of her phone breaks the moment between us and she tugs her hand free to grab it.

"Can you close your eyes while I read this?" she asks.

"What? Why?"

"Ugh, I don't want you to see me. I know this is crazy and we just met but isn't the mystery intriguing?"

"You won't peek at me?"

"No, I'll turn my back to you."

"Okay, I'll close my eyes." She shuffles around so I close my eyes as the light from her phone screen comes on before it disappears again and cloaks us in darkness.

"Darn it," she says, as she stands. I stand and face the direction she's in but it's pitch black in here so I struggle to make out the shape of her or any of her features.

"My cousin is looking for me. She stopped sucking face with her guy long enough to realise I was gone."

"Well it was nice meeting you Willow."

"It was nice meeting you too Reed," she says, as she moves forward to find her way to the door. Her body skims across mine and I can't help but grab ahold of the material which rests against her hip. She must be wearing a dress as it gathers easily in my hand. Her soft breaths puff out as I step into her body, causing her to shift right against the door. "Reed?" she whispers. Her body shivers as I run my fingers up her body. Her arm is bare and the goosebumps are evident on her skin as I caress the soft skin of her neck and under her chin, before I tilt her head upwards. An unknown force has come over me and I can't stop myself.

"Let me turn on the light," I whisper, as her body is pinned between me and the door.

"No!" she shrieks, making me step back. "Sorry. I don't want you to be disappointed," she mumbles.

"Willow, maybe the dark isn't too bad a place to meet your mystery man after all," I whisper, sliding my knuckles across her face. Her prominent cheekbones stick out and my finger bumps into glasses. She inhales softly. My fingertip finds her nose and glides along the slope until I'm met with her full lips. Her phone vibrates again and breaks the heated moment.

"I gotta go before she sends out a search party," she says, as her breath mingles with mine. My brain has left the building and my body is in charge now, it wants to have a kiss to remember this night. I press in closer before she speaks again, but her sudden words halt my movements.

"Wait, I've never been kissed," she stutters. I close my eyes, press my forehead against hers for a second and take in a breath. Her first kiss shouldn't be stolen by a stranger in the dark so instead I run my nose from her chin to her ear and breathe in her apple scent deeply.

I whisper, "Your secret is safe with me Willow," before my lips gently kiss her cheek, close to her mouth. She shivers again as I release her and step back from the door and away from her. "I'll turn around while you leave," I tell her. I keep my word and turn my back to her. The sound of the door knob turning before a strand of light enters the room is my only clue the door has opened. "Willow, I wouldn't be disappointed," I tell her, before the sound of the door closing behind her has me exhaling deeply. "Shit, her number," I mumble. Why didn't I ask for her phone number? My feet carry me from the room but stagger from the alcohol in my system as I begin the search for my mysterious stranger. The crowd surrounds me, the faces all blur into each other and I'm not met with glasses of any kind. Five minutes with no success is all it takes before I give up hope and decide to head home.

As I stumble away from the thrashing music, my feet kick at rocks along the way as I wallow. The first girl I've had a deep connection with has slipped through my fingers and there's no way to contact her. Regret stirs in my stomach the further I walk away from the party until the rundown wooden house I call home stands in front of me. My regret is replaced by dread. I blow out a determined breath and hope I can make it to my bedroom unscathed.

Chapter Two

Sully

"How was the party last night?" Logan asks, as he rides his skateboard along the short ramp.

"It wasn't too bad," I tell him, before my board drops to the ground and I place a foot on it. Logan raises his eyebrow at me. "Don't look at me like that."

"You hate parties. We only go to get you away from your house so there must have been someone who caught your interest. Am I right?"

"Fine. I met a girl," I admit, rolling my eyes before I skate away. His interest is piqued so he follows me.

"Come on. Don't leave me hanging. What happened?"

"We bumped into each other and got talking," I lie. Nobody, not even Logan, my best friend knows how bad my anxiety truly is. He doesn't realise I sneak away and hide out if it gets a bit much. He assumes I'm off hooking up with girls.

"What's she like?"

"She's funny and seems cool. She's new to the area."

"Did you get her number?"

"No."

"Damn. No worries, if it's meant to be she'll cross your path again," he tells me, as he pats me on the back.

"I wish I didn't have to go to my grandparents for the whole summer," I grunt. My mum ships me off to them every summer. I don't know if it's for my benefit or my parents so they can fight in peace. My grandparents are cool but I miss hanging out with Logan.

"Time will fly by and before you know it, it'll be our senior year of high school."

"Yeah you're right, it's gonna be epic man."

"It will be if you give up the grumpy old man act," he huffs.

"You know it's easier for me this way. I cope better if people don't think they can approach me so easily," I tell him for the hundredth time. He never understands my need to keep people at a distance. Small talk and normal conversations with people can be too much for me some days. The grumpy old man persona Logan refers to is one coping mechanism I use from a long list of strategies and it works pretty well for me.

"You talked to the girl at the party easily enough by the sounds of it," he says.

"Yeah well it was different," I explain, not mentioning I didn't actually see this girl and she didn't see me. If I told him I met this girl because I was hiding out in a dark room, I would never hear the end of it.

"How was your family dinner last night?" I ask, changing the subject.

"Same old crap. I'm sick of attending these fancy dinners for my parents. I feel like an idiot dressed in my penguin suit," he whines.

"The curse of being rich."

"Shut up doofus. Come on, let's have one last skate before you have to go."

We skate for the next few hours and ride around the jumps and rails until we've run out of fumes. We ride over to the local diner, Jimmy's and grab a shake each, laughing as we relive the funniest moments from school this year. As I drink my chocolate shake, Logan's eyes light up.

"Look," he says, as he points to the window beside us. A piece of paper which has 'Help Wanted' printed across it is taped to the window. "I should get a job here for the summer."

"Why? Your parents have money."

"Yeah but it wouldn't hurt to have my own. Plus you'll be gone so who am I gonna hang out with?"

I shrug my shoulders because it's the downfall of our pairing. When one leaves, the other is left alone. We know other kids from school but we've never had an interest in hanging out with them except for the odd occasion when Eddie skates with us.

"You could always make new friends," I joke, and he rolls his eyes at me in response.

"Yeah right, you'd have more to sulk about because if I made a new friend, I would force them into your life. I'm gonna do it," he says. Slamming the cardboard drink container on the cream tabletop, he says, "No time like the present," as he scoots to the edge of the red vinyl chair and walks away from the table. He strides over to the cash register and I can't help the bubble of envy shooting through me. My best friend's life is pretty much trouble free. Far from what mine is like. Logan's house is a safe haven of sorts when I need to get away from the bickering hell I call home.

It isn't long before he comes back, and his face sports a huge smile.

He slides back onto his seat and says, "Jimmy said I can have a trial tomorrow and if I'm any good he has work for me over the summer which is perfect." He looks at the paper in his hands Jimmy gave him like it's a golden ticket.

Glancing at the big black and white clock on the wall I let out a huff, "Time for me to go man. " The smile drops instantly from Logan's face.

"Come on, I'll drop you off on my way," he says. He picks up his empty container and I quickly slurp mine so as not to waste one morsel of the chocolate treat. We grab our skateboards we stowed under the table and throw the cardboard cups in the trash can as we leave. We hop onto our skateboards and travel along the familiar footpaths which lead to my house. Logan gives me a quick one armed hug before he waves goodbye and heads to his house without me.

Chapter Three

Sully

Like Logan said it would, the summer passed in a blur. Most of my days were spent cooking for my grandparents. They never asked me to do it, it's somewhat of a tradition I began a few summers ago. It gives them each a rest, so why not? I also helped my grandpa Henry complete all the odd jobs around the house he couldn't finish by himself during the year. They've mentioned to me a few times over the past summers they would take me in full time if they could afford it but they struggle to look after themselves and taking in a growing teen boy would add to their struggles. They are the one bright spot I have in my family so I wouldn't want to be an extra burden on them.

They live in a small modest little house two hours away in the small country town of Banya. Our small town of Fernbrooke is bigger than Banya but Fernbrooke is suffocating and I can't wait until the day I leave. If I could, I'd leave Queensland, Australia all together.

Don't get me wrong, I may complain about having to leave Logan during the summers but I thoroughly enjoy my time with my grandparents. It's nice to have a reprieve from the constant name calling and being treated like someone's personal punching bag. They keep me with them the whole summer. When I say the whole summer, I mean the day after school lets out until the day before school goes back for the next year. They dropped me off late last night so I'm going to Logan's house not having seen him since the day I left.

He exits his house and smiles at me as he closes the door.

"Hey Sully, how was your summer?" he asks, as he pulls me in for a hug.

"Same as every year. I helped my grandparents around the house and cooked for them. You know the drill. How was yours?" We fall into step next to each other.

"It was pretty crazy. I enjoyed working at the diner. The girl I texted you about who works there, uh I think I'm in love with her," he admits, which makes me throw my head back and laugh.

"Does she know you're in love with her dude?" I tease.

"Are you crazy? I didn't have it in me to ask her out but I'm gonna give it a shot. She's going to our school this year."

"Well if she captured your eye, you might want to get in fast before some other guy comes in and sweeps her off her feet."

"Okay. I'm gonna do it. I'm gonna ask her out," he decides. "Come on. I told her I'd meet her out the front of the school to show her where the office is." We say hi to a few of the guys from our year and give a few head nods as I brace myself for the noise about to hit me when we enter the school but Logan's voice interrupts my thoughts.

"There she is," he points, as I follow his finger. A bright shiny new green Volkswagen beetle car sits parked in one of the carparks.

"New car?" I ask.

"A gift from her stepdad to welcome her to the family apparently. Her mum eloped with some rich guy who lives in town. He's the reason she had to move here," he explains.

"She sounds a bit like a princess." We watch her exit the car and throw her bag over her shoulder. Her short black hair sits in a bob above her shoulders. She wears the blue and green pleated uniform skirt to mid thigh with her white shirt tucked into it and her long white socks sit below her knees. Her black shoes click against the concrete as she walks our way.

"She's pretty down to earth once you get to know her. Don't ruin it for me man."

"Me? Why would I ruin it?"

"Sully, I don't know how to say this but your people skills suck," he tells me, making me chuckle.

"You know people aren't my thing," I remind him.

"Well could you try to be less cold. For me?"

"I'll try but don't hold your breath."

He shakes his head at me and smiles, before he yells out, "Willow over here," which causes my back to straighten.

"What did you say?" I ask.

"I called Willow over. What's wrong with you? You look like you've seen a ghost."

"Nothing." She walks over to us as I grab the handles of my backpack, and pull it against my back for comfort.

"Willow, I want you to meet my best friend. This is Sully. Sully, Willow," Logan says, as he introduces us. She looks me over from head to toe. I give her a nod, not able to speak. Is this my mystery girl I dreamt about all summer? It would be a tragedy to find out she's the girl Logan likes and is off limits.

"Where's the office?" she blurts out to Logan, not acknowledging me in the slightest. If it is my mystery girl, she's right, I am disappointed. If this is her real personality, it's a big turn off and I thankfully dodged a bullet.

"Why are you in such a rush?" Logan asks her.

"Forget it. I'll find the office myself," she sulks, before she takes a few steps away from us.

"Come on, I'll show you," Logan says, before he jogs a couple feet so he can walk beside her. I walk behind them but my long strides eventually close the distance and I catch the end of their conversation.

"You can direct me if it's easier," she says.

"Don't want to be seen with us sweetheart?" I tease, annoyed she could possibly be the girl I got along with at the party and now she's slipping through my fingers. Logan turns to me and before she can see, he gives me a tiny shake of his head.

"Ignore Sully. You'll get used to him," Logan whispers to her. I roll my eyes, glance over her way and catch her watching me with wide eyes.

"I'm out. I'll catch you later," I tell Logan, making him huff.

"Fine Sully. Catch you later," he yells out, as I walk off and pull my bag straps tighter. My laboured breaths drum in my ears but I force myself to focus on the pressure of my backpack pushing on me as I feign a casual walk while inside a volcano is waiting to erupt.

Luckily the boys' bathroom is empty when I enter so I close my eyes, take deep breaths in and out and try to calm my racing heart. Cold tap water splashed over my face helps. Dragging my hands over the top of my hair, I use one of my thin black hair ties to gather my hair at the base of my neck and fasten it. Feeling more settled, I walk to my homeroom to grab my timetable for the year.

As I walk into my second class for the day, which happens to be English, the seat in the back right corner beckons my name. I've had enough of this day already. Logan was excited for us to be in our last year of school but I already wish it was over and we were graduating. As the class fills, Logan walks in and his smile brightens when he sees we're in the same class.

"Sully," he welcomes me with a handshake, as he slides into the seat next to me. "Your morning all good?"

"Not too bad," I lie, not wanting to affect him with my mood.

"Can you not wreck things with Willow man. She's cool."

I lean back into my chair, before saying, "I can't promise anything."

He lets out a huff before something catches his eye at the front of the class and his head whips around.

"Willow," he calls, as he waves her over and she walks down the aisle to him. He stands and holds out the chair in front of me for her to sit. She drops into the chair after she places her backpack on the ground. Logan gives me a wink before he slides into the desk beside her and leaves me to sit by myself.

I rest my chin on my forearms and breathe in deeply. The familiar apple scent tickles my nose as she looks over her shoulder at me. I jerk back in my seat because now I know it's her, the girl I thought I had a

15

connection with. My fists clench by my side as Logan whispers something in her ear. There she goes slipping through my fingers yet again.

She doesn't wear the glasses she wore at the party, although I never saw them so who knows what they look like. She mentioned she wished she wasn't invisible which confuses me as invisible is not a word I would associate with her. She's beautiful. Her light blue eyes and pale skin are a stark contrast against her shoulder length black hair. She would stand out to me even if she wasn't the girl from the party.

Logan turns to me, offers me a small smile and I respond with a head nod to let him know I'm okay. My heart sinks again because even though I felt I had a connection with her, there's no way I'll step on my best friend's toes. He's more like a brother to me and one of the only people I can rely on. I don't trust anyone fully but Logan comes close. There's no way I'll try anything with Willow now, not when he wants her. I let myself take one last look at her, breathe out a sigh, lean further back to get away from her apple scent and focus my eyes on the front of the classroom instead.

The bell for the end of class rings so I grab my things because I want to leave this room as soon as possible. Logan is already on his way out of the door, not realising Willow has turned back around with her books clutched to her chest. She glances at me as I fling my backpack on and pull my straps tight.

"Sorry, forgot my bag. I'm not used to carrying it around all day," she informs me.

"I never asked," I grunt, wincing inside as her face drops as she grabs her backpack and shoves her books inside. I walk to the front of the class and find Logan waiting outside the door.

"Willow still in there?"

"Yeah she's coming." I walk off, not in the mood to walk with the two of them.

"Sully man, give her a chance," he pleads, before I get too far.

"She rubs me the wrong way. She's stuck up if you ask me." Her black hair peeks out of the classroom door and I know she heard me. I don't want to hurt her but it's easier this way. She's the girl I thought about all summer but it can't be and it stabs me in the heart. To protect myself, I have to push her away. I'd never be worthy of a girl like her anyway so it's better this way.

"Sully," he calls out, but I continue to walk away and refuse to turn back this time.

Chapter Four

Sully

The week passes and the more it goes on, the angrier I become. Every time I catch Logan and Willow together, my blood boils. He insisted she join us for lunch every day which she accepted. It isn't until Friday lunchtime in the noisy cafeteria, the hairs on my neck stand at attention. Willow walks over to our table where I'm already seated with Logan. He offers her a wide smile, happy for her presence while I sit back, spread my legs and take a bite of my red apple. No smile appears on my face. As she takes the seat next to Logan he reserves for her, I notice the small girl behind her. She's not in our year level but a year younger.

"Guys, this is my cousin. Is it alright if she sits with us?" Willow asks, directing her question at Logan more than me.

"Sure she can. The more the merrier," Logan says, causing Willow's eyes to peek at me. She catches my hard expression before she averts her gaze back to Logan.

"This is Aurora but you can call her Lolly. Lolly, this is Logan and grumpy pants over there is Sully." I choose to ignore her remark, sit straighter and zone in on Aurora.

"Lolly? What a strange nickname," I say, as my blood runs cold.

"I guess. When I was little, my dad said I was as sweet as a lolly and it stuck. Soon enough all my family jumped on the bandwagon and called me Lolly too," she explains, as her cheeks redden.

"Do you have any other family at this school?"

"No, I'm an only child. Willow moved here at the beginning of the summer so it's been nice to have some family around," she explains. My eyes shift to Willow and I catch her eyes. She is the girl from the party and this confirms it. She doesn't wear her glasses so I assume she must wear contacts at school. Her brows pull in the longer I stare at her not saying a word and the awkward silence leaks into the air.

"Sully, you keen for a skate after school?" Logan asks, breaking the spell I was under. My gaze drifts towards him and he raises a brow at me because he knows I'm being more weird than normal.

"We skate every day after school, so why are you asking?" I snap at him, and he rolls his eyes at me.

"Girls, ignore Sully when he's in a mood which unfortunately is most of the time," Logan jokes, making the girls laugh. I slouch back in my chair and focus on my apple, which has become the most interesting thing at this table.

"I'm working tomorrow night's shift, are you?" Logan asks. My ears perk up as I wait for Willow's reply.

"Yeah I am. I've had a couple shifts this week too. Have you not been rostered on?" she asks Logan, as she takes a bite of her chicken avocado sandwich.

"Nah I asked Jimmy for the week off so I could settle back into school but he said he'll give me a shift or two during the week from Monday."

"I hope we get put together, it's always more fun with you there," she gushes at him.

"Is Billy Bob not fun enough for you?" Logan teases, and a laugh bubbles out of Willow as she lifts a hand to cover her smile from view. Why did she have to cover it when it lit up her whole face? My mood sombers when I realise it wasn't me causing her to laugh but my best friend. I force the bile to stay down as it burns my throat. I can't like the same girl as my best friend, he'd never forgive me.

"I can't stand his butt crack hanging out. I'm sure it's a health code violation waiting to happen," she giggles, making a smile spread across my best friend's face. The same glow I saw on her face has spread to his and I know in my heart, no matter what I felt for this girl from the time spent together in the dark, my best friend will always come first. They joke and carry on the rest of lunch while my foul mood swirls around me. Poor Lolly's eyes flicker back to Willow every time I catch her peeking at me. I can't pull myself out of the mood so it festers. It's easier than picturing Willow as the girl I had the connection with.

As soon as the bell rings to signal the end of lunch, I grab my trash and leave. Logan's voice calls out to me but I ignore it along with any feelings I had for Willow. I have to push them away because I can't hurt my best friend by pursuing the girl he likes. Logan's like a brother to me and there's no way I will get in his way, even if it's my heart paying the cost.

After school I catch Logan at his locker. He chose to purchase one this year as it's a privilege seniors are allowed. My parents probably wouldn't have paid for one for me even if I had asked. I prefer my backpack anyway.

"What's wrong with you today?" he asks, as he slams his locker shut.

"Nothing man. Drop it," I tell him.

"Is something going on at home?" he whispers, so no one else can hear. It makes me physically jerk that he'd mention my home life here of all places where someone could overhear.

"It's Willow. I don't like her. Why does she have to sit with us?"

"What's your problem with her?"

"She rubs me the wrong way. I call it like I see it and she acts like a stuck up princess," I tell him, and the sharp intake of breath behind me stabs at my heart because I know who it is without looking. Logan's expression tells me he hasn't spotted her yet so I carry on as if I don't realise she's there either. "I don't know why you like her so much."

"Give her a chance. You don't even know her," he argues.

"Whatever, I'll tolerate her for you," I tell him, knowing she's still behind me. Why hasn't she said anything yet?

"You'll see. You'll like her as much as I do soon enough." He smiles at me, not knowing it's the problem. I already like her more than him and it's in a way I'm sure he wouldn't appreciate.

"Hey guys," her cheerful voice greets us. She smiles brightly at Logan and moves to stand closer to him, further away from me I notice. She stands next to him but faces me and her smile drops for a second. She wants me to know she heard me and got the message loud and clear.

"We're heading to the skate park. You can come watch us if you like?" Logan asks her, but her gaze flicks to mine.

"Sully, is it okay if I come and watch you?" she asks, her chin held high as she taunts me.

"Do what you want," I tell her, and shrug my shoulders. Logan shoots me an annoyed look before he paints on a smile for her.

"Okay I'll come."

"Cool," Logan says, as he leads the way. After a few steps he says, "Shit, I forgot my history notes and need to write an essay over the weekend. I won't be a minute." He jogs back to his locker and out of hearing distance.

"If you weren't such a self centred asshole, you'd see I'm nothing like a stuck up princess," she bristles behind me.

"Just because you've got Logan wrapped around your finger doesn't mean I have to play nice sweetheart."

"You're a big dick."

"It's what all the girls say. Do you want me to show you so you can confirm?" I taunt. She blushes as her gaze lowers to my pants zipper before they snap back to my face at the sound of Logan's voice.

"Come on, let's go," he says, as he tosses an arm around her shoulder and leads her away. I can't help the involuntary twitch my dick does because Willow looked at it, he has a mind of his own.

Chapter Five

Sully

Every day I listen to my best friend drone on and on about Willow. He talks about all the fun they have while they work at the diner together and how he's gotten to know her on a deeper level. With every piece of new information he shares, it's like a shard of glass slices my skin open.

I've gotten used to her being around but I'm in more of a sullen mood than normal. Surprisingly enough she distracts me so much and takes all my focus at times, it makes everything else around me drift away. My anxiety caused by the hustle and bustle of the crowds isn't so bad if I have her to focus on. I focus on the sharpness of her jaw or stare at the two freckles at the base of her neck and it settles something inside of me. It shouldn't. I shouldn't let myself become so enraptured with a girl I hardly know, it's as if she holds a power over me she's unaware of.

All I know is with power comes pain. If someone holds power over you, they hold the ability to hurt you. Whenever a piece of her burrows it's way further under my skin, I get the same feeling. It makes me uncomfortable but at the same time I don't fight it. I should fight it but I'm a sucker for punishment.

Walking behind the pair of them like I usually do these days, they laugh together as if they are already a couple. I know Logan is biding his time before he asks her out. Is it wrong to hope she rejects him? I know it's wrong and I shouldn't want it to happen to my best friend but the part of me she has power over can't control myself.

"What do you say Sully?" her voice breaks through my thoughts.

"What?" I ask. I have no idea what she said as she smiles at me.

"Logan and I both have Saturday off work so we thought we'd catch a movie. You wanna come?" she asks, as her smile remains and flutters come alive inside me. Power equals hurt so I kill the flutters instead.

"No. It's bad enough I have to listen to you two love birds at school. I'm not listening to you on my weekend. Do everyone a favour and get a room already," I huff, as if I'm bored, but inside the flutters die as the smile leaves her face.

"Sully," Logan grunts at me.

"What?" I yell. Willow's shocked face looks between the two of us and confusion settles in. "I'll spell it out for you sweetheart. Logan here likes you and wants to ask you out. How about the two of you use Saturday as a date instead?"

"Damn it, Sully," Logan hisses, as I stare at her. Her eyes flick to Logan as her cheeks turn pink.

"Is it true?" she asks.

"Well uh yeah. I do like you...." Logan sputters. His words trail off as I walk away from them. My breaths pick up with each step. For a minute I wish I could rewind the clock and take back my words and replay the moment over again. There's no point in wishing though because wishes are for people who have hope and my hope died a long time ago.

I pull my backpack straps tight against my back and focus on deep breathing as I drop my board, press off the concrete and skate as far away as I can get so I don't hear her words. Deep in my heart I know she'll say yes to Logan and accept his date. Never in my wildest dreams did I think it would be me who helped push them together.

"What were you thinking?" Logan yells across the skate park, when he finds me half an hour later.

"Did it work?"

"Well, yeah it did."

"She's gonna go on a date with you?" I ask, as I turn my back on him.

"Yeah. After your blow up, I told her I liked her and she agreed to go on a date with me on Saturday," he laughs. I squeeze my eyes shut quickly to shut down the emotions so he doesn't see and skate away to compose myself before I turn around and skate back towards him with my mask firmly in place to hide my hurt.

"You owe me a thank you," I tell him.

"What? Why?"

"You've been umming and ahhing about asking her out for weeks now. I was worried you were never gonna do it so I helped you along. You're welcome," I tell him with a big fake smile on my face.

"You're a dick sometimes you know," he accuses, as he punches my shoulder and laughs.

"Well this dick got you a date so be grateful."

"Whatever, let's skate." We proceed to skate and blow off steam for the next few hours before we head home.

At home it's a miracle my dad isn't there so I get to my room without a fight. For once I'd welcome the distraction of his fists as they hit my skin because I wouldn't have to feel regret in the pit of my stomach.

Not able to get comfortable, I toss and turn all night. I consider going out into the hallway when my dad stumbles his way inside around midnight but come to my senses and don't move a muscle until his door slams shut. I dare not move in case he can hear my bed squeak in his drunken state.

A lock is attached to my door from years ago and it keeps him out but if he wanted in, nothing would stop him. Today gave me another reason to get out of this shit town. Willow can now be added to the list of people, along with my parents, I want to escape.

Lying in bed, I come to the conclusion that if Logan wasn't in the picture, I would never have been good enough for her. There's nothing I have to offer her so there's no point in pining after a girl I'll never be able to have or be worthy of. It's with these thoughts I fall asleep at two in the morning, determined to get rid of these stupid misplaced feelings.

Chapter Six

Willow

Logan picked me up ten minutes ago from my house and drove us to the movies. There's an action movie he was dying to see. He's paying for my ticket so I didn't want to disappoint him by telling him I don't particularly like action movies.

"Do you want some popcorn?" he asks, while we stand at the counter.

"Sure, I'd love some."

"Two large popcorns and two large cokes please," he tells the cashier. She gets our order ready, slaps the lids on top and places our food on the counter.

"It'll be fifty five dollars," she tells us. Logan pulls his wallet from his back pocket and taps his card against the eftpos machine. He tucks his wallet away, takes the tickets from the cashier and we each carry a drink and popcorn.

We walk over to the other cashier who mans the entrance to the cinemas. Logan hands over our tickets, receives the stubs back and the cashier directs us to cinema three. A light chatter greets us as a few people are already seated in the dark room. I follow Logan as he leads me to the back of the cinema. He shuffles across the empty seats until he finds us seats directly in the middle of the row where we sit and put our drinks in the cup holders.

"When was the last time you went to the movies?" he asks, as he pops open the lid on his popcorn.

"My cousin Lolly and I went over the summer. We saw the new horror movie with the baby who was going around killing everyone," I tell him.

"Was it any good? I don't like horrors," he confesses.

"It was okay I guess." I pull my drink out of the cup holder and take a large sip.

"Are you enjoying it here in Fernbrooke?"

"Yeah it's good. I miss my dad but it's fine."

"Have you made any friends? Apart from me of course," he says, as he smiles at me.

"Yeah I talked to this girl Kate in my calculus class. She's pretty funny and has told me to come eat lunch with her sometime. I have Sully, although I'm not sure if I would call him a friend."

"You get used to Sully after a while. He takes a while to warm to people," he says, as he takes a handful of popcorn and pops them into his mouth.

"I find it hard to believe. Sully isn't even warm to you."

"You know what I mean. He's less intense." Laughter explodes out of me. Sully is never not intense. Intense should be his middle name.

"Shh it's starting," Logan shushes me. I don't think I've been shushed by a guy in my life. It's only the credits for heaven's sake. His wide eyes stare at the big screen entranced by the ad about turning your cell phone off. I sit back, settle in to watch the movie and try to shake off the feeling of being shushed. I tell myself it's a date so I should enjoy myself and ignore the feeling telling me something isn't quite right.

Halfway through the movie, I grab my drink to take a sip. Loud explosions sound and Logan jumps in his seat, knocks my arm and makes my drink spill on my dress.

"Shit, sorry. Did it spill on you?" he asks, as he takes the drink from my hands. I can feel the cold liquid as it seeps through my dress.

"I'm gonna go get cleaned up," I tell him.

"Okay, I'll be here," he tells me, and turns straight back to his movie. He pulls out some of the unpopped kernels from the bottom of his bucket. His face screws up as a crack sounds out as he bites into the hard pieces. I turn away from him and shuffle out of the aisle to find the toilets.

I walk into the bathroom and find them empty. Lifting the front of my dress I inspect it, and see a big brown patch has soaked through. My decision to wear a white dress is now a regrettable mistake. I pull out some paper towels and wet them under the tap before dabbing at the coke stain. It doesn't look much better but I swipe it back and forth under the hot air of the hand drier. It doesn't take long at all to dry but it's not pretty with the brown stain. Hopefully I can salvage the dress at home.

The urge to return to the movie isn't strong as I leave the bathroom since I wasn't enjoying myself. Action films don't tickle my fancy and I would have preferred a romance. Checking my watch it's been over two hours so the movie shouldn't be too much longer. I decide to sit on the comfy looking bench seat they have outside the cinema and wait for Logan. It's fifteen minutes later when people exit and Logan joins me on the seat.

"The movie was awesome," he smiles at me, his excitement clear in his voice. "How's your dress?"

"Stained but hopefully it will wash out," I tell him. He grabs my hand and I freeze as he holds on. Walking away with my hand in his grip, my body automatically follows but I'm instantly aware there are no butterflies in my belly. There should be butterflies, right? Logan leads us to his car, the air cooling as the evening sets in. I glance at him before we get to my side of the car and can't help but notice friendship is all I feel when it comes to him.

"Logan?"

"This isn't working, is it?" he says, as he runs a hand through his hair.

"Not exactly. No," I reply, laughing which makes him burst into laughter with me.

"I thought we would be good as a couple but now we are on an actual date, it feels...,"

"Awkward?" I finish for him.

"Yes," he yells, making a smile break out on my face.

"I feel exactly the same. I love you as a friend but I don't think I have romantic feelings for you."

"Hey it's okay. I like you but I don't think dating should feel like this. Friends?" he asks.

"Friends." He pulls me in for a hug and I wrap my arms around his waist.

"Now that's out of the way, how about we go get ice cream as friends?"

"Sounds perfect," I tell him, as he walks around the car to unlock his door. We both hop in and he turns to me.

"Could you do me a favour?"

"Yeah sure."

"Could we pretend we are dating? At least for a bit. I don't want people to know I lucked out so horribly," he says, as a cheeky grin appears on his face.

"Yeah sure. I don't think I want a relationship right now anyway so it'll keep anyone from asking me out. It's a win-win situation."

"Perfect. Thanks Willow. You are a good friend," he says, as he turns the ignition.

"Are you gonna tell Sully?"

"Nah, I don't want him to know as he's the one who forced the date. He might think it's his fault if he knows I lucked out."

"It's fine. It'll be our little secret," I tell him, and click my belt into place.

"Yeah. Now let's get some ice cream."

He drives off and a sense of peace washes over me, something I haven't felt since Sully blurted out Logan liked me. I guess I didn't want his feelings ruining the main friendship I have in this town. The thought of losing Logan terrified me so I'm glad it's worked out the way it has. I settle back in my seat and the thought of ice cream brings a smile to my face.

Chapter Seven

Sully

Logan is working at the diner tonight. I should probably get a job too so at least I've got money to get out of this stupid town and never have to return to this forsaken place. Instead I choose to party and forget my troubles.

The amber liquid warms my throat as the music plays loudly around me and the other students from our year laugh and carry on. For years kids from school have come out to the field not too far from the school grounds to party. There are no houses around so the noise doesn't disturb any neighbouring properties making it the perfect place. It's a usual occurrence to come out here on a Friday and Saturday night for most of the kids.

Someone long ago brought big barrels into the centre to create a big fire to keep everyone warm while they drink and dance. My skin prickles as the girls dance and stumble, not a care in the world. I wish my life was as easy as theirs.

My seat on the back of Eddie's truck gives me an eagle eye view of everyone around me as the alcohol does its job. I want to feel numb or at least my face wants to feel numb because it aches like a bitch at the moment. My eye is swollen and bruised. I'm used to the beatings my dad hands out. Long ago I learnt if I let him get out his frustration with a few hits then he stumbles away. It's when I fight back he lays into me and keeps the fight going so I never fight back. My lesson was learnt the hard way. He doesn't care if he hits my face for all to see. No one would believe it was him or else they don't care. Logan knows but it's because the evidence is clear and he knows I don't get into fights so it leaves one explanation.

Logan has offered to talk to his parents about it but I told him not to. I try not to go around to his house when I'm bruised either so they don't suspect anything. Sometimes I have to go to Logan's house though to get a reprieve from my own house. I hide out in his room during those times so they don't see me and my body can heal in peace.

My cheek bone welcomes the cold feeling the glass bottle provides and hopefully it settles any swelling there. Through the flickering flames, I can see the big hay bales out in the field. There's livestock out further in the fields so sometimes they have these hay bales for them which they distribute later. It makes for an intimate space for people to use at these gatherings to hook up.

There's about twenty of the huge round bales, wrapped in green plastic and they sit one on top of the other in a circle. If you climb to the top of the bales, there's a big hole in the centre where about ten people can fit if they squeeze on top of each other.

It's not what captures my attention though. It's the two girls who are being led to the bales who draw my eyes. Willow walks towards the bales and holds hands with her friend Kate from school. Kate holds a bottle of some fruity pre-mix in one hand and there's a matching bottle in Willow's hand. Buck and a few of the guys from the basketball team sit on the bales at the top and hold out their hands to pull the girls up.

My hackles rise because there's only one reason they would want the girls to go into the bales. Before I realise it, I've jumped off the truck and am ready to spring into action. I gulp the remainder of my bottle, but never take my eyes off Willow. Her and Kate drop into the hole, out of sight and I throw my discarded bottle away while my steps pick up pace.

I climb the green plastic bales with ease until I'm at the top and drop myself into the hole. Buck's eyes widen as I stare at him. By now they should all know Willow was on a date with Logan last weekend, which makes her off limits. She shouldn't be in here. I suspect she has no idea what goes on in here since she's new to town.

"Hey Sully," Buck starts. My hardened eyes gaze at him and it makes him physically gulp. Most of the people in here are guys except for Kate and Willow and another girl who grinds away on one guy's lap, unaware of the standoff going on.

"Girls, are you alright?" I ask. They both nod in reply.

"See Sully, nothing for you to worry about. We were just being friendly," Buck starts again, but I don't release my gaze on Willow.

"Girls, did you want to hook up with any of these guys? It's why they brought you in here," I tell them honestly.

"Hey, hey, hey," Buck tries to argue, but one look from me and it cuts him off. Willow and Kate's eyes have widened and this time they both shake their heads. I stand, throw my legs over the top of the bales and walk around to the other side so I'm closer to the girls.

"Come on, let's go," I say to them, and hold my hand out. Kate takes mine first as I help her over and I grab Willow's hand to do the same. Heat flows through my hand at Willow's touch but I ignore it. I stand at the top and pull Kate's drink out of her hand and thrust it into Willow's grip.

"Here, I'll lower you," I tell Kate, and hold her until she hits the grass below. Once she's okay, I lean over the top of the bales while Willow hands Kate their drinks.

"If any of you fucks go near her again, I'll rip your fucken heads off. You hear me?" I all but yell at the group. It startles the couple enough they stop making out and wonder what is going on. They all nod except for Troy who is always begging for a fight.

"Bit feisty there for someone who isn't your girl Sully," Troy prods.

"You wanna go?" I ask, my hands fist at my sides. The fury from getting beat by my dad pulses through me. I'm ready to fight.

"Looks like you already lost today man, don't want you getting your ass beat some more," he taunts. I see red and lunge forward but Buck grabs hold of me before I can get to him.

"Forget him Sully, he's drunk. Sorry, we shouldn't have brought her here. It won't happen again," he placates me. Troy smirks at me as he tips his own bottle to his lips. I could force myself out of Buck's grip if I wanted to but the sound of her voice behind me makes the anger drip away.

"Sully?" The sound of my name on her lips causes the fight to leave me. I turn back to her and climb over the bale.

Troy smarts off again, "Pretty whipped there by someone who isn't your girl."

"Ignore him," she pleads, as her grip on my forearm draws my focus. I nod once, sit on the bale and jump off. She copies my movement and sits on the edge before she slides forward into my grip. I squeeze her waist and pull her down as her hands land on my shoulders. It's as if time stands still for a second as I draw her slowly against my body until her feet touch the ground. Her eyes lock on mine and we breathe for a minute before she breaks the trance.

"Thanks." I step back and glance around for her friend.

"Where's Kate?" I ask. We scan the crowd until she points to a group of dancing girls on the other side of the fire.

"There she is," she says. She steps forward but I stop her.

"I'm taking you home. I don't care if Kate comes or not but you are coming with me now," my jaw clenches. Her eyes blaze at me.

"You're not my keeper Sully," she lashes back.

"Someone has to be when you don't even know what stupid situations you are getting yourself into."

"What's up your butt? We were perfectly fine."

"Girls go there for one thing sweetheart and I don't think Logan would appreciate hearing about your little adventure."

"I wouldn't have done anything. I didn't know."

"Not all guys are nice guys Willow. Use your bloody head. How is climbing into a dark hole with a bunch of drunk guys a safe option huh?" I quietly yell at her. She steps back as if I have physically struck her. The hot tears shimmer on her lashes before she wipes them away. The sight of the tears causes a vice grip around my heart. "Go tell Kate you're leaving. If she doesn't want to come with us, make sure she stays with the girls and can get home safely," I tell her. I stand there and face the

34

darkness of the field surrounding us as she walks away. Ten big breaths help compose myself before I head back to Eddie's truck and wait.

Back at the truck, I watch her talk to Kate. Kate tries to thrust Willow's drink back at her but she shakes her head. She keeps doing it until Willow gives in and takes it. Tipping it back, she skulls the remainder of the pink liquid, which makes my blood boil. I storm over to her as she finishes the bottle. Kate is cheering her on until she catches sight of Willow's stunned face so she slowly turns and takes a step back. I don't blame her as the rage swarms around me.

"Let's go," I tell Willow, who rolls her eyes at me in response.

"You wanna come Kate? Sully's making me go home," she whines.

"Nah I'm gonna stay."

"Have you got someone to get you home safely?" I ask, as my attention turns to Kate. She falters for a second before pointing over to a couple of guys. One of them is Eddie.

"Yeah, Eddie's my neighbour. I'm sure he'll give me a ride," she informs me, and I nod.

"Let's go Willow," I tell her again. She blows out a breath before she hugs Kate goodbye. We walk around the barrels of fire over to where Eddie sits with a couple of his mates. I've known Eddie about the same length of time I've known Logan. At school we hang with different groups but Eddie hangs with Logan and me at the skate park sometimes. He's a good guy. He looks and smiles at me as I approach.

"You good Sully?" he asks, as the conversation comes to a stop. Willow stands behind me and peeks at the group.

"You know Kate?" I ask.

"Yeah she lives next door to me. How come?"

"She was in the bales but I pulled her and Willow out," I tell him. His jaw clenches and his eyes shift to where the bales sit.

"Where is she now?"

"Over there dancing with the girls," I say, as I point her out and he nods once he catches sight of her. "I'm taking Willow home but Kate said she'd catch a ride with you. Are you good if I leave her here?" I ask, because if he's not okay with it I'll drag her home too. I'm not about to leave a friend of Willow's or any girl here with no way home.

35

"Yeah I've got her man. You head out. Don't forget your board is in the truck. It's unlocked," he tells me, and holds out his hand for me to slap.

"Thanks man. See ya," I tell him, and walk back towards his truck. The passenger door opens with a squeal so I grab my skateboard from the floorboard and tuck it under my arm as the door slams shut. Willow stands and waits for me and I walk off into the darkness of the field knowing she'll follow me. Her wobbly feet are unsteady so I slow my steps and let her fall in line beside me.

"It was nice of you to worry about Kate," she says, as we trek the familiar path back towards school.

"Yeah well you probably wouldn't let me hear the end of it if I didn't make sure she could get home safe. Eddie's a good guy. He'll take care of her."

"Can you not take a compliment without making some snarky remark?" she grunts, before she hiccups loudly.

"No," I reply, as she hiccups again.

"You're so infuriating."

"You're so dumb. You need to think before you do stuff."

"I'm sorry. I didn't know what was going on in there. Can you blame me? Everyone else is drinking and having fun. Why did you have to kill my fun?" she whines.

"Fun? You think it's fun having some sleazy guys grope you or possibly worse and you can't fend them off?" I stop in my tracks and stare at her, my chest heaves at the thought of anyone hurting her.

"They're guys from school. They wouldn't hurt me." I roughly thrust her chin to look at me.

"I'll tell you again. Not all guys are good guys. Just because you know them from school doesn't mean they won't hurt you. Alcohol changes people." My dad is the perfect example. She doesn't say a word and we stand there silently in the dark, my knuckles pressed against her chin. I close my eyes, and take a breath in to calm myself. "I need you to be more careful in situations like this, okay?"

"Okay," she softly replies, before she hiccups again. We continue our trek and once we arrive at the edge of the school grounds, the few outside lights shine our way.

"What happened to your face?" she asks, as she inhales sharply. She obviously didn't get a good look at my shiner around the fire.

"Nothing."

"It looks bad."

"You should see the other guy," I joke, moving the topic along.

"Hey," she says, as she pulls on my arm and halts my steps. "You sure you're okay?" she timidly asks.

"There's no need to worry about me sweetheart. I can take care of myself." I force my feet to move. She's fallen behind again by the time I arrive at the school gates. We'll never get home at this rate so I drop my skateboard to the concrete. It's nearly midnight if the time on my phone is correct. Logan will be finishing at the diner soon so we may be able to catch him if we hurry. "Come on, we should be able to catch Logan at the diner before his shift ends so he can give us a ride home," I tell her, which makes her eyes light up.

"Good idea, my feet are killing me," she complains.

"How did you and Kate plan to get home in the first place?" I ask, the anger rises in me again. Why do a lot of things she says bring out this reaction in me?

"Kate said she had it sorted so it was probably with Eddie," she tells me. Her response helps fight the rage brewing inside and I place a foot on my board.

"Climb on and I'll skate us there."

"Are you serious?" she squeals.

"Yes. You're about to collapse and I ain't carrying you." The thought of carrying her floats through my mind and I instantly want to take back my words.

"You won't crash?" she asks.

"Who knows. Hop on and let's find out." I tap my foot against the board and feign frustration.

"You're a jerk you know," she huffs, as she sits and pulls her knees to her chest.

"I know," I softly reply, before saying, "Hold the board and scoot forward a bit." She does as I ask so both my feet can fit on the board and we can cruise for a bit. I place one foot on the board and push off with the other, and slowly but surely we gain momentum. It takes a bit more effort to find my groove but I eventually do and for a moment the shitty night is forgotten as her laughter reaches my ears. A foreign smile crosses my face at the sound.

"This is so much fun," she screams, as we glide along the dark quiet streets. A light chuckle leaves me as I steer us in the direction of the diner. When Jimmy's comes into view, I remember who it is I'm taking her to. My best friend who likes her and the smile falls from my face. I need to get a stronger hold on these feelings she ignites in me. Every time I push them away, it's as if they come back stronger and hit me with more force.

I pull up in front of the large windows and she gets off. Her wind whipped hair surrounds her and the biggest smile I've seen tonight shines from her face.

"I've never ridden a skateboard before. It was awesome," she tells me, and the familiar grip on my heart squeezes at being her first for something.

"Hey guys, what are you doing here?" Logan's voice causes Willow to turn from me, and she throws her arms around him. He easily hugs her back and jealousy spikes in me. I wish I could touch her in the same way.

"I was with Eddie at the Hill and saw Willow there with Kate. I was leaving so I dragged her with me because I knew you'd beat my ass if she didn't get home safe." The incident at the bales is not mentioned. With her arms still wrapped around his neck, her eyes find mine in a silent thank you.

"Thanks buddy." He smiles my way and the suspicion he had on his face when he saw us together disappears.

"Could you give us a ride home?" I ask.

"Of course. I just finished so it's perfect timing. Come on, I'm parked around the side," he tells us. Willow moves an arm around his waist and he throws one over her shoulder so he can kiss the top of her head. My skin itches and I nearly make an excuse to skate off alone but bite my tongue instead. He unlocks his car and I slide in the back with my board across my lap so Willow can take the front seat.

"Was it packed at the Hill?" he asks, as he pulls out of his parking spot and heads to the main road.

"The same as always for a Friday night."

"Did I miss anything?" he asks.

"Nah, it was pretty tame. I'd had enough but Eddie stayed to watch Kate so we had to walk half the way," I explain. Logan glances beside him as loud snores fill the car, which cause us both to laugh.

"Shit, she snores like a man," I joke.

"Did she have a lot to drink?" he asks.

"I'm not sure. She was drinking those girly premixes."

"Thanks for looking out for her mate," he says. I didn't want to say anything in front of her to him but I was always going to tell Logan about the bales.

"A few of the basketball guys got her and Kate into the bales," I tell him.

"What?" his anger lashes the air.

"Calm down before you wake her. She's fine. I didn't know she was there until I saw them climbing the bales. I went straight over and got them. Don't worry, nothing happened."

"Thanks man," he sighs.

"She said she didn't know about the bales man so take it easy on her."

"You've changed your tune about her," Logan says, and suspicion laces his voice.

"Not in the slightest but I don't want to see any girl get hurt especially by those basketball dickheads." He nods and accepts my explanation.

"Sorry man, yeah. She's mentioned she's never really partied before. I should have better prepared her when she said she was gonna go there tonight with Kate." My hackles rise as he knew she was going out there and anything could have happened if I wasn't there. I tamper my anger, not saying anything before I yell at him.

We arrive at a large two storey property when Logan gently shakes Willow to wake her.

"Babe, wake up," he says, causing her to stir. "You're home now," he tells her, as she wriggles from where she was propped against the window. "Do you need me to walk you to the door?" he asks.

"No, I'll be okay," she says. "Text me when you get home." She pushes the door open and steps out, before she pops her head back in. "Thanks for tonight Sully." I nod my head in reply. She quietly closes the door and staggers her way along the footpath to her door. We watch as she opens it and disappears inside before Logan pulls away and heads towards my house.

"Can I crash at yours?" I ask, which causes Logan to take the next right turn, automatically heading towards his place.

"Course man, anytime."

"Thanks."

"How drunk was he this time?" he asks, referring to my dad. He would have seen my black eye as soon as we rocked up to the diner but he never acknowledges my bruises in front of others and I appreciate the small gesture more than he realises.

"Mum said he cut out of work around lunch and had been drinking since. I walked in the door at five. He got me as soon as I'd changed out of my uniform so I left straight afterwards. I met Eddie at the skate park and we headed to the Hill," I explain.

When we arrive at his own huge house, I jump out and take my board with me. The house is quiet as we move through it. His parents are probably already asleep as Logan was working at the diner and not out partying like I was. His mum never sleeps on nights he goes to parties. Worried about him and not able to sleep until she's heard from him or he's home safe. My own parents have never cared when I come or go. A party is nothing to them.

As we enter his familiar room, I drop onto my usual side of the king size bed, kick off my sneakers and lie down. He moves around the room before he heads to the bathroom to shower. I close my eyes and will the images of Willow out of my mind before I fall asleep.

Chapter Eight

Willow

It's the Tuesday after Sully dragged me home from the Hill. Ugh I can't believe he went all caveman on me. He was so scary. With the look in his eye, I believe he would have taken on the whole basketball team. I didn't want him to get hurt so I called out to him which thankfully stopped him from doing anything stupid.

After Sully's little tirade to Logan a few weeks ago about me, I stopped eating with them every day at lunch. I told Logan I needed to make some other friends and I have Kate now so something good came out of my pathetic excuse to get away from Sully.

I sit in our usual spot at a corner table we managed to find in the cafeteria. We can see Logan and Sully's table and as I eat, Logan gives me puppy dog eyes from across the room. He told me to bring my friends to their table but I said Sully probably wouldn't like it. He told me to leave Sully to him but I didn't want to encroach on Sully's space any more than I already have. I don't want to give him another reason to add to his long list of why he doesn't like me.

I still don't understand his hatred towards me but I have noticed it isn't just me. Sully dislikes a lot of people or doesn't like them might be a better term. He talks to Logan and rarely laughs. It always catches me off guard when he chuckles. Every time I try to catch sight of his smile, there's nothing there. His normal uninterested face always stares at me. It's as if I imagine the laugh in the first place and it sometimes makes me question my sanity.

"You know if you hadn't gone on a date with Logan and his friend wasn't such a sourpuss, I would suggest going after Sully," Kate says, as she takes a seat next to me and realises where my focus is.

"What?" I screech at her. She's lost her mind.

"What? He's hot. Don't tell me you don't wanna run your hands through his thick hair. I sure do," she says, as she bites her bottom lip and looks in their direction.

"Why don't you ask him out?" I ask, and as I do, a niggling feeling in my belly flares, but I'm unsure what it means.

"Willow, girls don't ask out Sully. Have you seen the death stare he directs at everyone?" she states, and I can't help the laugh that bubbles out of me because her description of him is perfect.

"I'm glad I'm not the only one scared of his death stare," I say, as I grab a couple fries off my plate.

"You must admit it was hot how he saved us on Saturday night," she says, turning to face me.

"Did you know what happens in the bales?" I ask, having wondered if she knew the secret of the bales.

"Hell no. I've hardly been out to the Hill and no one has mentioned it before. They'd talk about the hook ups out there but I didn't know they meant in those bales," she states, as she stares at me in the eyes. I didn't tell her what Sully said to the group in the bales. I know it was me he was talking about when he yelled at them and I didn't want to draw attention to it. He was just being a good friend to Logan.

My eyes wander to the table where the guys are seated and heat warms my skin. It's not Logan I catch looking at me this time. It's Sully. Logan has disappeared so Sully holds my gaze now I've caught him. He always does the opposite of what I expect and throws me off balance. He's unpredictable. A normal person would be embarrassed if they got caught staring but not Sully. He doesn't care what anybody thinks. Ever.

He turns away from me a few seconds before Logan returns to his seat.

"Have you ever considered Sully might like you?" Kate whispers, causing me to jump. I had almost forgotten she was next to me.

"What? No," I argue.

"I saw the way he was looking at you girl. If he gave me the same look, I'd run across the room and jump into his arms," she states, and fans her face with her hand.

I laugh at her antics, "You're an idiot. He doesn't like me, he loathes me. His face is saying he'd like to wrap a hand around my neck and squeeze."

"Yeah squeeze while he's fucking you," she squeals, making us both erupt with laughter as I whack her arm.

"Oh my gosh, I can't believe you said that."

"Hey, nothing wrong with some rough love," she tells me, winking at me before she takes a big drink of her orange juice. I laugh at her joke before my eyes flicker back to the boy's table. "It's so unfair having so much hotness wrapped up in a pair of best friends," she says, as her eyes follow mine again.

"You think Logan is hot too?" I ask.

"Yeah, they're both hot. Don't you think so?"

"I guess. Sully would be if he smiled more," I say, which makes us laugh.

"What happened with you and Logan? I thought you'd make a good couple." I confided in her on Saturday how Logan and I weren't together but didn't go into too much detail.

"We went on a date but it felt more like friends. He felt it too when we were alone outside of school and work. He didn't want to tell anyone he lucked out so we aren't confirming anything," I tell her. It's the story Logan and I agreed to. Logan is a great friend but there were never any romantic feelings towards him.

"It's a shame, he's a decent guy. Don't worry my lips are sealed. I won't tell anyone you guys aren't together," she tells me, while she continues to drink her orange juice.

"Thanks. There weren't any butterflies, you know?

"Oh yeah. If it's not there, you can't force it."

43

"Exactly. Better we know after one date anyway instead of a year down the track or something," I tell her.

"Yeah true. Now we can find you someone else," she tells me, which makes me shake my head at her.

"I'll focus on school for a bit. It's far less distracting."

"I'm here for all the distractions. Please," she says, making us howl with laughter. We spend the rest of our lunch break, chuckling at Kate's jokes. I can't help every so often my eyes flicker to where Logan and Sully sit. Neither of them look my way again and I can't help but wonder which boy causes the sudden feeling of disappointment.

Chapter Nine

Willow

Last night I got hit with the worst news. My dad called and told me my grandpa had passed away. He was my last grandparent alive and he has been since I was six years old. My other grandpa died before I was born. Both of my grandmothers passed within a year of each other when I was three years old so I don't remember them. My grandpa Joel was the best. He would take me out for ice cream every Sunday when he'd come see me. Even though he was getting older, he still made time for me every Sunday.

Part of the reason I didn't want to move here was because I didn't want to leave behind my dad and grandpa. I bet if it was just my grandpa around I could have convinced him to move so he was closer to me. He stayed so he could keep my dad company so I didn't even entertain the idea. I don't know what went on between Mum and Dad but she got him to agree for me to move here for my last year of high school. It's the first year of her new marriage, shouldn't they be in their honeymoon phase? Having a teenager around makes no sense to me. To say I'm unhappy about the whole situation is an understatement.

Dad called me last night to tell me about grandpa Joel and as he said the words, I swear my stomach dropped. It's the same feeling you get when you are at the top of the rollercoaster and it heads over the

45

edge for the first plummeting dip and your stomach drops right out of you. I still haven't recovered.

I was a ball full of tears last night. Mum had to take the phone off me and talk to Dad so she could understand what was going on. To my embarrassment, well I would be embarrassed if I wasn't so catatonic, her new husband had to carry me to my bed. Mum snuggled under the blankets with me and I fell asleep in her arms to her singing random songs to try and quieten my sobs.

She tried to keep me home from school today, telling me one day wouldn't hurt but I didn't want to sit around the house feeling sorry for myself. I don't think I could handle any more tears as the crying gave me a blinding headache this morning when I woke up.

I find myself in a daze, standing at my open locker as the bustling atmosphere of the day buzzes around me. My mum got me a locker after the first day of school when I told her I kept forgetting my bag as I wasn't used to carrying one around with me due to having lockers at my old school.

Here I stand. I can't remember what day it is or what my first period is. The bell sounds in the distance and lockers bang shut, laughter surrounds me and my books in my locker become a blur the longer I stare at them. I have no idea how long I've stood here, unmoving but the noise has softened. Part of my brain registers the squeaking of sneakers against the linoleum but the other part of my brain is floating away with other thoughts, too distracted to focus on the task at hand.

"Ooh is little miss perfect late for school today?" His taunt carries to my ear as if he whispered it to me. Blinking, I know it's unlikely as he never gets too close to me. His feet continue on their journey until they stop. My face is hidden from him by my locker door but I know he's stopped. I can feel it. My breathing picks up because he's the last person I want to see me like this. I hastily grab whatever book is on the top and move to close my locker.

"Shoot," I say, as he's standing right behind my locker door as I push it closed. His brows pull together as he inspects my face. I lower my eyes because I know if I look into someone else's eyes right now I'll break. His hand whips out and snatches my textbook from my hands.

"What are you doing?" he accuses, as he places my calculus textbook back, finds my art history book instead and places it in my hands.

"Thanks," I mumble under my breath.

"What's wrong with you today?" he huffs, his irritation towards me shows. I keep my eyes to the floor and watch as the lines blur. I gently shake my head as my throat clogs with emotion. I swallow to push it away but it doesn't help. The rattle of my locker door as it closes makes my heart spike as his sneakers step into view. His firm fist is cold against my chin as he forces my eyes to meet his gaze. His furrowed brows soften when he sees my face.

"What happened?" he asks, his softer tone catches me off guard as I hold his gaze. The bruising on his cheek doesn't go undetected.

"My...my...my...," I gasp. The words don't come out. "My grandpa...grandpa...died," I manage to get out but my breaths become a fight. As I pull one in, another is close behind and Sully's eyes widen.

"Shit," he cusses, as he grips my forearm gently and tugs me behind him. My feet follow his long strides, before he pulls me into the janitor's closet. He flicks on the light but my breathing won't slow. "Willow, you're having a panic attack. I need you to slow your breathing. You're perfectly safe here. No one can see you now," he tells me, but thoughts of my grandpa flash through my head and my breaths remain erratic and fast.

"Fuck," he says. He shrugs his backpack off and rummages through it. He pulls out a brown paper bag and turns it upside down so his lunch falls into his bag. He roughly pushes the opening over my mouth while he holds the back of my neck and stares into my eyes. "Slow your breaths. In and out. You're about to pass out and I can't be caught with an unconscious girl in the janitor's closet. Come on. Breathe in, five, four, three, two, one, and out, five, four, three, two one. Keep going and again, five, four, three, two, one." His soothing voice calms me as I follow his instructions, and bring my breathing back to a normal rate. His tight grip on my neck remains and as I raise my eyes to his, the reason for this situation hits me full force. My grandpa died. The tears fall before Sully cusses again.

"Come here," he demands, the grip he has on my neck pushes my face into his firm chest where my sobs release and fill the air. I wrap my arms around his waist as I need to hold on to something, not even caring it's the boy who hates me. He rubs my back, as he patiently lets me cry out all the pain. "I've got you," he softly whispers at one point, but it could have been my imagination.

Once I gather control over my crying attack, I whisper, "Thanks."

"Do you want me to get Logan?" he asks, and I shake my head as I release the tight grip I had on his waist. I step back and give us both some space.

"No. Could we please not tell Logan about this?" I rush out.

"You sure? He'd want to be there for you," he says, but I shake my head again.

"Please. I won't be able to get through the day if I tell him. I need to get through the day," I whisper, more to myself than him.

"Whatever you say, but it's Thursday not Tuesday," he states, which makes my own brows furrow. "You had Tuesday's first period book out before but it's Thursday," he says, and my slow brain catches onto something.

"You know my schedule?" I query.

Without missing a beat, he rolls his eyes while he says, "Do you know how often Logan goes on about what class you must have or be in when you're not around. It's drilled into me now. It's not like I want it there," he tells me, as he taps the side of his head.

"No need to get snarky, it was just an observation," I point out, and my hands land on my hips. He always knows how to push my buttons.

"Well since you aren't blubbering all over my shirt anymore, let's get out of here because it stinks," he says, as he wrinkles his nose.

"I wasn't blubbering," I whisper. My eyes drop to his shoes again as I fight to hold the tears back. Dammit, it's going to be a hard day.

"Hey," his gentle voice prompts, as his fist lifts my chin for the second time. "I'm just teasing. It was only a slight blubber," he says, as his lip pulls into the first smile I've ever seen cross his face. A deep dimple pops out of his right cheek causing me to draw in a big breath.

He's gorgeous when he smiles. How have I never noticed his dimple? Right, silly me, I forgot. It's because he doesn't smile around me.

"Why do you hate me?" I ask, my brain thinks this is the right moment to blurt the question out. His eyes widen as the smile drops from his face and I regret my outburst as it ruined the moment and took the light right out of his face.

"I don't hate you."

"Yes, you do," I state.

"I don't. Can we drop it?" he asks.

"If you don't hate me, why are you so horrible to me?"

"I'm horrible to most people," he says, as he rolls his eyes again.

"I'm pretty much a part of your friend group, shouldn't you at least be a bit nicer to me?"

"No," he flat out states.

"Why not?" I demand. As his eyes close, he raises a hand to squeeze his forehead, as if he's getting a headache.

"Please can you drop it?" he begs this time.

"Why can't you tell me the reason you don't like me?"

"Drop it alright. I'm not telling you," his frustration leaks out, as his voice raises.

"Why the hell not?" I yell back.

"It's too hard, okay?"

"What's too hard?" As the words leave my mouth, he pushes me against the wall and crowds my space. My shallow breaths come now because of another reason. We stare at each other and I'm confused about what is happening. One moment I'm crying, the next moment Sully has me pressed against the wall, and he looks at me like he wants to take a bite out of me.

"Ask me again," he whispers, as his warm breath fans my face.

"What?" I stammer.

"Ask me the last question again." I rack my brain trying to think of what I had asked him moments ago until it comes to me.

"What's too hard?" I whisper back. I gulp to try and ease my sprinting heart.

"It's too hard to look at you with him. It wasn't supposed to be this way," he says, which makes my brows pull together. Is he telling me he likes me in some weird way?

"You hate me though," I tell him.

"Far from it sweetheart," he sighs, as he lowers his forehead to mine and breathes me in with a serene look on his face.

"Sully?" I softly ask, causing him to pull back. His gaze falls to my lips before his thumb swipes ever so gently across my bottom one.

"Has he kissed you?" he asks, holding my gaze as his thumb continues to caress my full lip. For some reason I find myself being honest with him as I shake my head. His own chest beats in time with his breaths.

The silence stretches before he says, "Forgive me?"

"What?" My words are cut off as he closes the gap between us and slides a hand from my neck into my hair. He tilts my head and before I know it, his lips are on mine. Tender and sweet. I automatically close my eyes. His full lips pull my bottom one between his and gently press against me. He doesn't do anything else before he pulls away, and leaves me shaking. He leans his forehead against mine again.

"For stealing a kiss," he says, my lips on fire from where he gave me my first kiss. I won't admit it out loud though.

"You're forgiven," I whisper. He lets out a sigh before he steps back from me. A serene look is on his face for a beat before he breaks the moment.

"Shit. Logan," he cusses, causing my eyes to widen. Before I can process anything, his lips press to my forehead as gently as they had touched my lips then he walks out the door and leaves me standing alone in the janitor's closet, wondering what in the hell is going on. I had my first kiss with a boy who hates me. Or doesn't hate me. I have no idea. All I know is I've felt more alive in the last ten minutes than I have this whole summer, excluding my time with the mystery guy I met in the dark.

I stand in the janitor's closet confused and try to wrap my head around everything until the bell rings for the next period. I catch sight of my forgotten text book I must have dropped during the commotion.

I grab it, open the door and walk to my locker in a daze before the hall fills again.

Chapter Ten

Sully

It was stupid and my body acted before my brain could stop it. I shouldn't have kissed her. A sliver of regret gnaws at my gut but there's also some satisfaction mixed in with it. I've never wanted anything in my life as much as my heart wants Willow. My life doesn't breed hope so I've never wanted anything for myself. Why would I when all it does is cause me to hope for things. I gave up hoping for anything of my own a long time ago because all it left me with was disappointment. Disappointment at least is constant these days.

The day I met Willow in the dark, hope bloomed for the first time in a long while until the end of summer when Logan's confession about his crush on Willow snuffed it out. This leads me back to my present predicament. I felt bad about stealing a kiss from her. When she confirmed she hadn't kissed Logan, my brain went haywire and I couldn't think of anything else except my lips had to touch hers. For once I took what I wanted. I felt I deserved it as I'd met her first. Hanging out today with Logan, I felt the guilt eating me from the inside because she's not mine and she probably never will be.

I made a pact with myself to give her this small peace offering before I shut the door on us. I can't allow myself to think of her as anything other than my best friend's girl. I know she hasn't told Logan about her grandpa dying otherwise I wouldn't be here standing outside her house, looking like a pathetic loser.

My grandparents gave me some cash when I left their place over the summer. They know my parents aren't the greatest at taking care of me so every summer they give me a small envelope of money for me to hide away when I get back to spend on clothes or essentials. I usually do too. I don't think I've ever bought something that wasn't a necessity but this time the girl in this house needed something more and I wanted to be the one who gave it to her.

Staring at the two storey house, I wonder if I'll ever live in something as nice as this. Logan and Willow make a good match as they both live in nice houses with good families. Nothing like mine where I avoid getting the life beaten out of me when my drunk dad walks through our broken home.

Logan showed me which room is Willow's when we skated here so he could drop off some homework to her one day when she was sick. The light shines from her window on the second floor behind the white lace curtains. I search the grass below and find a couple of tiny pebbles to throw. I pull my arm back, and launch one as gently as I can to hit the glass.

No one comes to the window so I throw another one and wait. A few minutes pass and still no one comes so I throw a third and listen out for the familiar tinkle. A rattle follows so I step back and look to see Willow has pushed open the window and is looking for the source of the sound. Her wide eyes convey the shock at seeing me. I motion for her to come to me and she pulls the window shut.

It's a few minutes later when she races around the side of the house as she ties the cord of her purple satin robe tight around her waist in a bow. It hits her mid thigh and I have to force myself to avert my eyes. Now is not the time to be ogling her.

"What are you doing here?" she puffs, as if she ran straight from her room.

"Did you tell Logan?" I ask. Her eyes drop before she shakes her head.

"Why did you do it?" she asks, her question catches me off guard. The kiss. That's what she's referring to where I was asking if she had told him about her grandpa. Talk about crossed wires.

"Because I could," I say, hating myself for the words because I don't mean them and wish I could take them back as she flinches away from me.

"You're a real piece of work Sully," she huffs. Anger laces her tone. I can handle anger when it comes to her. It's familiar and safe.

"Please don't tell Logan." She wraps her arms around herself to protect herself from me. I'm not good for her and I probably never will be. Plus she's with my best friend. It is what it is.

"Is that all you came here for? To try and convince me to keep your secret from your best friend?" she spits with venom, and it's my turn to wince but I do it internally. I never let people see when things get to me. My armour was built a long time ago.

"No, it was one of the things. Can you promise not to tell him? What's the point in wrecking your relationship and my friendship over a silly mistake which is never gonna happen again?" Words flow out of my mouth, and they cut my tongue like barbed wire with every lie spilling out.

"Yeah a mistake. It won't happen again. I got it."

"I uh came to give you this," I say. I step towards her and hold out the black velvet jewellery bag I had hidden in my pocket.

"What is it?" she asks, as she takes it and pulls the drawstring apart. She tips the contents into her open palm and my hands sweat. This feels like a dumb idea now.

"A ring?" she asks, as she holds the silver ring between her thumb and index finger so she can inspect it. I take a deep breath and close the gap between us. I snatch the ring out of her grip and pull her right hand towards me so I can slide the thick banded silver ring on to her middle finger where it fits best. I hold her hand to her face so she can see, and with the tip of my finger I tap the side of the ring and make the centre part of it twirl around. I do it again and watch as her top lip twitches as if she's holding in a smile.

"It's an anxiety ring or like a fidget spinner ring. I thought it might help with the panic attacks," my voice trails off before I say, "It's dumb."

"No, no it's not. It's thoughtful and sweet of you. Thanks." She smiles at me, and the sight makes my heart swell.

"I hope it helps," I say, as I step back away from her and get ready to make a run for it. I've never given someone something like this before and the way she's making me feel is uncomfortable.

"Can I ask how you know about these rings?" she says, as her eyes find mine. I hold her gaze for a couple of beats before I lift my hand to show her my two rings. I hold my thumb so she can see in the dark. My black ring is hard to see but I tap against the side to make the centre spin and with it, her smile grows. I worry if I stay I will do something else to make the guilt in my stomach grow so instead of being mature and talking through things, I do the next best thing and dash off into the darkness before she can get a word out.

Chapter Eleven

Sully

It's been several weeks since I stole the kiss from Willow. Betrayal eats away at me and I find myself close to confessing my sin to Logan. Skating around our usual haunt, I fly down one of the ramps and glide up another to meet him where he sits on the bench seat. Since his date with Willow they act closer, they always hug or laugh together and it makes my skin crawl because it's not me in his place. He takes a sip of his water as I flick my board before taking a seat beside him.

"I've given up on my crush I had on Willow," he says.

"Why?" I ask, as my heart beats faster.

"We're better off friends I reckon. I gotta confess something. Don't get mad okay?" he says, as he swallows more of his water.

"What?"

"Our date wasn't as great as I made it out to be and we may have been fake dating the past few weeks," he confesses. My heart hammers in my chest.

"Come again?"

"We both realised we are better off as friends after the date and I didn't want you to feel bad about pushing me to ask her out so I asked her if she could pretend to be my girlfriend for a bit," he explains.

"You've been pretending this whole time?"

"Yeah. Are you mad?" he asks.

"Let me get this right, so you guys have never been a couple? Nothing happened between you two? You didn't kiss her?" I rapidly fire my questions at him.

"No, we were never a couple and nothing ever happened, not even a kiss. Happy now?"

"Okay," I reply, my heart slows, and the guilt disappears as I realise I never betrayed my best friend. I've been beside myself for weeks thinking I'd gone behind his back in the worst way but I in fact hadn't.

"Okay," he replies.

Feeling lighter I ask, "Who's the new girl?"

"What?"

"The new girl you have your eye on. I'm your best friend, you idiot. You move on from one girl to the next, so who's the new girl? The fact you are telling me you and Willow were never a thing must mean you are wanting to make yourself available for her," I say, as my heart slows at the realisation he's not interested in Willow anymore. It doesn't mean I can have her now though, I'm not good enough for her.

"Her friend Kate," he says, as he smiles at me. I chuckle lightly at him.

"You've got to be kidding me."

"What? She's hot," he adds,

"Have you told Willow about this?" I ask.

"No. Why would I?"

"She might not appreciate you creeping on her friend."

"Hey. I'm not a creep," he argues.

"Yes you are, you big creeper," I joke, and offer him a small smile feeling lighter than I have in weeks.

"Shut it, you egg. I shouldn't have told you," he laughs.

"Come on, enough girl talk. Let's skate," I suggest. I drop my board back to the ground and skate off with a rare genuine smile on my face.

Chapter Twelve

Willow

"I'll see you later Logan," I call out from the back of Jimmy's.

"Are you gonna be okay getting home? Why don't you ring your parents to come and pick you up? It's raining pretty heavily out there now," he tells me, as he glances towards the large glass windows in the front of the diner.

"It's just water Logan. I'll be fine. Plus my parents are away for the weekend, remember?"

"Oh yeah I forgot. I wish I didn't have to work, then I could have kept you company tonight," he says.

"Next time. I better go before it gets any worse," I tell him. He walks towards me and gives me a quick hug goodbye.

"Bye Willow."

"Bye," I say, before I open the back door and pull the hood over my head. The rain pelts against my face so I wrap my arms around my waist to try and add some extra warmth for the walk home. I should have driven my car today but I didn't think the rain was going to be this bad. There was a light drizzle when I left this morning and my jacket was enough to keep me dry. It's five o'clock on a Saturday night so it's still fairly light out but the darkening sky makes it appear later than it is. Logan arrived at work an hour ago and will be there until midnight again.

After about five minutes of walking, I glance across the road and notice the shop fronts along the strip offer a bit more shelter from the rain. Cars zoom past and I decide to dash across so I will be drier on my journey home. I wait for the road to clear, but this time of day is always busy around here with people headed out to dinner and events. When there's a lull in the traffic, I make a run across the road. My hood flies behind me as I dash out onto the road. Bright headlights shine at me so instead of stopping in the middle of the road, I quickly rush to the other side. My work shoes don't have the best grip and I slip as I'm about to get to safety, stumble over the curb and twist my ankle.

"Shit," I scream. The puddle I land in quickly seeps through my work dress and chills my skin. Tears spring to my eyes as my ankle throbs. I push myself to stand but the pain from my ankle is excruciating. I hop to the front of a sewing shop which has closed for the day, drop to the cold wet concrete, let the tears flow and feel sorry for myself. I unzip my jacket and pull out my small bag hanging across my chest. Finding Logan's number I press call and hold the phone to my ear.

"Willow? Everything okay?" he asks.

"I slipped over and hurt my ankle. I can't walk. Would you be able to come and take me home?"

"It's rush hour now and we are swamped. Billy Bob is telling me to get off the phone because customers are waiting. Don't worry, I'll get someone to come and help you. Where are you?"

"I'm sitting under the awning at Sewing World," I tell him.

"Sit tight. I'll send someone okay," he tells me.

"Okay," I say, before he ends the call. I put my phone back in my bag and zip my jacket closed. The tears flow freely as my ankle throbs more.

A few minutes later a car slows and parks in front of the sewing shop. I lift my head from where I have it resting on my bent knee to see who it is. The driver gets out and comes around to the front of the car.

"Hey, are you okay?" he asks. As he kneels in front of me, I take in his face. I recognise him as the guy in the bales who taunted Sully. Logan wouldn't have sent him to help me, would he?

"I'm Troy. You're Willow, right?" he says, smiling at me.

"Yeah. Did Logan send you?" I ask,

"Logan? Ah yeah. Why are you sitting in the rain?" As I stare at him, a feeling in my gut simmers similar to butterflies but not in a good way. It's my instincts telling me something isn't right. Logan wouldn't have sent Troy and as I realise this, the whizz of skateboard wheels approach us. My heart thunders in my chest as he skids to a stop in front of me causing Troy to stand and take a step back from where he was crouched next to me. Sully lifts his board and holds it by the wheels. Looking at him, his nostrils flare as he stares at Troy.

"Did you not get the message last time or are you dumb?" Sully speaks to Troy, whose eyes harden as he watches Sully. His eyes flick to Sully's board as if he's worried Sully will hit him with it. I don't think he would risk breaking his board though.

"I saw your girl here sitting in the rain so thought I'd do the gentlemanly thing and stop and see if she needed help," Troy taunts. Why is he calling me Sully's girl?

"She's fine now so off you go," Sully barks, making Troy laugh as he walks back around to the driver's side of his car. "Next time, even if she's in a burning building you drive the fuck on, you hear me?"

"Yeah whatever," Troy replies, before he hops in his car and presses the gas as he speeds away. Sully's shoulders heave as he watches Troy's car until it disappears from view.

"Umm for your information, if I was in a burning building I wouldn't mind him stopping to help me," I tell him, raising my brows at him. His gaze comes back to me before he crouches next to me.

"Don't be silly, you don't need his help when I'll always be there," he says the off handed comment, and my heart beats faster. He runs a hand through his wet locks which are untied and hang past his shoulders. "Give me your phone," he instructs, so I get it back out of my bag and hand it to him.

"What for?" I ask.

"What's your password?" he asks.

"Six, zero, zero, six," I tell him automatically, not even questioning why. He raises a brow at me, before his dimple shows as the faintest smile appears.

"Are you serious?" he asks.

"Why? What's wrong with it?"

"Your password is boob?" His smile widens as my cheeks burn.

"What? No it's not."

"Well that's what it looks like," he teases, as he types it in.

"Well it's not. Ugh give it here, I'm gonna change it now." I try to grab my phone but he holds it out of reach while he types.

"All done. Now you have my number saved. You can call me directly if you need help or if you are in a burning building," he says, as he hands back my phone which I put in my bag. I take in a deep breath, and remember his lips on mine for a second. His eyes drift to my lips before he stands and I wonder if he has the same thought. "Now. You can't walk?"

"No, I was barely able to hobble under the shelter," I tell him. The rain has increased the longer I've been stuck here.

"Come on, I'll lift you onto my board," he tells me, and I laugh.

"You're gonna skateboard me home? You couldn't bring a car or something? Did Logan not tell you I was injured?" I huff, because I doubt he can skateboard me home with my leg like this and the wetness seeping through my clothes is making me cranky.

"Sweetheart, I don't have a car and I don't know how to drive. Logan called me knowing this. How about we hurry and get out of the fucken rain because I'm getting cold," he grunts.

"Fine," I grunt back, wondering why we always end up at each other's throats.

"Fine," he replies, as he touches my ankle and inspects it.

"Ouch that hurts," I tell him, as he prods at it.

"It's swollen."

"No shit Sherlock," I huff.

"Do you want my help or not? I can easily head back home where I was dry and leave you here."

"Well Troy could have given us a ride," I say, which by the murderous look on his face was the worst thing to say.

61

"What did I fucken tell you about thinking before doing dumb shit? Troy is not a good guy no matter how much he may look like a knight in shining armour," he yells at me.

"At least he had a car."

"Good to see all you think about are the material things princess," he says, as he picks his board off the ground. "Find your own way home if I'm not good enough to rescue you." He turns his back on me and skates back the way he came. He must be playing a cruel joke on me and plans to return any minute but the minutes stretch on and the sky darkens as I sit there. My mood shifts from angry to depressed as I sit there and wait but he doesn't return. The tears start again as I shiver from the cold. I'm soaked now as the rain changes direction and pelts me from the side.

I suck up my pride and pull my phone out. My fingers numb from the cold, find it hard to swipe but I manage to find his name. As I hold the phone to my ear, my teeth chatter as I wait for him to answer but his answering machine comes on. The hot tears run down my face so I drop my face into my hands. My sobs become uncontrollable and I fear a panic attack is coming so I try my best to focus on breathing deeper into my lungs. I'm so consumed in my crying episode and trying not to let panic set in, I'm startled when firm hands slide around me, one under my legs and the other behind my back. I stare into his hazel eyes as he stands effortlessly while he holds my weight.

"Don't cry over me sweetheart. I'm not worth your tears," he says, which makes the tears run faster. "Can you hold my board?" he asks, bending to pick it up. He stands on the edge and flips it so it's easier for me to hold onto it. I hold it by the wheels like he did, even though my fingertips are numb.

I jostle in his arms as he walks away from the place where I've been stuck for over an hour. My tears won't stop and I don't know what part of tonight's events are the reason for them. I'm a bundle of pain, confusion and nervousness all rolled into one. Sully makes it to the end of shops and he bravely steps out into the rain without any buildings for protection. His strong arms hold me close to him while my legs dangle over his other arm. Every so often my ankle hits the side of his body making me wince but it can't be helped.

"Shh. I'm sorry," Sully whispers, before he plants a kiss on my forehead. "I told you not all guys are good, including me," he states, which causes a few more tears to escape. We walk past a house with a pretty gardenia plant and Sully stops to pick a couple of the white flowers before he hands them to me.

"I know they aren't sunflowers but hopefully they'll make you feel better," he says, as he continues his trek to my house.

"Sunflowers?" I ask.

"Your favourite flowers."

"How do you know they're my favourite?" I ask, as my brows pull together in confusion and he visibly gulps.

"I must have heard you talking to Logan or Kate one day," he explains. I bring the flowers to my nose and inhale the sweet flowery fragrance.

"Thank you," I say, a hint of a smile appears on my face at his small peace offering.

We get to my house after what feels like the longest walk ever and we are both drenched. Sully continues to hold me on the doorstep while I get my house keys out of my bag. We are way past numb as the feeling in my fingers has gone. It takes a couple of tries to get the key in the lock but I manage it. Sully turns his back on the door and pushes it further open so I don't hit it with my leg. He closes the door with little effort as he stands and drips in the foyer while still holding me in his arms.

"You can put me down," I tell him, but he cuts me off.

"Where's your bedroom?" His hazel eyes look into mine as the rain in his hair drips down his face.

"Upstairs," I say. I flick my head behind me to show him where the stairs are. He moves with ease, carrying me to the landing at the top of the stairs and I point to my bedroom at the other end of the hallway.

"This is me," I tell him, as we get to my door. In the small space he manages to turn around and open the door, all while he holds me steady in his arms. His expression never changes as he walks into my space, his impenetrable wall holds firm. The only difference I notice is the deep breath he takes the further he walks into the room, as if he's breathing my scent in. His gaze sweeps the room before he strides over to my dresser where he chooses to deposit me. My fingers are so weak from the numbness, the skateboard falls out of my hand and onto the cream carpet. I place my freshly picked flowers safely on the dresser next to me before they are dropped too.

Our eyes stare into each other and neither of us says a word. He leans both hands on either side of me as he fills my space. My heartbeat stampedes in my chest due to our close proximity and it's like his eyes can see into my soul. One of his hands pushes the hood of my jacket away from my head. The same hand slowly moves to my zip and opens it, all the while holding my gaze, never wavering.

I pull my arms out of my jacket and let the soaked material pool behind me. Sully lifts the cord of my bag over my head and sets it aside on the dresser. A twitch of his eye is the only clue a thought has gone off in his head. He steps out of my space, grabs my bag and takes my phone out. He unlocks it and types out a message as he holds it one handed before he places it on the dresser.

"What did you do?" I ask, unable to stop the curiosity.

"I texted Logan and said you got home safely and you'll talk to him tomorrow," he tells me, as he leans back into my space.

"Okay," I say, noticing how my voice comes out breathy.

"You're so wet," Sully's voice drawls, and the sound hits right between my legs and he isn't even touching me.

"I am," I reply, shocking us both as his pupils dilate.

"We should get you warm," he states. I turn my head to the closed door on my right.

"The main bathroom is through there. It's connected to my room," I tell him. He pushes away from me and as he goes through the door, I draw in a big breath. What am I doing right now? He hates me, doesn't he? I can't explain it but there's something about him which sets me on fire. I don't think I'm strong enough to resist the flame and fear he may burn both our worlds to the ground.

The sound of the bath running draws my attention before he comes back into the room. His eyes sweep over my uniform as the teal green dress clings tightly to my skin. I don't second guess my decision as I unbutton the huge white buttons. Sully stands back, his fists clenched at his sides as his eyes enjoy the show and help me to undress. I undo the last button, pull the dress open and reveal myself to him. I pull my arms out and the material sits on top of my discarded jacket. Both of our laboured breaths fill the room as his eyes flicker across my body, my white lace underwear now see through from the rain.

Sully closes his eyes for a second before he walks back into the bathroom. The running water stops. The tension, thick in the air when he returns, causes me to take another deep breath, and I wonder what I'm doing. The thought is fleeting and my body pushes it away quickly. He steps closer to me and peels my shoe and sock off my uninjured foot.

"How's this one feeling?" he asks. In all honesty, I'd forgotten it was injured.

"It's numb so I can't feel it at the moment," I tell him. He nods once, carefully undoes the laces and stretches the shoe open as much as he can before he pulls it off. He drags my sock slowly off as well. All the while his t-shirt clings to his skin and showcases the outline of his abs.

"It's swollen and bruised," his soft voice says, as he runs a finger over my skin. His touch leaves a trail of heat behind. His eyes look into mine and I wish he would give some clue away to what he is thinking. His stony expression remains and gives nothing away. He moves closer between my legs, and invades my space again.

My chest heaves and his eyes drop to follow the movement. I close my eyes as I burn up from his gaze on me. I close my eyes as his hands ever so gently run along my thighs until he cups my butt. My eyes flash open as he pulls my body flush against him. I feel how hard he is through his pants where my centre meets his body.

My fingers grip the bottom of his soaked black shirt and my hands slide under it to feel his skin. His shallow breaths signal my touch does affect him. I move to take it off but his hand grabs my wrist and halts my movement. My brows pull in and he shakes his head softly, telling me no. My brows pull in further as I resist against his hand but he holds firm and doesn't budge. He shakes his head again. I let out an angry puff at being denied a look at his body I desperately want to see.

His own brows pull in and the wall he always holds so firmly around him drops away and I'm left staring at a vulnerability I never would have associated with Sully. His forehead drops to mine with his eyes closed and he breathes in while his grip remains on my hand, stopping it from wandering.

Thunder sounds from outside causing him to move his head and look into my eyes.

"You'll be the death of me Low," he whispers, before he kisses my forehead again and releases my hand. Low, he called me. Not sweetheart or princess but Low and I like it best of all. He nods, giving me permission to remove his shirt. I push the damp material away from his cold body and drop it next to my discarded uniform.

He doesn't give me a chance to look him over as he swiftly plants his hands under my butt again and lifts me against me. My arms automatically move around his neck to hang on. He walks me to the bath as he holds me in his arms. He squeezes the handfuls of skin he holds in his grip, causing an involuntary moan to escape from my mouth as it brings me closer to his hardness. He closes his eyes as he gently moves me up and down against him, making me moan again.

At the sound, he burrows his head into my neck and holds me against him as if he's scared to let me go. I let my hands skate along his muscular back, where goosebumps appear from the chill of his skin. I shiver in response and he must take it the wrong way thinking I'm cold, but wrapped in his arms, I'm anything but cold. My body is on fire from his touch.

He slowly lowers me into the tub. The hot water burns my numb skin at first making it sting until it heats. He manages to manoeuvre me while he avoids hitting my ankle on the edge of the tub. I sigh as my body relaxes and he releases me.

"Wanna join me?" I ask him, not ready for our connection to be severed and not sure where my bravery comes from.

"I don't think it's a good idea," he tells me.

"Come on, a quick dip so at least you aren't shivering anymore. Unless you want to hop in the shower and get warm. I don't want you to get sick," I tell him, a white lie on my part. I'm being brazen and selfish.

He watches me from where he sits outside the tub, his body obscured by the porcelain. He pulls off his sneakers and socks before he stands with his back to me. I can't take my eyes off him as he peels his wet jeans from his legs. He stands in his navy coloured trunks, his muscular legs matching the rest of his physique.

"Scoot forward," he demands, so I wriggle forward the best I can without hurting my injured leg and he steps in behind me. He puts his hands under my arms and lifts me so his body can slide underneath me and I am pressed right against him. The water rises with our combined mass and covers us to my shoulders now. My head falls back against his chest and I can feel his heart gallop in his chest. He may act cool and collected but his heart beat gives him away. He uses a hand to rub hot water over his face and through his hair a few times before he relaxes.

"Mmm this is so much better than freezing," he mumbles. I'm unsure if he meant to share his thoughts out loud. I relax into him, close my eyes and let the warmth wash over me. I've been frozen for what feels like hours so my body is happy it's finally warm. Sully turns on the tap to add more hot water. I'm thankful this bath is bigger than normal so the pair of us can fit easily.

When the water touches my chin, he turns it off and sinks himself further under so more of his body is covered. The warmth of the added water seeps into my skin and relaxes me further. His hand tucks my hair behind my ear before he lowers his arm to rest along the side of his body. His other arm slowly traces patterns along my shoulder and arm before he wraps it over my chest and holds me tightly to him.

I let out an audible sigh. It feels like heaven to be held in his arms as the warm water surrounds us after being cold for so long. I like Logan but as a friend, he's never made me feel on fire like Sully does. It's as if Logan is the calm and Sully is the storm. As we sit there content to let ourselves soak in the heat, I break the silence because I want to get to know Sully better. The real Sully.

"Can I ask you something?"

"You can ask me anything but it doesn't mean I'll answer," he says, right by my ear. His sultry voice causes my toes on my good leg to curl at the sound. Gosh if he could bottle his voice, he'd have a million dollar business right there. I don't say anything for a beat as I'm too wired from the sound of his voice but he must think it's because he said he may not answer. The hand wrapped around me loosens and he begins running his fingertips lazily along my collarbone and arm. My chest rises and falls with his touch.

"Ask your question sweetheart," he whispers, sending a jolt straight to my core.

"Do you like me?" I blurt out, and squeeze my eyes tight as it's not what I wanted to initially ask but his touch distracted me and made my brain short circuit.

"I don't like anyone," he says, his fingers move along their path to my collarbone before they move between my breasts.

"You like Logan though?" I remind him, and his hand stills.

"Sweetheart, let's not mention another guy's name when my hand is on you," his firm tone demands. I nod, not able to reply. "Good girl," he says, as his wandering fingers move again. "He's the exception. He's like a brother to me."

"What about me?"

"I definitely don't think of you as my brother," he says, a hint of a smile in his voice. I want to turn to see it but don't want to break the moment. I'm worried any movement will scare him off. His smiles are such a rare sight, it's a tragedy to miss one.

"What do you think of me?"

"I think of you as many things," he says, his touch makes me press back against him.

"Like what?"

"Well at the moment I think of you as a mosquito."

"A mosquito? That doesn't sound very nice."

"Yes, a mosquito. You know in the moments when you're in your room in the dark of night, head on your pillow and you're about to fall asleep but then you hear it. Right in your ear is the incessant buzzing of a damn mosquito coming to ruin your peace and quiet," he tells me. I want to throttle him but he anticipates my reaction. He knew his response would make me lash out so he grabs my injured leg by my knee and presses it against the porcelain.

"Watch your leg, we don't need you hurting it more," he says, his firm pressure on my knee makes my anger drip away.

"I'm not a mosquito," I huff, as I settle back against him. He releases the pressure on my knee when he's sure I won't lunge at him again. His fingers now run a lazy trail under the water. At the same time, he slides his legs straight underneath me which moves more of my body out of the water. With one leg hanging out of the bath, my legs are spread open for him and heat rushes to pool in my centre. My hungry breaths become louder in the quiet room.

"Give me your hand," he whispers in my ear, as he shifts me so I'm lying on top of him. I join my hand with his where it teases my leg and he runs the pad of his fingertips all over my hand. My senses are on overload. "Have you ever made yourself come?" he asks, and I shake my head. I'm so inexperienced and never knew much about sex until last year. Some would go as far to call me naive. "Do you want to come?" his voice asks, as the sultry notes sink right into the spot between my legs again. I nod against his chest so he grabs my hand and leads my fingers between my legs. He plants them on the top of my underwear line and holds them there.

His other hand grabs my hand resting beside my body. He sits his fingers on top of my hand and makes me glide mine along my skin until he touches the bottom of my bra cup.

"Tell me to stop," he whispers, both our breaths loud now.

"Why?"

"Because I shouldn't take what doesn't belong to me." His confession causes me to squeeze my eyes shut.

"What if I want to belong to you?" I sigh, and his heart rate beats faster behind me.

"It's stupid to wish for things especially if they have no chance of coming true," his soft voice says, but I wince in response.

"Let me be stupid," I reply, as I inch my fingers along my underwear. He takes over and moves my fingers for me. He holds the index fingers of both hands with two of his fingers and directs them where he wants them. He runs the pad of my fingertip against my nipple which can be seen through my white bra. The sensation sends a shock between my legs. He swipes my finger back and forth which causes tingles to run through me. Our breaths fill the air and he hardens underneath me. He moves my finger right to the spot I need his touch and through my underwear he makes me rub small circles.

"Don't stop," he says, before he bites my ear lobe and moves his hand so he can grasp my thigh and pull my legs further apart, giving me more access to the delicate spot. He continues to swipe my finger back and forth over my nipple as the shock waves course through me.

"Sully," I moan, as the sensations become too strong.

"Keep going sweetheart. Nearly there," he says, as his voice sends another spike of lust through me. He releases my hand at my breast but I keep rubbing back and forth, knowing he wouldn't want me to stop. He adjusts my body over his and switches the hand rubbing at my centre. I'm unsure why until he grabs my other breast and squeezes, before he pinches the nipple hard. I cry out from the pleasure. He demands more from my digit, teasing me by speeding up and slowing down several times, before a burst explodes out of me. My moans fill the air as he continues to work me with my finger until my sated body sags against him.

My laboured breaths are the only sound in the room. He doesn't remove his hands like he knows if he moves, it will break the moment. I twist my head to look at him and find his hazel eyes as they flicker back and forth between mine, searching for something. He blinks and the spell is broken, and I'm unsure if he found what he was looking for.

He removes his hand from between my legs and the one holding my breast. He wraps both arms around my waist instead as he drops his chin to my neck. For some small reason this feels more intimate than what we did and I long for him to hold on to me like this forever. I relax in his arms, even though the hot water has long since turned cold but I don't dare move, not knowing if the version of this boy will be present when we leave our peaceful cocoon of water.

He presses his lips to the curve of my neck and I store it in my memories, worried for some reason it may be the last time his lips are on my skin. It's hard to explain but it feels like he's pulling away, both physically and mentally.

"The water's getting cold. Let's get you dry," he says, as he loosens his grip. He moves me so my butt slides onto the bottom of the tub and he can step out without me hurting my leg. "Towels?" he asks, with his back to me.

"Under the sink," I tell him. He walks over to the cabinet and retrieves two white towels. He places one on the sink while he scrubs his hair roughly to dry it quickly before he dries himself off and wraps the towel around his chest. My brows scrunch because it's an odd way for a guy to wrap a towel but I don't say anything.

He turns back to me, catches my eye but doesn't say a word as he brings the towel to me and pulls out the plug. We wait for the water to drain before he slides his arms under me and lifts me into the air. He carries me back to the dresser and places me back in front of my long forgotten uniform.

"Clothes?" he asks, and I point him to the top drawer on the right.

"Grab a nightie, it's probably the easiest thing for me to get on," I tell him. He pulls the drawer open and holds a bright red satin nightie in his hands which barely covers my butt when I wear it. "No, choose another one," I tell him, as my cheeks heat and turn a similar shade to the nightie. His lip twitches before he shoves it back in the drawer before he pulls out a pale purple one with a bear on the front. My cheeks darken some more as he holds my pyjamas. I grab the towel he placed beside me and hold it to cover my body, feeling self conscious all of a sudden.

"I'll let you get dressed," he says, before he exits the room. I unclasp my wet bra, peel it off and pull the nightie over my head. I have to wiggle my butt to get my underwear off without hurting my ankle and manage it after some work but they drop to the ground before I can catch them.

A knock on the door has my eyes glancing at Sully as he pokes his head in. Seeing I'm decent, he walks in with an ice pack in his hand he found in my freezer. He throws it on the bed and walks into my bathroom. He comes back with a face cloth and he throws it on the bed as well.

When he turns back to me I say, "If you open the drawer at the bottom, I have an old oversized Oasis t-shirt which should probably fit you. You can chuck your clothes in the dryer if you like and have a towel around your waist," I say. He follows my instructions, finds the t-shirt and pulls it over his head. Once it hangs low over him, he turns his back to me and pulls the towel out. He wraps the towel around his waist and pulls his briefs off.

"Where's the dryer?" he asks, picking his jeans and t-shirt from the floor.

"Down the hall, last door on the left," I tell him, and he exits. A few minutes pass before he comes back and heads straight to me. He steps between my legs and my arms wrap around his neck, our noses are centimetres apart but neither of us closes the gap. He lets out a sigh as he slides my nightie under one butt cheek then the other before he lifts me off the dresser. He walks me over to the bed and lowers me carefully so as not to hurt my ankle. He turns back to the dresser and grabs my wet underwear, uniform and jacket. He carries them into the bathroom and comes back empty handed. He grabs the ice pack and face cloth he dropped on the bed earlier and moves to lie beside me.

Looking at my ankle the skin is mottled blue and purple and swollen like Sully said.

"It looks bad. You don't think it's broken?" I ask.

"I'm not sure but I'd guess it's more than likely sprained. You might need to ask Logan to take you to get it checked out tomorrow," he says.

"Logan?"

"Yeah he's got a car. It would be easier for him to get you there," he states.

"Right." He lays the flannel against my ankle before he places the ice pack on top.

"Hopefully if you keep icing it, it'll reduce the swelling a bit." The silence drags between us until Sully lies back on my pillows. "Come here," he says, as he holds his arms out for me. I shuffle forward, place my head against his chest and he wraps his arms around me. Ever since the bath, the mood has changed. I don't know what made him change but it's as if his walls are half way up again.

"What's wrong Sully?" I ask, not expecting him to answer.

He lets out a sigh before he answers, "I'm being stupid for a minute," as he squeezes me tighter. I squeeze my eyes shut as I don't understand why he doesn't think we can be together. I don't want to push it though, afraid he may run scared. I slide my fingers under my shirt he's wearing, wanting to feel his skin especially if it's the one chance I am allowed to do it. I do what he did and trace lazy patterns across his toned stomach. As I move to touch higher, he grabs my hand. I twist to look at him and he looks back at me. I get a sense of deja vu, because he's acting exactly the same as earlier when I tried to remove his t-shirt.

I stare into his eyes as I wait and hope. He stares back for so long, as though we might never move until his eyes close and his grip loosens. I trail my hand upwards and feel smooth skin all over so I don't understand his hesitation. It isn't until I notice the slight hitch in his breathing when my hand slips across his ribs. Jagged skin mars the side of his body. I can't figure out what would have caused the scarring.

I lean on my elbow and look at him. His eyes are firmly shut, his breaths heavy in the air and my heart cracks at the sight.

"Sully?" I whisper, and his vulnerable eyes look at me. "Can I see it?" I ask, and again he stares at me for the longest time before he gives a slight nod. I wriggle the t-shirt up, not knowing what to expect. I pull in a breath at the sight and let it out slowly. I run my fingers over the bumpy skin. There are some thick lines as if he was cut and stitched back together. There are a few other scars which look more like burn marks than anything else.

"What happened?" I ask the question, but I already know I won't like the answer.

He closes his eyes again as his shaky voice says, "My dad. One night when I was eight, he didn't think punching me was enough so he grabbed a kitchen knife and cut me a few times. When he got bored of cutting me, he held the same knife against the stove top flame before he pressed it to burn against my skin. I passed out and woke up in the emergency room with my mum. It's the one time I remember her doing anything for me."

His eyes flick to mine and I don't realise I'm crying until he wipes away a tear with the pad of his thumb.

"I told you I'm not worth your tears, sweetheart," he softly says, causing the tears to fall silently on my face. He slides his hand into my hair and brings my face to his chest as I release my tears for the small boy who had to go through that and for the grown boy lying beside me who has his walls so firmly in place it's no wonder he doesn't let anyone in. There's no doubt in my mind now the bruises on his face which frequently appear are from his dad. He holds me until my tears lessen and my eyes become hard to open.

The last thing I remember before I fall asleep are his lips as he kisses the top of my head and whispers, "No more being stupid now for either of us, Low."

Chapter Thirteen

Sully

Sitting on the back of Eddie's truck with Logan, we both take skulls of the amber liquid he stole from his parent's alcohol cabinet. It's top shelf for us tonight.

The Hill is quieter this Friday night as one of the basketball players is having a party. Logan and I always avoid their parties as nothing good ever comes from them.

I tip my head back as I skull a bit more and let it simmer in my gut. It's been weeks now since Willow hurt her ankle. It healed and I was right, it was a sprain and luckily was not broken. We haven't talked about what happened and she's been in a sullen mood ever since. I don't blame her. I shut myself off from her after the night we spent together. Letting her in past my walls was too much for me to handle and I backtracked like a coward. I don't deserve her so it's better this way.

Logan snatches the bottle from my fingers, tips his head back and swallows his own mouthful. His phone rings and interrupts our laughter as he pulls his phone out of his pocket to answer it.

"Hello?" he says. "What, I can't hear you?" There's silence while he waits and listens to the person on the other end. "What do you mean she's missing?" My hackles rise as Logan looks at me and a pit in my stomach forms. "Okay we're on the way. Stay put," he says, before he ends the call. He stands and yells out, "Eddie. We need to go."

"Who was that?" I ask, as we watch Eddie race over to us.

"What is it?" Eddie asks.

"It was Kate. Willow, Kate and Lolly went to the basketball party but they can't find Willow. They're worried so they rang me," he tells us, and the pit in my stomach grows.

"I'm good to drive. I haven't been drinking," Eddie tells us, and he rushes around to the driver's seat while Logan and I sit in the back of the truck bed, holding on to the sides as he races out of the paddock.

"Do you think she's okay? Kate sounded worried," Logan says.

"She better fucken be," I mumble, as my rage begins to boil. He looks at me but doesn't say a word as Eddie drives the ten minutes which would usually take us double the time to get to Chris's house where the party is. Another rich boy with his large house has people pouring out of it by the time we get there. Willow could be anywhere.

"I'll call Kate," Logan says, as Eddie parks and we jump off. "Yeah hey, we're here. Any sign of her?" Logan shakes his head and instead of waiting to get more details, my legs march through the party goers, not caring if they are in my way or not. Logan and Eddie call behind me as they chase after me but I don't stop. My only thought is to find her.

As I push through the front door, swarms of drunk people surround us. A smoky haze fills the room as the heat from all the bodies packed together in the tight space steals the oxygen from the room. The alcohol I drank not long ago has worn off in my desperation to find her. Logan and Eddie catch up to me as I've slowed because it's getting harder to push through the throes of people.

"Through here," Logan yells to me over the music, directing us to the kitchen where we find a scared Lolly and Kate.

"Where did you see her last?" I ask the girls, as my fury leaks into the air.

"She was dancing with me until she went to find Lolly in the bathroom. Lolly came back but Willow never did. We searched the bathrooms but she wasn't in either of them," Kate explains.

"Where are the bathrooms? Lets start there," Eddie says, coming up with a plan. We follow Kate and Lolly as they push through people to show us a long line of people waiting along a hallway. I walk to the front of the line and as the door opens, I quickly push in but there's no Willow in there. I ignore the groans of the pissed off people waiting and we follow Kate to another area of the house where the second bathroom is situated. The line here is shorter but Logan pushes through this time to check and there's no sign of her.

"Did you check the bedrooms?" Eddie asks, and my face whips around to face him. His eyes widen at whatever he sees on my face. "She may have wandered in there by accident or to sleep or something buddy, chill."

"Did she have much to drink?" I ask the girls.

"Yeah she did. She was taking shots before we even left my house. She was in a funny mood and wanted to get wasted," Kate says, as my anger rages. The girl never bloody listens. She's always doing dumb shit, now she's who knows where.

"Should we split up?" Logan asks. I'm about to reply when the voice behind me speaks and it stops me dead in my tracks.

"Aww if it isn't big bad Sully coming to rescue his girl," Troy taunts. I'm in front of him so fast, I hold my forearm against his neck and make his eyes bulge.

"Where is she?" I calmly ask, even though I'm anything but calm.

"Let him go Sully," Buck says, as he tries to get me to back off but it ain't happening. A few of the other basketball players gather around to take in the show. Troy's hateful eyes stare into mine.

"Where the fuck is she?" I yell, and cause the room to go silent.

"Sully, ease up man," Logan softly whispers, but all it does is make me press harder against Troy's throat.

"Who are you looking for?" Dexter, one of the few guys on the team I can stand, asks.

"Willow?" Have you seen her?" Logan asks, as my focus is still on Troy.

"Uuuuhhh," Dexter drags out.

"Fuck man if you know, spit it out before he murders someone," Buck turns and talks to Dexter.

"Troy mentioned something about her being in the room he's crashing in tonight," Dexter says. My vision blurs for a second before I see red. Hands grab at me and pull me back as I lunge at Troy. Blood pours from his nose and lip and his eye is already swollen.

"Fuck, stop Sully. You've done enough damage," Logan says, but I don't even remember punching him. My throbbing hand proves otherwise. I stop fighting Eddie, Buck and Logan who are all restraining me.

"Which room is it?" I yell. Buck and Dexter leap into action and run up the stairs as I keep pace behind them. Logan yells out to Eddie to stay with Lolly and Kate as he follows after me.

"Move," Buck bellows through the hallway, and everyone steps to the side as they let us race past. He runs all the way to the last door, opens it and turns on the light. I rip into the room, and my eyes search everywhere but she's not there. The bed is untouched and she's not on the floor.

"Where is she?" Logan asks, as he enters. I gaze around, until I notice the door with the light shining underneath. I stride to it, and turn the knob but it won't budge.

"Shit it's locked. Willow?" I yell, as I pound on the door but there's no answer. I drop to the ground, peek through the gap at the bottom of the door and can see the material of a red dress on the ground but can't make out much else. I can't tell if it's Willow or not but whoever is in there isn't in good shape.

"Go ask the girls what colour Willow's dress is," I say to Dexter, and he dashes off.

"We need to get in there," I say to Buck and Logan, as I run my hands through my hair and panic starts to set in. My breaths come faster so I shake my head as now is not the time for a panic attack.

"Here, I'll try this," Buck says, as he pulls his wallet out of his back pocket. He takes out a credit card and jiggles the handle while he swipes his card to jimmy the lock open.

"Sully, what's wrong man?" Calm down. You're freaking me out," Logan whispers to me, and I notice my breathing is faster and louder. I raise my hands to my head and force deep breaths in and out as best I can.

"Panic attack," I manage to say to Logan, causing shock to register on his face.

"Deep breaths. I'm sure she's okay," he tells me. Dexter races back in the room with Kate, Lolly and Eddie on his heels now.

"Her dress is red," Kate tells me, forcing me to close my eyes tightly.

"Shit. It's her," I say, the panic consumes me as my hands tingle. "Fuck I'll break the door down. Buck watch out," I tell him.

"You can't. What if you hurt her?" Logan argues, and he's right. Damn it.

"Got it," Buck says, and I leap to the door as he opens it and my heart hits the floor and splits in two. I rush to her side and quickly examine the situation. She's got vomit all over herself. It's all over her dress and on the floor. I lift her head, push her hair off her face, and gently shake her to try and wake her.

"Willow?" I call, but there's no response. She's passed out cold.

"Shit, what do we do?" I turn to look at all of them for answers as I'm out of my depth.

"Should we call an ambulance?" Dexter asks, unsure of what to do. She's floppy in my hands and her skin is clammy. I check her pulse at her neck to see if it's still beating.

"Willow? Come on," I plead, as I shake her some more. I can't take it anymore and shake her a lot harder.

"Low, wake the fuck up now," I scream, causing some of the others to step back. Willow's eyes flicker open before she leans over and vomits all over me. I move her so she's over the toilet, but a good chunk got me and I'm going to reek from it. I hold her hair back while I rub circles on her back, and wait it out as she purges the alcohol from her system.

She stops, her head flops back, and her eyes barely open when she peeks at me.

"Did anyone hurt you?" I ask, but she shakes her head.

"Felt sick. Troy tried to come in but I locked myself in the toilet," she mumbles.

"Okay Low. You're safe now," I tell her.

"Sully?" she whispers, before her eyes close again.

"Yeah?" I ask, before adjusting her so I can cradle her in my arms.

"I wanna be stupid again," she mutters, making my heart jolt before she's out cold again. I turn around to find the others staring at me as I hold her effortlessly to my chest.

"Let's go," I tell the girls, Eddie and Logan. "Thanks," I say to Buck and Dexter, who nod at me as I hike Willow higher against me. I hold her tightly and make sure her dress is tucked tight underneath her so no one sees anything. The others lead the way and when the party goers see me carrying Willow, they move out of our way so we can get through the house faster. We make it back to the truck without seeing Troy, which I'm thankful for as I don't know what would have happened if I'd caught sight of him again.

"Where to?" Eddie asks.

"Let's go to mine. My parents won't care if we all crash there," Logan says, and the girls agree.

"We were supposed to crash at mine but I'll text my mum and tell her we are crashing at a friend's house," Kate tells us.

"Are you alright with her in the back?" Eddie asks.

"Yeah man. I don't wanna risk her spewing in your truck," I tell him. The girls jump in the front with Eddie.

"Here take her for a minute," I say to Logan, as he grabs hold of her. He holds her tightly while I climb into the truck bed then passes her carefully to me before he climbs in. Logan sits opposite me as Eddie drives away. Her soft snores reach my ears and I gaze at her to make sure she isn't vomiting or anything. I slide a finger across her forehead and move her fringe to get a better look at her face.

"When did this happen?" Logan asks, looking at me.

"What?"

"When did you fall for her?" he asks, and my heart sinks. I let out a sigh, not sure what to say so I start at the beginning.

"She's the girl I met at the party before I went away for the summer. She doesn't know it was me," I tell him, watching as his eyes widen. "It's a long story. I'll tell you later." Knowing I'll have to tell him everything now and hope he won't hold it against me.

The drive to Logan's is quiet and the street is peaceful as Eddie's truck parks in his driveway. Logan jumps out of the truck bed and holds his arms out for her so I can get out but I jump down, squeezing her to my chest so as not to jostle her too much. I don't like the thought of letting her go and don't like the feelings it brings out of me.

"Thanks Eddie," Logan says, as the girls hop out of the truck.

"Yeah thanks man," I say.

"No problem. I hope she's all right," he says. "I'll catch you guys later," he says, as he reverses his car out of the driveway and heads off home. The girls trail behind us as Logan unlocks his door and leads the way through his house. He walks into his room and he flicks the light on.

"Girls, you can take the bed. I've got a spare room Sully and I can crash in," he tells them, as they look around and take in his room. I stand and hold the unconscious girl in my arms, scared to release her. "Do either of you want some clothes to sleep in?" he asks the girls, but they both shake their heads.

"Willow could use a shower or something. She's stinking up the room already," Kate says, which has Logan laughing lightly.

"What should we do?" he asks. "Hose her down?" he jokes, as he smiles at me.

"She's not a damn dog," I snap, causing the smile to drop from his face.

"Shit Sully. Get a grip would you," he hisses at me, which makes the girls step back and sit on the bed.

"I can try to shower her," Kate says, as her eyes flick between Logan and I.

"Okay," Logan says. "I'll grab her some clothes and let my mum know I'm home and you guys are crashing here. Sully, show Kate where the bathroom is," he tells me.

I walk out of the room as Kate follows behind me. I stand back so she can open the bathroom door and we walk into the huge space. Logan's bathroom is bigger than my bedroom. I sit Willow on the vanity, pull my phone out of my back pocket and place it next to her.

"Did she have her phone on her?" I ask Kate. She steps forward and feels around the front of Willow's dress, avoiding the vomit until she finds Willow's small bag I didn't notice was slung over her. She peels it over her head, pulls out her phone and gives it to me. I take it from her fingers and type in the code to unlock it. Luckily she hasn't changed it as the screen brightens. My heart stills at what shines back at me. My name and number. She must have been about to call me before she passed out. Sighing, I make the screen go black before I place it next to my phone.

"How are we gonna do this?" Kate asks. The girl in my arms has barely moved at all since we found her. Logan enters, carrying some clothes with him and a handful of towels.

"What's the plan? Lolly's already gone to sleep," he tells us.

"Kate and I should be able to manage it," I tell Logan. We're gonna have to get Willow's dress off and Logan is not going to see her in her underwear. Over my dead body.

"Whatever you say man. I'll be in my room if you need me," he says, before he walks away and closes the door.

"Can you help me get her dress off her? I'll hop in the shower with her and hope we can get rid of as much vomit as possible." "Okay," Kate says. I move Willow so her body is turned into me and Kate can unzip her strapless dress. As she peels it away, she halts.

"Umm Sully she isn't wearing a bra?

"Shit," I mutter. "If this was you Kate, what would you want me to do?" I ask her.

"What do you mean?" she asks, as confusion crosses her face.

"If it was you this wasted covered in vomit, what would you want me to do?" I ask. Her eyes light up with understanding.

"Leave the dress on. We'll shower her with it on and I'll change her afterwards," she firmly states. I nod in agreement.

Kate opens the shower door, turns the water on and steps back out so as not to get wet. She steps back to me and peels Willow's heels off while I kick my own shoes off. I step into the shower stream, and let it soak through our clothes. She doesn't stir at all and I wonder if she needs a hospital.

"Can you grab Logan? I'll get him to carry her to the room and you can change her there," she nods, before she walks out. I use my hand to rub water over Willow's face gently. I put water in my hand and thread it through her hair strands as she's got vomit in her hair. I grab the shampoo from the built-in shelf on the shower wall, squirt it onto her hair and lather it.

"Damn it Low," I whisper, hating she let herself get in this state and I wasn't there to stop her. I've pretty much ignored her for weeks so I feel responsible for her drunken state. I remove the shower head from the wall and rinse her hair out, holding her the best I can with one hand. I spray her dress too and remove all the vomit visible to my eyes. I move the shower head to my other hand, quickly squirt a bit of shower gel on her collarbone and hope it takes some of the putrid smell from her skin.

Kate and Logan step into the room.

"Is she okay?" Logan asks.

"She hasn't even stirred man. Can you take her so Kate can change her in the other room?" I ask.

"Of course." He grabs one of the towels and opens the shower door. I transfer Willow to his arms and have to stop myself from grabbing her straight back. He wraps the huge towel around her. "I brought you some clothes so you can change too," he tells me, and I nod in thanks. They leave the room and a funny feeling washes over me as if they took a piece of me with them. I shake the feeling and peel my clothes off now I'm alone before quickly scrubbing body wash over me and my hair as well, hoping the remaining smell washes away. I turn off the water, dry myself and chuck my soaked clothes in the basket. I pull on Logan's t-shirt and shorts and hurry back to the room to find Logan waiting outside the closed door.

"Everything all right?"

"Yeah, Kate's changing her. You have got some explaining to do tomorrow," he tells me, as he crosses his arms over his chest and stares at me. I scrub a hand across my face before nodding. Kate opens the door before he can say anything else.

"She's decent," she tells us, taking Willow's soaked dress and towel to the bathroom. I step into the room and find Willow asleep on her side of the bed. She looks peaceful as if she's sleeping and not drunk out of her mind. Kate comes back into the room and steps over Lolly into the middle of the bed. One of them has placed a bucket on the floor in front of Willow in case she vomits some more.

"Come on Sully, let them sleep," Logan coaxes me from the door.

"Yeah I'll come soon," I tell him, as I drop my butt on the carpet beside Willow's side of the bed. Logan flicks off the light and the door closes. Kate shuffles around getting comfortable as I turn my head to watch Willow. Her face peeks out from the blanket they've covered her with. A soft glow through the curtains gives me enough light to see her face in the dark room. I sit and watch her serene face as long as I can before sleep takes hold.

"Sully," someone calls, which jolts me awake.

"Yeah?" My eyes open and I'm disorientated for a minute, as I find myself seated on the floor.

"It's me, sorry. Willow's making funny noises," Kate says from the bed. I turn onto my knees and inspect Willow as she moans and grunts.

"Willow?" I say, but her eyes are still firmly shut. I stand and flick on the lamp sitting on the bedside table. "She's going to vomit," I tell Kate, before grabbing Willow and pulling her onto the floor with me. "Willow?" I call again, and her eyes shutter open. I thrust her face over the bucket right before she heaves the contents of her stomach into it. Rubbing her back, I hold her hair back as she gets it all out. Kate jumps off the bed, walks out the door and returns a minute later with a partly wet towel.

"Here, use this to wipe her mouth," she tells me, as she hands it to me.

"Thanks," I tell her, as Willow continues to empty her stomach. It turns into a lot of dry heaving when there's nothing left. "If you can't sleep with this going on, I'm fine to watch her if you wanna go to the spare room where Logan is," I tell Kate, as she looks as exhausted as I am

"You sure?"

"Yeah, I've got her. Go out the door, turn right and it's the next door," I tell her. She leaves and gently closes the door behind her. Willow's heaving eventually stops. I use the dampened towel Kate gave me and wipe her mouth. Her eyes are still closed so I'm not even sure if she realised she was vomiting.

I pull her into my lap and hold her against me for a few minutes, her gentle breaths return once again as she sleeps. I stand and tuck her into bed, before taking the bucket and tipping it into the toilet. I quickly rinse it out before I take it back to the room. She hasn't stirred so I sit back on the carpet to keep a watchful eye over her.

Drifting off again, I hear my name called out.

"Sully." This time it's Willow's voice.

"Willow?" I ask.

"Sully," she groans, but I realise she's still asleep when she doesn't say anything else. I tuck her hair behind her ear and the selfish voice in my head speaks to me. I climb around Willow, and lie on top of the blankets so as not to disturb Lolly who hasn't stirred since her head hit the pillow. I wrap my arm around Willow, wiggle my other arm under her head and bring her back to my front as I spoon her. I leave the light on this time, as I have a feeling she probably will need the bucket again. I know I shouldn't be doing this but this girl pulls me in with her power over me. I love it and hate it all at once and I'm not sure what emotion will win the battle in the end.

Chapter Fourteen

Willow

My heavy eyes struggle to open. The quiet talking hits my ears before I can scan my surroundings.

"Kate?" I softly call out. My throat is dry and my tongue heavy in my furry mouth. The banging of my head causes me to wince against the light shining in through the foreign window.

"I'm here," she says, before she steps into view. Crouching in front of me she looks me over. "How are you feeling?"

"Like a truck ran over me. Where are we?" I ask, scanning the room while trying not to move my head which isn't an easy feat.

"Logan's."

"Good morning," I hear, before a yawn greets me from the other side of the bed.

"Hey Lolly," Kate says.

"Why are we at Logan's?" I ask, as my head hits the pillow again and I close my eyes.

"Because you got drunk and we lost you. I rang Logan because we were worried and I didn't know what to do," she explains.

"Ugh did he come to my rescue?" I ask, embarrassment taking over. She sits on the end of the bed by my feet and crosses her legs.

Lolly sits next to her and pulls a pillow into her lap so she can hug it. "What?" I ask, their creepy smiles are weirding me out.

"Logan did come to your rescue but I wouldn't say he was the main culprit," she says, wiggling her brows at me while Lolly giggles.

"What are you saying? You're not making much sense."

"Sully," Lolly squeaks out, and both their smiles widen as my face drops in horror.

"What? He came to find me?"

"Gosh girl, he stormed through the house like he'd burn the damn thing to the ground if he couldn't find you," Kate says, fanning herself.

"He did?" I ask, finding it hard to believe.

"You know how he always has this bored expression on his face like nothing can penetrate it?"

"Yeah?"

"Well shit girl, I think you broke him," Kate says, making the pair of them laugh.

"Broke him how?"

"He beat the crap out of Troy thinking he'd done something to you. When we did find you, you were behind a locked door and I swear I nearly cried looking at his face. He looked so distraught when he couldn't get to you. When we got the door open, you were covered in vomit and he picked you up and it didn't even phase him when you spewed all over him," she explains.

"Ugh I didn't?" I moan, wishing the world would swallow me whole.

"Yeah sorry girl but you sure did." I slap my forehead, mortified as I sit and copy Kate's position.

"Did anything else happen?" I ask Kate.

"We had to shower you because you were covered in vomit. Don't worry your dress stayed on and he was so cute about the whole situation. Oh I changed you by the way so no one saw you naked except me. Sorry," she says, shrugging a shoulder like it's no big deal, while my face burns. "He sat by the bed while you slept. He was worried you might vomit again, which you did by the way. He sent me to go sleep in the other room and he stayed and looked after you," she tells me.

"Oh my gosh I'm so embarrassed. Where is he now?" I whisper, in case he's close by and can hear me.

"He left," Lolly fills in.

"What?" Kate and I say in unison.

"Yeah it must have been an hour or two ago because I woke up and he was spooning you. When he realised I was awake, he freaked out, and jumped out of bed. He told me to go back to sleep so I did and he walked out of the room," she tells me.

"I don't remember any of it," I whine, wishing I could remember him holding me at least.

"Yeah I'd be gutted if I couldn't remember being held by Sully too," Kate says, her damn brows wagging at me again.

"Shut up," I laugh, throwing the pillow behind me at her. She falls back on the bed, clutching it as she laughs. Knocking on the door has us quieting before Logan's head pops around it.

"You girls okay? Willow?" he asks, coming into the room. Kate's cheeks turn pink as Logan comes to stand beside her but I move my focus to him.

"Hey, I'm so sorry about last night. The girls filled me in. I hope I didn't wreck your night or anything?"

"Nah, you didn't wreck anything. I was happy to help. Glad you're okay but can you do me a favour and not drink so much again?" he asks, and now it's my turn for my cheeks to pinken.

"Yea sorry. I was being dumb."

"Be careful in the future, especially with alcohol," he tells me, and for some reason I feel like I've failed him.

"I will."

"Are you feeling okay?" he asks.

"Yeah but I have a killer headache brewing and my throat is dry."

"I can help with that," he says, before leaving the room. He comes back a minute later and hands me a glass of water and two painkillers. I quickly swallow them, being an obedient patient which earns me a smile from him.

"Thanks."

"No worries. Now are you girls ready to head home? I can drop you off or you can hang here longer if you want? My parents have left to go to some luncheon so the house is empty," he says, looking around at each of us.

Kate answers first saying, "I don't mind hanging for a bit. I've got nothing better to do if you guys wanna stay too?" I glance at Lolly who nods.

"Okay I guess we are staying," I state.

"Awesome. Movie?" Logan asks, looking around again.

"Sure," I say. "Where's your bathroom?"

"Oh come and I'll show you. You probably don't remember being in it last night when you were out for the count," Logan tells me, walking away. I fling the blanket off and follow after him.

"Am I wearing your clothes?" I ask him, as I meet him in the hallway.

"Uh yeah your dress was pretty trashed. Kate changed you though so your modesty is all intact," he tells me, smiling.

Wringing my hands in front of me I look at the ground, "Uh is Sully coming back?" The silence stretches so I look at Logan's face and catch the smirk on his face.

"Is he the reason we didn't work?" he asks, with a smile still on his face.

"Not at first. I honestly think we are better suited as friends. You're a great guy Logan, it's just...." my words trail off

"I'm not Sully," he finishes, making my face turn red I'm sure. He laughs at my expression. "It's fine Willow. It's hard to compete with the stone cold exterior of his. It drives the girls wild." My face drops at the thought of other girls chasing him and Logan must notice because he backtracks, "Not that he's got any girls chasing him at the moment. No girls. Nada, Nope. None."

"I got it Logan," I laugh, grabbing his forearm to halt his rambling.

"Okay. Good. I'll let you go," he says, moving out of the way so I can pass him to go to the bathroom. "Oh and I'll message Sully to come back if you like?"

I nod, smiling before walking to the bathroom.

"Oh and Willow?" I turn back to him, with raised brows waiting.

"Take it easy on Sully. He may act like this hard guy who doesn't let anything affect him but he's not as tough as he makes himself out to be," he mumbles.

"Okay," I whisper. He nods and leaves the room.

I relieve myself before washing my hands and look in the mirror. My hair is all over the place. I use my fingers to brush it the best I can. My eyes feel dry from falling asleep with my contacts in. I pop them both out and chuck them in the bin. Grabbing some toothpaste on my finger I brush my teeth the best I can. Twice. My mouth feels gross and I hate to think how much I vomited. Cupping water in my hands, I rub it over my face, freshening up a bit.

Feeling better, I catch sight of the clothes I'm wearing. A huge black t-shirt and a pair of shorts have been rolled over on the top to hold them in place. My underwear is missing but I'm guessing they got wet with my dress.

I guess this is the best it's gonna get today. I leave the bathroom and make my way back to the bedroom but voices call to me from downstairs. I change direction and head to the living room instead. Logan's house layout is similar to my stepdad's house. I still haven't been able to settle in their house. I miss my dad but I promised I would stick out this year with my mum. I would be off to college, wherever I decide to go, so I wouldn't be at either parents house soon enough.

Lolly, Kate and Logan are all sprawled out on the L shaped couch so I sit on the side where I can stretch my legs out. Logan's huge eighty five inch television screen hangs in the centre of the room. Logan flicks through the latest movies asking what preferences we have. I tell them to put on whatever as I'm not fussed. We end up with the latest action movie. Logan leaves the couch to go make popcorn and Kate goes to help him. Lolly does a side nod to where they disappeared into the kitchen. My brows pull together but she flicks her head a couple of times and smiles at me.

"Kate and Logan?" I mouth at her, and she nods excitedly before a giggle bubbles out of her. My eyes snap to where they went and I realise I missed a lot last night. They walk back in several minutes later and there are no clues to signal something is going on between them. Kate hands me a bowl of popcorn and a can of coke while Logan hands some to Lolly. When they take their seats on the couch, they sit closer than I'd expect them to. Well they are both single and they'd make a cute couple.

Logan presses play on the movie and we're all quiet as we munch on our snacks and drink our sodas.

"Do you know where my bag is guys?" I call out.

"Oh it's in Logan's room on the side table next to where you were sleeping. Your phone is there too," Kate says. I leave the couch and walk up the stairs to find my bag. My phone is useless, the battery has died so I leave it there and grab my spare pair of glasses. Putting the black frames on I'm thankful I take them everywhere with me. I decided this year to wear my contacts with it being a new school and all. I thought I could reinvent myself but my eyes are so sore from falling asleep with the contacts in, I need some time without them. I have my eye drops too so I quickly drop a couple in each eye before placing the frames back on my face.

Walking down the stairs I take the seat where I was before. They are all entranced with the movie until Logan speaks.

"I didn't know you wore glasses Willow."

"Oh yeah. I usually wear contacts. My eyes are hurting a bit because I fell asleep with my contacts in so I'm wearing my glasses," I tell him.

"Lucky you had them on you," he says.

"Yeah another reminder not to get so drunk next time too," I tell him, shaking my head at my own recklessness.

"Good plan. The smell of vomit will haunt me for a week," he teases.

"Shut up," I squeal, lunging over to hit him.

"It was pretty bad," Lolly joins in, making us all laugh before Logan's phone dings loudly. He checks it and lets out a huff at whatever he reads. He types out a reply before he tosses his phone to the side. It dings again and he repeats the process. Whoever he's messaging is making him mad. He catches me watching him and winces.

"Sorry I don't think he's gonna come," he whispers, so the girls won't hear. I shrug my shoulders at him as my stomach drops. I don't know why Sully took off this morning without even talking to me after they all said he took care of me. Why won't he face me? It's been weeks now since he made me come and I felt like we were getting somewhere but there was always part of him holding himself back. He shut me out and ignored me more than usual. He gives me whiplash with his constant changing of moods.

Part of the reason I got so drunk last night was to forget about him. I wanted a night to forget and be free. Well I sure got a night of forgetting. I can't even remember arriving at the party or what happened afterwards. When Kate was telling me what happened, I was sceptical but with all three of them saying Sully acted like a he-man then I've gotta believe it. I wish I could have witnessed it for myself.

Losing myself in my thoughts, movie forgotten, my hungover body pulls me back to sleep. Distant murmurings sound in the background as I drift in and out of sleep, not fully able to relax but managing to rest at least.

"Willow, are you cool to stay for another movie?" Kate asks, shaking my shoulder to wake me.

"Yeah I'm happy to stay as long as you are. Wake me when you want to go if I'm still sleeping," I tell her.

"I will," she says, smiling. I wriggle around, getting comfortable again.

"Willow, do you want a blanket?" Logan asks, popping his head out from the kitchen.

"Yeah I'll keep it here in case I get cold," I tell him. He walks to a cupboard by the bottom of the stairs, pulls a fluffy grey blanket out and puts it next to me on the couch. "Thanks," I tell him.

"You're welcome. Do you want a drink or anything?"

"Nah I'm good," I tell him, burrowing into the couch and closing my eyes again.

Muffled voices pull me out of my sleep, but my tired eyes won't open, trying to drift off again. Someone lays a warm blanket over me, before the couch jostles as someone sits next to me. I want to pull myself out of sleep to see who it is but my tired body has other ideas, pulling me back into my slumber.

Gentle strokes through my hair feel nice as I wake from my sleep. My head lays sideways on a firmer surface than the couch. I rub the side of my face against it, trying to find the most comfortable spot and the stroking stills. I flutter my eyes open, and there is Sully, hair hanging around his face as he looks at me. I bolt upright as my face was rubbing awkwardly on his thigh, close to his crotch.

We sit silently looking at each other as my deep breaths fill the silence. I notice the television is off and the rest of the room is quiet. I notice Lolly is fast asleep on the other side of the couch.

"Kate and Logan are out on the back verandah talking," he tells me, knowing I was wondering where they'd gone.

"When did you get here?" I ask.

"About an hour ago," he says and I assume it was him putting the blanket over me. He pushes the centre of my glasses so they sit properly on my face. "I like your glasses," he tells me. My cheeks blush at the compliment.

"Thanks. I owe you a big thank you for taking care of me last night and for rescuing me," I tell him, dropping my gaze to my lap. He lifts my chin in what I've realised is fast becoming a habit with the two of us. I will admit a thrill runs through me whenever he does it. Staring into my eyes, his own flicker back and forth for a few seconds before he talks.

"I don't ever want you being so dumb again. Do you hear me?" he scolds. I nod gently as he still has his hand under my chin. "I mean it, Low. You have no idea what..... Seeing you like....how I felt....," his words trail off, one incomplete thought runs into another, his frustration leaking out. I latch on to his final sentence.

"How did you feel?"

"Scared damn it. I felt scared. Is that what you want to hear? I was scared something had happened to you and I was too late to get to you. You were behind a locked door and when I did get to you, you were lifeless Low. I've never been so shit scared in my life," he growls at me, his voice rising with his anger. "Don't ever do it again. I don't care if I'm around or not. Don't you dare put yourself in the same situation again," he's yelling now, and I can't help the tears dropping onto my cheek. His temper always does something to me. It's as if it calls to the angry part of myself I have buried deep inside.

"I wouldn't have drunk so much if you'd talked to me instead of ignoring me for weeks," I yell back.

"Don't put this on me. You're the one who drank too much. You can't blame me for your decisions," he yells.

"Well I can blame you for making me feel like this. It drove me to drink," I fire back.

"Grow up. You can't have a tantrum every time things don't go your way," he huffs.

"And what about you huh? You didn't like what was happening between us so you chose to ignore me, without even talking to me or thinking about how it would make me feel after what happened with us. Well you know what? It made me feel cheap and used," I scream, puffing out of breath as I hold his gaze.

The fire behind his eyes ebbs and the anger drips away. He reaches for me but I smack his hands away. He continues to try to grab me and I keep smacking him until I smack harder. He manages to pull me into his chest as I fight.

"I told you I'm not worth your tears, sweetheart," he says, wiping my tears with his thumbs. I cry against his chest as he holds me against him.

"Stop pushing me away and making me cry," I force out between sobs.

"I'm sorry," he whispers into my ear, before he kisses the tip and cradles me to his chest until I stop crying. When I finish crying, he cups both my cheeks and holds my face. He uses his thumbs to wipe away the remaining moisture under my glasses. Gazing into my eyes, he pulls my face forward and I close my eyes, anticipating his lips meeting mine.

"Is the coast clear? You guys wanna watch one more movie?" Logan's voice breaks our moment, as I jump back out of Sully's reach.

"Yeah one more won't hurt. What's the time?" I ask.

"It's three o'clock," Logan says, looking at his watch. Logan and Kate squish back on the couch forcing Sully to move closer to me. Logan picks something, asking if it's okay with everyone. I can't even answer or tell what the movie is as I'm too engrossed by Sully being in my space. He wraps an arm around me, pulling me back to place my head where it was resting on his leg. I snuggle and get comfortable as he adjusts the blanket so it covers my body and his legs which lie on the

94

couch beside me. We settle in to watch the movie and this time I try my best to stay awake to enjoy this moment with him.

Chapter Fifteen

Sully

I've tried not to push Willow away. It's hard. My mind and heart keep fighting this inner battle and I'm waiting to see who will be named victorious. My mind always comes back to how I don't deserve this sweet girl. Often I will look at her and wonder what it is she sees in me. What is it about me that holds her attention?

It's been weeks since I confessed everything to Logan. He wanted me to confess to Willow and tell her I'm the guy from the party. I told him how we had met in the dark and she didn't know it was me as she knows that guy by Reed. I told him it was a moot point now since we were kind of together already. Though I have no idea what that actually means.

I'm not sure if she suspects there's a war raging in my head. She never says anything but her face can be easy to read at times. Her brows furrow when she assesses me, trying to figure out the inner workings of my mind. It's a wasted effort on her part because even I don't have the answers in my head she desperately seeks.

Logan is circling around Kate as well. He hasn't come out and told Willow or Kate how he feels but it's obvious. You can see it in the way he talks to her and always wants to be around her. He's biding his time, not wanting to get friend zoned like he did with Willow. He reassures me Willow never looked at him the way she looks at me. I have to believe it means something, right?

We spent the day, the four of us, at Logan's house watching movies again. Willow insisted on some romance to combat the action movies Logan loves. I don't care for movies usually as I've never been able to sit still long enough to enjoy them but with Willow, I could sit around doing nothing and it would feel like the most productive use of my time.

I walked Willow home and now I'm on my way to my own house. Thoughts of Willow and how she looked today in her navy blue sundress fill my head. Her glasses framing her bright blue eyes is probably my favourite look on her. It's with these thoughts an unannounced smile crosses my face and again Willow distracts me from reality.

The familiar creak of the verandah as I walk up the stairs should register with my brain that I'm home but it doesn't. Turning the brass handle I let myself in. You would think the familiar musky smell would wipe the smile from my face but it doesn't. No, it's the blow to my temple I don't see coming which takes my smiles away, as I'm distracted by her again. Home sweet home is what crosses my mind as my vision blurs.

"You piece of shit." A swift kick to the ribs as I fall to the ground has me grunting. "What have you got to smile about, you good for nothing sack of crap." Another kick forces the wind from my lungs. Breathe in. Breathe out. My hazy vision from the first knock to my head leaves my movements lethargic. I cover my face the best I can but not before I catch sight of my mother's feet as they walk past. Not slowing, not stopping, not concerned. Just their normal everyday pace as her feet take her along the hallway and away from where her husband beats his kid. Her kid. Their kid.

"You'll never amount to nothing. You hear me? You aren't worth shit." The stale smell of tobacco and beer lingers as he hovers over me, laying punch after punch to my barely covered face. Breathe in. Breathe out. "You little fucker," he shouts, as his foot reels back and he stomps on my ribs. The pain from the blow is excruciating but it's not as if he cares. "You're pathetic," his voice grows distant, as his footsteps do too.

Breathing is hard now. Short, shallow breaths are all I can manage. Ringing in my ears disorientates me longer than I like but I am able to stand. Opening the door I came through, I exit and flee. I stagger along the footpath under the cover of night making my way to where I feel safe. I've run this route so many times I know it like the back of my hand. It's just this time it's not Logan's house I stand in front of. It's Willow's.

With one hand holding my ribs, the other fumbles through my jeans finding my phone. I scroll to her number and dial.

"Sully?" her small voice answers, and my body wants to take a deep breath in reaction to the sound but my body rejects it, causing me to wince in pain.

"Low, can you come outside please?" I beg, knowing the sound of my voice is a sign something isn't right.

"What's wrong?" She senses something is horribly wrong, panics for a second before she hurries to get to me. I drop onto her porch steps to wait and focus on breathing tiny breaths instead as they don't hurt as much as the bigger ones. The door flings open and lets the light from inside shine on me as she gasps. I drop the phone from my ear now she's here and she crouches in front of me. "Sully?" she whispers, as the two outlines of her sway in front of me. I blink, trying to clear it but my head is still blurry from his first punch. "Was it your dad?" she asks, and I nod but I can't be sure because I'm so sore and stiff. "Come, let's get you inside. My parents have gone out to dinner so no one will see you," she tells me, grabbing my forearm and helping me stand.

I stagger forward as my feet hit the porch but she slides herself under the arm not holding my ribs and takes my weight as I'm struggling to stay upright. We slowly make it into her room. She follows my lead and slows to my pace, helping me to the bed.

"What do I do?" she begs, and my droopy eyes lift to hers. Tears slide down her face, dripping off the end of her chin.

She's so beautiful and I want to say it out loud but instead I croak, "Not worth your tears," which makes them flow faster. I wish she could see I'm not worthy of her and I never will be. I've never been shown kindness behind the walls of my own home so it's a struggle to believe a person would offer me kindness for no other reason than she wants to and she can.

My short, sharp breaths fill the space as I fight to keep my eyes open to watch her. She breaks my gaze, fiddling with her phone before she holds it to her ear.

"Logan! It's Sully. He's at mine. His dad beat him pretty bad. Can you come? I don't know what to do. Okay, see you soon." Her words rush into the phone, as I realise she's called for help. No one apart from Logan has ever helped me. Or hurt for me. "Logan's coming. You'll be okay," she reassures me, as I sit clinging to my painful rib. She sits beside me, the bed jiggling with her weight. Her hand on my thigh is the only sign of her touch. She gently squeezes it to reassure me. We sit side by side as my harsh breaths break the silence of the room.

A distant knocking makes her leap from the bed and rush from the room before Logan appears in my view moments later. I blink a few times to try and clear my vision.

"Where bud?" he asks the familiar words. He's helped me so many times over the years and sometimes I can talk, sometimes I can't. All he asks now is where the injuries are so he knows how to help me. My best friend. I've loaded so much onto his shoulders over the years and I can't help as guilt churns my stomach at doing it again.

"Ribs, face, my head. He got me good in the temple. Vision blurry," I croak out. He nods as I talk, recalling all the google knowledge he's had to accumulate over the years to help me. He's probably bandaged more injuries than a first year paramedic.

"I reckon you're concussed. Did you vomit?" he asks.

"No," I tell him.

"I'm gonna feel your head okay?" he tells me, but I don't answer, letting him do his thing. His gentle fingers probe around my head, scanning for lumps or bumps but he finds none.

"You said your vision is blurry. Are you feeling dizzy?"

"Not now. I feel sluggish," I tell him, as my limbs feel heavy now.

"Let me check your ribs." I drop my hand away for him so he can lift my shirt. Willow's gasp reminds me I'm at her place and not his this time. She was out of my view so I'd forgotten for a minute. "Willow,

99

can you grab some ice packs please?" Logan directs her way. Her steps fade. "Bud you're bad this time. Do you wanna go to the hospital?" he whispers to me, while Willow is out of ear shot.

"No," I say. He lets out a heavy sigh before Willow's steps sound again and she thrusts some ice packs at Logan.

"I'm not sure if your ribs are broken or not, so do you want to sit or lie down? What do you think would hurt less?" he asks me.

"I'm unsure but it doesn't hurt as bad at the moment," I tell them.

"Okay how about we get you seated against the headboard so you can try to rest?"

"Okay," I reply. My sluggish feet try to kick off my shoes but I can't. Willow catches on to what I'm trying to do and she unties my shoelaces and slowly peels my shoes off for me. She moves them by her door as Logan helps me stand and moves me gently so I can sit in the middle of the bed. Willow puffs pillows on either side of me, while Logan hands me the ice packs to hold against my ribs. Willow scoots in as close as she can get without hurting me and places an ice pack against the side of my head.

"Have you got some ibuprofen?" Logan asks Willow. "Yeah. It's in my bathroom in the cupboard behind the mirror," she directs him. He goes into the bathroom and comes back out with a glass of water and dumps the two pills into my palm. Flinging them back, I gulp the water to swallow the pills, hoping they can give me some relief from the pain.

"Try to rest Sully. You're safe now," he tells me.

"Yeah you're safe Sully. We won't let anything harm you." Willow's soft voice has me closing my eyes and drifting to sleep.

Willow

Sully's soft snores fill the space as I continue to hold the ice pack against his split cheekbone. My tears dried a while ago when they ran out. My heart physically hurts for him. I don't understand how his own father could do this to him and not care he's hurting him.

"How long has this been going on?" I ask Logan.

"Since before I met him when we were thirteen," he says, as he breathes out a sigh. He sits on the other side of Sully holding the ice packs to Sully's ribs because when he fell asleep his hands went limp and dropped them.

"Has he asked for help?"

"He tried once but nothing ever happened except him getting beaten worse the next time so he stopped trying to seek help. He usually escapes to his room if he can now but if he knows he's in bad shape, he makes his way to my place," he tells me.

"You're a good friend," I tell Logan. I'm glad Sully has had someone in his corner all these years and can't imagine if he had no one to help him through all this.

"You're good for him too, you know."

"I don't feel like I've helped much at all tonight," I confess.

"I'm not talking about tonight, I mean in general. Sully's always been stuck behind this stone cold exterior and it's hard for anyone to break through but you soften his edges. He smiles more than I've ever seen him smile and he's happier. To what his usual sense of happiness is anyway," he tells me.

"I don't think we are talking about the same Sully. I still don't see him smile often."

"You're not looking hard enough. They are there."

"I doubt it," I say, and roll my eyes at him.

"Hey, I mean it. He seems lighter lately. Trust me when I say it's your doing, not mine," he says, removing the ice from Sully's ribs. "You got any more ice packs?"

"Yeah, I'll go grab some," I tell him, taking the one he holds out for me. I take them to the kitchen, place them in the freezer to cool again before walking into the bathroom where our first aid kit is. I grab two more of the disposable ice packs and give them a squeeze to set off the chemical reaction to make them cold. By the time I'm back upstairs with the boys they feel ice cold in my hands. Handing one to Logan, he places it back on Sully's ribs as his head rests backwards against the headboard. I take in his serene face covered in cuts and bruises. I wrap the ice pack in a face cloth before laying it against the opposite side of his jaw this time.

"You should try to rest too. It's getting late," Logan tells me.

"I'll ice this part of his face and I'll close my eyes for a bit. Are you gonna rest too?" I ask.

"You rest first and I'll wake you after a bit to switch and we can take turns keeping watch on him and switching the ice around. I don't want his face to be too swollen tomorrow."

"Sounds like a good plan."

"It's nice to have someone to do this with. Don't get me wrong, I'm not complaining and I love Sully, but it's nice not to have to worry about him alone."

"I know what you mean. It's been hard on you too. Well I'm here now and happy to help," I tell him.

"Okay, pass your ice pack and you get some rest now. I'll wake you when I feel sleepy," he tells me. I pass over the ice pack and snuggle next to Sully, resting my head half on his thigh where he isn't injured because I don't want to cause him any more pain. He could be bruised on his legs for all I know but I can't see because of his jeans so I wiggle my head off him not wanting to hurt him if he is in fact bruised there too. I let the pain for what he's been through wash over me and as I close my eyes, a few tears escape. Even though Sully's repeated words, "Not worth your tears," run through my head, I can't help but feel I would give him all my tears if they could keep him safe.

Chapter Sixteen

Sully

A dull ache in my side makes my eyes blink open. Turning makes me wince from the pain. My body feels stiff. I inspect my surroundings and realise I'm sitting and Willow's head is resting on my thigh. I gently slide the hair away from her face so as not to wake her. Snores on my other side catch my attention. Logan sleeps with his back to me. Breathing out a sigh, guilt builds in my stomach at them having to tend to me. It's bad enough Logan constantly helps me but now I've dragged Willow into my mess too.

My head swirls but it's still foggy from the blow I received. I remember wanting to feel safe and my feet must have brought me to Willow's house. It's still painful to breathe too deeply so I focus on keeping them short before I close my eyes and drift back to sleep. My hand rests on Willow's shoulder, holding her to me.

Voices talking drag me from my sleep. I'm not sure how much time has passed since I last opened my eyes.

"Hey Sully. How are you feeling?" Logan asks, standing beside the side of the bed.

"Like I got hit by a train," my cracked voice says, as a yawn takes over. Willow appears from the bathroom holding a glass of water out to me.

"Here. More pain killers," she tells me, dropping two pills into my palm.

"Thank you," I say, as I pop the pills in my mouth before draining the glass. She takes it from my fingers and walks back to the bathroom. "What's the time?" I ask, turning my head to Logan. Pain slices my side but I hold in my reaction, not wanting to give Logan anything else to worry about.

"It's after twelve now. I've gotta get going because I have a shift at the diner but can you do me a favour and stay here to rest for one more night. Willow said her parents left again this morning and won't be back until tomorrow night," he tells me. I take in my best friend. The worry lines cross his forehead as his eyes wince at me, waiting for my reply.

"Yeah I can do that man." The small smile on his face indicates I said the right thing. I hide out at Logan's house whenever I'm in a bad condition so for him to worry about me this much, I must look bad.

"Sweet man. I'll check in later but I'd say you're in good hands with Willow. I gotta go."

"Thanks man," I tell him, before he pops his head through the open bathroom door where Willow is. They talk for a minute before Logan turns around to face me.

"I'm headed home now so I'll grab you some of my clothes to change into on my way to work."

"Appreciate it," I tell him, before he waves goodbye and leaves. The sound of the front door closing sounds throughout the house. Willow pops her head back out of the bathroom.

"I'm gonna have a shower. Do you need anything?"

"No. I'm good for now."

"Okay. I won't be long," she tells me, before she closes the bathroom door. The sound of the shower water turning on pricks my ears. I wish I wasn't in this helpless state because right now I'm highly aware of the fact Willow is getting naked behind the door, twenty steps from where I sit.

I try to wriggle myself over but the pain in my ribs is still as strong as it was when I woke up. My head pounds in my ears as well. I've been hit hard enough in the head before so I've experienced a concussion. Rest is what I need so I take Logan's advice and close my eyes again. The sun shining through the window doesn't help my headache either.

The shower water shuts off but I keep my eyes closed, not opening them until the door squeaks. Willow's wet hair hangs around her face and she's wearing her glasses today. She's got a pink t-shirt and some light blue jean shorts on. We stare at each other until the knocking at the front door can be heard.

"It's probably Logan," she says. I nod and she dashes out of the room. A minute later she's back carrying a plastic bag. "Here's some clothes if you want to shower and change."

"Thanks Low," I whisper. I manoeuvre my legs off the bed but this time I can't hide the pain streaking across my face.

"Hey easy," she urges, as she rushes to my side. Crouching in front of me, she looks into my face and I can see sadness for me radiating behind her eyes. She's not good at hiding it. "Do you think a bath might be better?" she suggests.

"Yeah. The heat on my ribs might help loosen them, they feel a bit stiff now," I tell her. She nods before walking back into the bathroom. She turns on the water quickly before she's back by my side.

"Come on I'll help you," she says, hopping under my arm on the opposite side to my hurt ribs. I press my weight onto her to steady myself as I stand. Hobbling to the bathroom, the bath is still filling when we get there. "Can you get in alright?" she asks, lowering me to sit on the side of the porcelain.

"I should be fine," I tell her. She shuts the water off before walking out to her room and coming back in with her chair from her desk, placing it beside the bath.

"I'll sit here to be sure," she says. I nod before I undo the button of my jeans and lower the zip. Her eyes widen while she watches me undress. My dick twitches, entranced by her. I stand on wobbly feet and manage to push my jeans and stomp on them as I try to wrangle my feet out. "Let me help," she offers.

"No," I shout, causing her to step back in alarm. "Sorry. I already feel helpless enough, please don't get on your knees for me," I softly say, letting my walls go for a minute and being vulnerable with the girl who has stolen my heart. It shouldn't be this way. Her helping me. It shouldn't fucken be this way.

"Okay," is all she replies, as we both stand there breathing heavily. I continue to struggle to get my jeans off but she holds her ground, doing what I asked and not helping. I finally get my feet out, and am now standing in front of her in my boxers and t-shirt. I realise with the pain in my ribs I'm gonna need her help. Taking a deep breath, I push the unwanted feelings swirling in me away.

"Could you help with my t-shirt?" I ask, as my eyes drop to the floor.

"Sure." Her apple scent from her shampoo invades my senses. I lower my hand I've been keeping on my ribs, holding them as if they might break. Who knows, maybe they are already broken. She slides her fingers under my shirt and makes quick work of removing it all while avoiding my sore rib. She glances at my chest and the painful expression crosses her face as she catches sight of my ribs for the first time. My fingers take her hand in mine to reassure her.

"I'm okay," I say, but she shakes her head as the tears pool along her lashes. "Come here," I sigh, and pull her gently into my embrace. She comes willingly but keeps her arms at her sides. I tilt her face to look at me with my knuckles under her chin. "You can hug me back you know," I tease, giving her a genuine smile.

"I don't want to hurt you."

"You could never hurt me sweetheart," I tell her, as I lean and press my lips gently to hers. She wraps her arms loosely around me and I rest my cheek on top of her hair, breathing in the apple scent of her shampoo. It's true, she could never hurt me physically but now I fear for my heart. She alone holds the key to hurt me.

I reluctantly let her go and she does the same. I use her shoulder for balance as I lift one leg into the tub followed by the other. The hot water stings my feet but I lower myself slowly, needing the heat to loosen my muscles. Willow offers her forearm so I grip it while I gingerly lower myself. Releasing a hiss, I sink under the water and sit while I stretch my legs out in front of me.

"You okay?" Willow's voice pulls me from my thoughts and I glance at her before I nod. Forcing myself to take a deeper breath, it has me wincing as the pain is still there. Wishful thinking had me hoping the pain may have magically subsided within the last few minutes of me being in the bath.

"I'll loosen up soon," I tell her. "Could you dim the lights? The brightness isn't good for my head with the concussion."

"Of course." She jumps off her chair and flicks the switch off by the door and suddenly we are bathed in dimness which feels much better.

"Thank you," I tell her. She takes my fingers in hers and squeezes.

"We've got some arnica cream I can look for after you're out to help with the bruising." Her soft voice drifts over me as my body relaxes in the warmth. I sink lower, and close my eyes.

"Sounds perfect," I reply, as all my body wants to do is rest. Willow's fingers continue to grasp mine between hers as my mind slowly drifts away.

"Sully?" Willow's voice gently calls to me, waking me. I startle at the feel of water around me. "You're in the bath. Sorry you drifted off and I let you rest but the water is getting cold now."

"Sorry."

"Don't be sorry. It's fine. Let's get you out." She pulls the plug out and drains the water. She holds out both hands for me to take and I use her to balance as I pull myself to stand. My ribs are a dull ache now so the bath definitely helped. She continues holding my hands as I step over the rim onto the bath mat. She releases my hands before she grabs a fluffy white towel by the sink and holds it out to me. I wrap it around me the best I can. "Will you be okay getting changed?" she asks.

"Yeah, I'll manage," I tell her.

"I'll go hunt in the cupboard for the arnica cream. Yell out if you need me." She steps out of the room and closes the door behind her. I lower myself onto the seat she was using. The plastic bag with Logan's clothes sits by the sink. Using one hand, I scrub my hair to dry the wet ends. Luckily most of it is still dry. Rubbing the towel across my body as gently as possible, I dry myself the best I can. I lift my butt to peel my now soaked boxers off and use my feet to get them off. With heavy steps I make it to the sink, and pull out what Logan bought for me. There are a couple t-shirts, some boxers, a pair of shorts and a pair of grey sweat pants. Clutching the pants in my hand I stumble back to the chair. Placing the towel on the seat, I sit and wiggle my feet into the holes and I'm able to pull them to cover myself as they hang low on my waist.

"You alright Sully?" Willow calls through the door.

"You can come in," I call back, and she pushes the door open. Her chest heaves with the deep inhale she takes while looking at my naked chest.

"I got the arnica," she says, holding the tube of cream in her hand. "I can rub some on before I help you with your t-shirt."

She steps forward and squeezes a generous amount onto her fingertips. The cold temperature of her fingers makes me wince as she slowly rubs small circles over my ribs gently so as not to hurt me. She adds more cream diligent in covering the whole bruised area.

"I'll put some on your face too," she says, and I nod. She closes in on my space, adding more cream to her fingers. Her soft touch slides over my cheekbone and my jaw, working the cream into my skin. She does the other side of my face too, adding more to my temple and around my eye. Screwing the lid back on, she picks one of the t-shirts out of the bag and pulls it over my head and arms without too much wincing on my part.

"Thank you." She walks into her bedroom with me following slowly behind and we make our way back to her bed. She walks into the bathroom with a cream linen basket, collects all the towels and clothes before disappearing.

"I put your clothes in the wash and I'll put them in the dryer later," she tells me, when she reenters the room. Now knowing I have an aversion to light, she walks over to the curtains and pulls them shut so the room is cloaked in darkness. Turning the television on, she brings the remote with her to the bed and flicks through the channels. "Do you think you can lie down and rest now?"

"Yeah I'll try," I tell her, manoeuvring around and lying on my good side. It isn't as bad as I thought it would be to breathe lying down which I'm grateful for. She puts on one of her romance movies but I'm not paying attention. My eyes are already feeling heavy. "Low?" I softly call, my voice sounding distant to myself.

The bed jiggles under me before she says, 'Yeah?"

"Come closer, I won't break." She wriggles closer, shifting the blanket around so it covers us from our shoulders to our toes. She shuffles close enough I can smell the apple but not close enough she'll hurt me by accident. I lift my heavy eyes, stare into hers before I stretch forward to place my lips on her forehead in a light kiss.

"Sleep," is all she says, before I'm out like a light.

Willow

Staring at his bruised and cut face, while he gently snores, I can't help the anguish which stirs inside me. I know he's safe at this moment but what happens the next time he goes home? What happens if his dad goes too far the next time? My heart tears and pulls as sadness consumes me. No one should have to endure what he does. How many times has he been sporting a random bruise or cut he's laughed off or ignored me if I've questioned him about it? How many times has he held the hurt in he must feel?

The movie I pressed play on is long forgotten. I haven't taken my eyes off the boy in my bed. My phone vibrates so I pull it out of my pocket. It's Logan wanting an update on our patient.

Logan: How's he doing?

I quickly reply, not wanting him to worry.

Willow: He's okay. He managed a bath and is in bed asleep.

Logan: Do you want me to come over after my shift?

Willow: Yeah could you bring us some food from the diner. We haven't eaten all day.

Logan: Sure. I'm finishing in half an hour. See you soon.

I place my phone on the bed beside me before returning to my post watching Sully. The time passes quickly and before I know it my phone is vibrating again.

Logan: I'm here.

I carefully move the blanket off me and slide off the bed. I fling open the front door to be greeted by a smiling Logan.

"I bring food," he says, holding the brown paper bags in his hands.

"You're a lifesaver. Thank you. I've been so worried about Sully I haven't even thought about food," I tell him, as I grab one of the bags and lead him up the stairs.

"How's he really been?" I stop outside my bedroom door and turn to Logan.

"He's slept most of the day. He seems quite weak, is that normal?" I ask. He nods.

"He needs rest to recuperate then he'll be right as rain. I can take him back to mine tomorrow. We usually hang out in my room when this happens and my parents don't bother us."

"Alright," I say, walking into the room. Sully is in the same position when I left him a minute ago.

"I might wake him to eat and he can go back to sleep afterwards if he wants," he says, walking over to the side of the bed Sully rests on. Shaking his shoulder gently he tries to coax him awake. "Sully? It's me man."

"Logan?"

"Hey man. I brought some food. Have something to eat then you can go back to sleep." Sully yawns before pushing himself into a sitting position and his face gives nothing away. He must be good at keeping his pain a secret.

"Thanks guys," he says, rubbing his eyes with one hand.

"Here, get this into you." Logan passes him a wrapped burger and some fries. He grabs some fries, pops them into his mouth before he unwraps his burger and takes a huge bite. Satisfied he's eating easily enough by himself, I unwrap my own burger and take a bite. The yummy combination of beef, tomato, lettuce and cheese ignites my taste buds. I can't believe I've gone all day without eating. No one talks as we eat. Everyone is too hungry to stop for conversation. Sully and Logan finish, tossing their rubbish into the bag. It takes me longer to finish off my remaining fries. I take the rubbish and walk to the kitchen bin so the smell won't linger in my room overnight.

Walking back into my room, Logan helps Sully keep steady as they walk to the bathroom. I decide to head to the laundry to check on his clothes. Emptying the washing machine into the dryer, I program a quick dry cycle for forty minutes, hoping it does the trick. By the time I make it back to my room, Logan is helping Sully back to bed. He helps lay him down and pulls the blanket over him.

"I'm gonna head off but I'll come back in the morning," Logan says.

"I got a spare room if you want to crash here?" I hope he hears the pleas in my voice. I'm not doing much but it would be nice to have the back up.

"Sure. I can do that," he says, nodding at me. I smile before going to my drawers and grabbing a satin pyjama top with matching purple shorts. I quickly duck into the bathroom, strip out of my clothes and replace them with my nightwear.

Opening the door I gesture for Logan to follow me. I lead him to the door next to mine and push it open.

Flicking on the light I say, "Thanks for staying Logan. It's nice to know you're here in case something happens. I'm afraid I'm out of my depth."

"You're doing great. I know it's overwhelming."

"Yeah it is a bit," I confess.

"Why don't you go and try to get some sleep as well. It's been a long night and day. I'm sure you must be tired," he says.

"Thanks Logan, I will." Walking out I close the door behind me and head back to Sully. He's already fast asleep so I crawl into bed beside him, trying my best not to disturb him. I examine his face, wanting to touch him but I hold myself back. Losing track of time, eventually my eyes get heavy and sleep finds me too.

The morning light peeks through a small gap in the curtains and surprises me. Stretching, my body feels rested but my mind feels like it went to sleep only moments ago. Glancing at Sully, his hazel eyes stare back at me, catching me off guard.

"Hey," he whispers, a rare but real smile shines across his broken face. Damn he's beautiful when he smiles.

"Hey." He lifts his arm so I scoot forward and press my face to his chest as our legs tangle together. If he's not worried about me hurting him, I'm not going to worry either, especially as I don't want to deny him a hug. He plants a kiss to the top of my head, making my smile grow where my face is tucked against his shirt. Wrapped in each other's arms, content not to talk at all, we lie and our unspoken words fill the silence.

Twenty minutes later, knocking on the door has me pulling away from Sully although it's the last thing I want to do.

"Come in Logan," Sully calls out. The twisting of the door knob squeals as he opens the door and his head pokes in.

"Hey guys. How are you today Sully?" he asks his best friend.

"Better. The rest helped. Feel as though my head isn't as groggy as it was," he confesses.

"Do you want to head out now or you wanna go later?" he asks, and my heart sinks at the thought of Sully leaving. I'm not ready for him to be out of my sight. Fingers grasp my chin and pull my gaze to his. His eyes flicker back and forth as he searches for what he's looking for.

"Can we hang a bit longer and head out later?" Sully asks, and my heart thumps at the prospect of him being around a bit more today.

"Yeah sure. No problem man," Logan replies.

"I might go make us some breakfast," I tell them, as I jump from the bed. Turning I talk to Sully. "Stop trying to get up, you're not helping. I'll be fine."

"Yes boss," he says, his wide smile shining through again.

We spend the rest of the day lounging around and watching movies. I actually hear Sully laugh once too. It's at a scene in a movie which I don't even find funny but he laughs. Once I get over the shock that he's capable of laughing, I see the lightness in his eyes while he chuckles and I can't help but join in.

In the afternoon the boys get ready to head to Logan's house before my mum and stepdad arrive back. Sully is more stable on his feet now so he can walk easily enough down the stairs.

"I won't be at school tomorrow. I'll probably hang at Logan's for a few days to heal but I'll come later in the week," Sully says, causing my heart to sink.

"Okay. I'll see you when I see you, I guess," I tell him.

"See ya Willow," Logan says, opening the door and walking out.

"See ya."

"I'll meet you in the car?" Sully says to Logan, and Logan nods in reply before he walks away. Sully pushes the door closed and leans against it. He tilts his head to the side while he watches me.

"What are you doing?" I ask, as his eyes stay on me with his stone cold expression in place. He offers me his hand and he pulls me to him. My arms automatically wrap around his hips. His knuckles tilt my head back and my neck cranes to see him. His open palm swipes across half my face moving the hair away, before holding my chin in his grip with his thumb and index finger. I have my contacts in today so my glasses aren't in the way.

"Thank you for showing me kindness even when sometimes I haven't shown it to you," he says, a slight furrow between his brows.

"You're welcome," I say, not knowing what else to say to the compliment as my cheeks heat. It's upsetting to think this boy has rarely been shown proper human decency.

"I should tell you to run," he says, as his eyes flick to my lips.

"Why?"

"Because I'm no good for you Low," he says, as he lets out a sigh. My words abandon me as I don't know how to reply so I tighten my grip around him, scared he will run away. "You make me selfish," he continues, and my own brows furrow. He sees the question in my eyes because he says, "You make me wish for things I shouldn't." Without warning he pulls my chin towards him and moves his hand to the back of my head, holding me prisoner as he tastes my lips with his. I cling to him as he turns us around and pushes me into the door, not letting go of my lips. Our tongues dance as he pushes all the words he can't say into the kiss. His movements slow as he finishes with a soft press to my lips, before pulling away. My eyes remain closed as he presses a swift kiss to my temple, opens the door and leaves. I lean back on the door and open my eyes. I lift my fingers to my swollen lips as a small grin spreads. The kiss was amazing but I can't help the thought which flitters in the back of my head. Somehow it felt like goodbye.

Chapter Seventeen

Willow

The weeks turn into months and the end of high school fast approaches. Sully and I are still us, whatever that is. We never labelled it. We are together or as together as someone can be with someone like Sully. He still has his walls firmly built around him. There are moments when he lowers them, usually when we are alone or when it's me, him and Logan. Not even Kate gets to see the side of Sully like we do, which I find rather sad. The world doesn't know what they are missing out on when it comes to him.

He still has bruises every now and then. He tells me not to worry but it's hard not to when I know what's going on in his home. He said it's not much longer and he'll be off to college. He's been applying for scholarships all over the place so he can go to college and escape the wrath of his dad. My mum and stepdad have said they will pay for me to go to college so all I have to do is apply and get accepted.

I'm currently sitting at my desk filling in another application while Sully lounges on my bed. I opened a letter from Davenport University I applied to but it was a rejection. Their rejection has only made me more determined to keep applying. Sully stands right behind my chair and picks up my rejection letter with his fingers. I turn to gauge his reaction while he reads over it. I should know by now there usually isn't any reaction on Sully's face to look for. His blank stare reads it over, before placing it back on the desk. He wraps his arms around my neck and leans his chin on my shoulder.

"Have you applied to Belmont?" he asks, as his hot breath tickles my ear.

"Not yet. I'm considering it because Kate is going there. Why?" I ask.

"I was thinking we could go to college together. I got offered a scholarship there." His soft words make my heart jump. I turn in his arms and he releases me.

"Really?" I squeal.

"Yeah. I got the letter this morning." His shy smile shines at me. I jump into his arms and he catches me effortlessly.

"That's amazing Sully. I'm so proud of you." His cheeks pinken with the compliment and I take his lips in mine. He takes control and walks us over to the bed. I remain seated on his lap while my hands slide into his hair he wears loose today. I love his hair and whenever I give it a light tug, it elicits a moan from him. His lips press harder, as I tug his hair and he pulls me closer to his body. He hardens and I move against him to gather the friction I need.

"That's it sweetheart. Take what you need," he whispers, while he peppers kisses along my jaw. He palms my breast, gently squeezing as it strains against his hand. He grabs one side of my butt, helping me find my momentum and rock against him.

"Nearly there," I moan. He flips us around so I'm lying on my back. He crawls over me, putting pressure on my core as he takes over the movement. He roughly pushes away my shirt and bra to release my breasts. His warm tongue slides against my nipple before he takes it between his teeth, gently biting it before sucking and releasing it with a pop. His hips continue their motions and the heat builds before I explode with his name on my lips. He silences me by taking my lips between his, slowly kissing me while I ride the wave out. With my eyes closed and a smile on my face, he puts some distance between our faces.

"Okay, I'll apply to Belmont college if you promise to wake me up like that every day," I tell him, which causes a loud laugh to sound out of his mouth. My eyes flash open as I take in this gorgeous boy with his head hung back, laughing as his hair hangs around him. His sparkling eyes shine at me before he kisses me hard once more before peeling his body off mine. Offering me a hand, he leads me back to my desk.

"Fill in the application," he whispers in my ear, before taking his spot on the bed and tuning back into the movie. I can't help how my smile widens at the thought of us being at college together next year. My stomach swirls with giddy butterflies as I research Belmont on my laptop to find out about their application process.

Chapter Eighteen

Sully

"You're worthless. You think someone is gonna love you? You're nothing and you'll always be nothing." His hurtful, twisted words penetrate through while I become numb to his punches. I withdraw into the secret space inside, only I know exists. It's where I hide from him. Where I turn everything off and where I stay until he walks away. Until the hits stop and the words stop being thrown my way. I gave up fighting back a long time ago. Fighting back never got me anywhere. Asking for help never got me anywhere. Hoping never got me anywhere. "You think I don't know you're seeing someone? You're never home anymore. You think she's gonna love you? Why would she love you when you're so pathetic? You've caused me nothing but misery boy."

His words burn my skin this time. Why did he have to mention her? His words, although they always penetrate my walls, today for some reason, dig deeper and hurt longer.

"You'll never be worth shit kid and the sooner you realise it the better," he taunts me, as he kicks my side. This time a crack sounds in the hallway and I fight for breath. Short and sharp. He staggers away while I fight the pain to breathe. He's broken my ribs this time, it feels much worse and the fact I can't take a deep breath without excruciating pain is like a neon sign warning me. Run. Run far away and don't come back.

Lying there torn and broken, I realise I've mentally been fighting a losing battle. I was never going to win this war. Self loathing pours over me as I struggle to breathe. This time I don't want to feel safe. I want to feel free. Pushing to stand, I flee through the door that has led to my hell since the day I was born. Feeling shattered, I stumble along the sidewalk, my feet taking me as far as I can before I can collapse.

Pulling my phone from my pocket I scroll through my contacts, and dial the person I need most right now. The voice inside me is telling me to run. I just wish running didn't mean breaking not one but two hearts.

Chapter Nineteen

Willow

The day of graduation has arrived. It feels like this year has blown past but in other ways it's stood still, at times sluggish even. I can't wait for today to end and for Sully and I to spend the summer together before we head off to college. I never thought coming to stay with my mum for the year would change my life so drastically.

I may have come here for her sake but I ended up staying for myself. Dad thought it was because she wanted to rebuild our relationship before I went off to college but rebuilding a relationship would require effort on her part. Being left alone for weekends at a time has shown me the complete opposite. She made time for me when I was forced to eat dinner with her and her husband at the table, otherwise I was rarely home, especially this last half of the year where I spent as much of my time as I could with Sully, Logan and Kate. Even Lolly, my own cousin, couldn't understand what the motive was behind my mother dragging me here. I guess I may never know. It was a faulty plan she never fully saw through to the end. I'm glad she did though otherwise I would never have met Sully. My dad has begged me to come spend the summer with him but I want the time with Sully before we get pulled into our busy college lives. I'm hoping our schedules at least sync so we are able to spend time with each other. We need to break out of this town to find our feet as a couple in the world.

Dressing in my navy gown, I carry my cap with me downstairs to meet my mum. She's coming to my graduation which I'm surprised she made time for. Walking down the stairs, I nearly trip on the last step as I catch sight of the dark haired man, waiting for me.

"Dad?" I squeal, righting myself before I jump into his open arms. He squeezes me tightly in his arms and the distinct smell of peppermint and lemon hit me.

"Hey kiddo," he says into my ear, as the tears rush to my eyes.

"I've missed you."

"I've missed you too. Let me look at you," he says. "You're so grown now."

"Why didn't you tell me you were coming?"

"Then it wouldn't be a surprise now, would it?" he says, flicking the end of my nose while I roll my eyes.

"Sorry to break up the reunion but we need to get moving so we aren't late," my mum tells us. I link arms with my dad as we walk out to the car. My stepdad is already in the driver's seat so I sit in the back with Dad while Mum sits in the front.

Dad fills me in on everything he's been doing since I've been away. As we are sitting in the back seat, he pulls a small jewellery box out of his pocket and places it in my hands.

"Your grandpa bought this for you last year. He said he saw it and he had to buy it for you for your graduation. He would have been so happy to see you today," he tells me, the tears shining in both our eyes. I flick open the black rectangle box and the item in the box forces the tears to rush to my eyes. It's a white gold chain with an ice cream pendant on the end with pink and blue ice cream. It's a reminder of our Sunday ritual and a flash of memories wash over me.

"Can you put it on?" I ask my dad, turning my back to him. He fastens the clasp of the necklace and I finger the pendant with a sad smile on my face. "I wish he was here," I whisper.

"Me too," Dad says, clutching my hand in his.

Pulling into a parking spot, we exit the car and my parents head in to find seats, while I head in the direction of the other students. We have allocated seating and have to sit in alphabetical order. It's all a frenzy so it's hard to see any of my friends or Sully. I know I'll see them afterwards so I don't worry too much.

We get moved into the hall into our seats and nervous energy floods through me. I can't believe today is finally here. We listen to the principal's speech and a few other speeches are delivered before our diplomas are handed out.

Once the students' names get called out, silence hits the hall. When a name is announced and they walk across the stage to receive their diploma, the people who are there for them scream and it makes me smile. Logan is the first name called in our group and I let out a whistle as his parents cheer from the other side of the hall. I do the same for Kate who has a bigger cheering squad as her siblings and parents hoot and holler for her.

When my row is called, I stand and bounce on my toes as I patiently wait my turn.

"Willow Reynolds," they call out. With a huge smile I walk across the stage, shake hands and receive my diploma. The cheers from my dad are so loud, it feels like he's right beside me. Walking down the stairs I take a seat and wait for the rest of the names to be called. It isn't until the last row of students stands I realise I haven't seen Sully and I don't even know Sully's last name. For a minute worry takes over me because how could I not know his last name. I'm sure I haven't missed him either unless he was in the first group of students who were called when I wasn't paying attention. All my worry is for nothing when the next name is called.

"Reed 'Sully' Sullivan." He should be walking across the stage but he's not there. My heart beats faster and for some reason my stomach drops when I don't see him.

"Reed?" I whisper to myself, that's his first name and not Sully. A memory comes flooding back to me and I realise why the name feels so familiar. The guy from the party who I met in the dark. It was Reed. It can't be a coincidence it's Sully's first name as I've never encountered another Reed. The guy from the party vanished into thin air, never to be seen or heard from again.

Cheering around me erupts as caps are flown into the air, but my butt remains planted in my seat. My breathing escalates and I have to get out of here. I dash out of the hall through the side door and draw big mouthfuls of air into my lungs. I thrash the graduation gown aside to get to my small bag and pull out my phone. My thumbs fumble with the letters as I type out my text.

Willow: Are you the Reed from the party?

I don't confirm which party because if it's him, he'll know. I try to pull my breaths in as I wait patiently. A few seconds later my phone vibrates.

Sully: Yes.

Willow: Did you know it was me this whole time?

Sully: Pretty much.

Willow: Why didn't you tell me?

Sully: You said you didn't want me to be disappointed and it was true what I said. You could never disappoint me. It should have been me saying those words though because I'm nothing but a disappointment to you. You deserve the world Low and it's more than I can give. I'm sorry.

Willow: You're not a disappointment. Where are you?

Sully: Gone.

I type quickly through my blurry gaze as my breaths come out short and sharp. People call my name but I don't register who it is.

Willow: What do you mean gone? You promised me we'd go together.

Sully: I lied.

Logan catches me before I fall, as another text comes through.

Sully: I told you not all guys are good, especially me. Remember I'm not worth your tears sweetheart.

Logan's horrified face looks at me as he wipes my wet face, pulling me into his chest as my anguish is released. My brain realises what my heart already knows. He left me and he's not coming back.

Chapter Twenty

Willow

Don't ask me what happened over the past summer. I hardly have any recollection of it at all. Kate became my drinking buddy and my caretaker when I'd drink too much. Her and Logan became a couple and instead of being happy for them, I shut myself off from them and would spend days in my room, hiding away from the world and my heartache.

My phone calls and texts to Sully went unanswered or straight to voicemail. I know he hadn't blocked me yet as sometimes it would still ring. Those times I'd picture him somewhere, looking at his phone, torn about whether to answer it or not. One day I'm hoping the part of him I know loves me will answer.

Love. Such a fickle word at times. We never told each other the exact words but we felt it, didn't we? I've never been in love but I'm sure it's what I felt. Why else would I be so inconsolable since he left.

I'm currently in my room packing for college. The college I was supposed to go to with Sully. After my breakdown when he didn't show up at graduation, I managed to talk myself off the edge because he couldn't avoid me when we were going to be at the same college. Boy was I wrong. Logan informed me the next day he'd managed to get Sully to answer his call and Sully told him he accepted an offer to another college across the country. Davenport University to be exact. It's the college I never got into so there was no way I could follow him.

Not being able to follow him was what broke me. He purposely chose a college knowing I couldn't go there. After receiving the news, the drinking started. I wanted to drown out everything. My mum even called my dad as she was concerned with the amount I was drinking. He tried to drag me back to his place for the remainder of the summer but I didn't want to leave. I thought he might come back for me, so I waited. Got drunk and waited. Moped and waited then waited some more.

I have a few days left here before Kate, Logan and I head off to the same college. Without Sully. I've talked to Logan about it too and I can see he's hurt as well but he pushes it to the side. Sully didn't leave me without a goodbye, he left Logan too which leads me to the angry cycle of my grief. It isn't a straight arrow where you go from one stage to the next either, it's more of a boomerang effect slinging back and forth, depending on what my mood is like when I wake in the morning. It's ridiculous I'm so heartbroken over someone who obviously didn't care about me. I try telling my heart and mind not to care, unfortunately they don't tend to listen.

We are all headed out for one last party tonight before we leave this town for the next four years of our lives. I don't know what the future holds, all I know is it doesn't include Sully which breaks me all over again.

Chapter Twenty-one

ONE YEAR LATER

Willow

My head is woozy all of a sudden. I finish off my tequila sunrise I ordered at the bar before slamming my empty glass on the table. A splitting pain behind my eyes and the lights in the club blind me. My stomach swirls as nausea hits. I haven't even had much to drink or the last drink had more alcohol in it than I thought.

Grasping my forehead, I shuffle my way to the back of the club where the bathrooms are. I came out tonight with a couple of girls from my accounting class but they were on the dance floor. I'll text them once I'm in the bathroom. People bump into me as I stumble my way along the hall.

"Hey pretty girl, where are you going?" a nasally voice says too close for my liking. I pull away from his grip on my waist but I have no energy. He leads me to where the bathrooms are situated. The women's are on the left and the men's are on the right. He's tugging me now, pushing my weight towards the right.

"No," I say, but I can hardly hear my own voice.

"Nearly there sweetheart," he says, as his voice sends a cold chill across my back at the use of the nickname I once held dear. A girl about my age walks out of the bathroom so I sluggishly grab her as she walks past.

"You okay?" she asks, glancing back and forth between me and the stranger.

"She's fine," his slimy voice says, pulling me with him towards the men's toilets but the girl holds my arm tight.

"Chelsea you alright?" she says to me louder, as another girl walks out of the bathroom.

"Chels, there you are? Who are you?" this new girl directs to the guy holding my waist.

"You know her?" he asks the girls.

"Yeah, she goes out with my cousin. Who the fuck are you?" girl two yells at him, and it's enough to get him to drop my waist. Girl one catches me as I stagger into her and the guy takes off as girl two cusses and yells after him.

"Let's get her into the bathroom," girl one says. They help me back through the same door they came out of.

"I'm gonna be sick," I mumble, so they shuffle me into the first stall where I release the contents of my stomach.

"Babe, what's your name?" girl one asks.

"Willow," I croak out, between gagging over the toilet. "I'm Rose," girl one says.

"And I'm Shonnie," girl two tells me. "I've seen you around campus. We have an economics lecture together," she says. My pounding head tries to concentrate but I find it hard, and the blinding lights of the bathroom aren't helping.

"You had a lot to drink?" Rose asks, and I shake my head.

"She's nearly comatose," the two Shonnie's say to the two Roses.

"Why Chelsea?" I ask, not able to get my question out properly.

"Oh, we've had this plan. If we saw a girl we thought was in trouble, we'd call her Chelsea. This way we could act like we know her to make sure she's okay without it being obvious to the guy. This is the first time we've had to use it, I'm glad it worked," Rose explains.

"Yeah as soon as I heard the word Chelsea I knew there was bad mojo going on," Shonnie says. My heavy eyes droop and I force them open but they're soon closing again.

"Shit, you got a phone Willow? We'll call someone you know," Rose says, her voice sounds faint now. I lift my bag slung over me, well I attempt to, but my body feels heavy and relaxed. "Six, zero, zero, six," I tell them, before my eyes close again.

"Oh my gosh, the bastard slipped her something I reckon. See who her last calls are to and try them," one of the girls says, but I can't discern who it is now, their voices fading fast.

"Ugh none of them are answering," one girl says.

"Leave a voicemail on the next one," the other girl says.

"Hey, my name is Rose. Please help. We have a girl here named Willow and she's passed out. We think she's been drugged. There was a sketchy guy. Shit the voicemail cut off. Do you think we could get her to our dorm?"

"Oh my gosh it's ringing. Answer it," Shonnie squeals.

"Hey…. Yeah I'm Rose…. Yeah I'm still with Willow but she's pretty much out…. Her eyes open randomly but I don't think we can move her…. We're at The Nightingale…. Women's bathroom….. Okay."

"Are they coming?"

"Damn, whoever that was sounded hot. He said he's not too far away so will be here soon. Boy did he sound angry."

"You think she's gonna be alright?" Her question is the last thing I hear before I'm out for the count.

Sully

I didn't even want to be in this city but Logan promised me I wouldn't see Willow. He wanted to see me for an early birthday celebration for him and I couldn't deny him after I'd been a shit friend and upped and left him. I couldn't risk telling him my plans before I left so I had to leave him along with Willow. The girl who has tormented my dreams this past year. I don't regret leaving her as it was the best decision I could have made for her. I was never going to be worthy of a girl as precious as her. All I was going to do was tarnish her with my filth and wreck her life like my dad had said.

I'll never go back to the town where I grew up. The reason I agreed to meet Logan tonight was because it wasn't back home and I was on break from college and didn't have anything better to do.

Stepping out of the taxi, Logan catches sight of me from where he is leaning against the brick wall of the restaurant. His warm smile spreads as he steps forward, and pulls me into a hug.

"Good to see you man. Thanks for this," he says. I give him a genuine smile, having missed my best friend this past year.

"Well I did miss your crazy ass." He pats me on the back as he directs me to the restaurant. Telling the host about his reservation, she leads us to a table at the back and gives us a minute to look over the drinks and dinner menu. When she returns I order the steak while Logan orders the chicken parmigiana along with a bottle of wine. She works fast and it isn't long before she is filling glasses of white wine for the two of us.

Taking a sip of my drink, Logan asks me about college.

"It's good. I enjoy it there and I've made some good friends," I tell him. We fall into easy chatter about college. Our food is delivered and our talk stops for a bit while we dig in.

"How are things with Kate going?" I ask, as I cut another bite of steak off before popping it into my mouth with my fork.

His face changes with the smile that appears, "Things are going good man. Real good."

"I'm glad. You deserve to be happy."

"So do you."

"Don't start Logan."

"I'm just saying. You could be happy too."

"Who says I'm not?" I challenge.

"If you were, you wouldn't have to hide away from your best friend for a year." I close my eyes, and release a sigh before opening them. "Fine, I'll drop it."

"Thank you," I tell him. The ringing of his phone breaks the conversation as he pulls it from his pocket. He glances at the screen before silencing it and putting it back unanswered. "You don't need to get that?"

129

"No, it can wait. It's not every day I get to see my best friend, you know," he says, his smile appearing again. We finish our meals and refill our glasses before Logan excuses himself to go to the bathroom. While he's gone I pull my own phone out to check it. I put it on silent before dinner so it wouldn't distract from my time with Logan.

A text message icon shows a new message from moments ago so I open it and see I have a voicemail message. Quickly I dial my voicemail without checking who called. Logan takes a seat as an unknown voice speaks.

"Hey, my name is Rose. Please help. We have a girl here named Willow and she's passed out. We think she's been drugged. There was a sketchy guy." A flush runs over my body as my stomach drops.

"What is it?" Logan asks, seeing the look on my face and the urgency at which I dial her number back.

"Willow," is all I say.

"Shit," he says, pulling out his own phone to check it. The phone connects and the girl from the voicemail answers.

"Who's this? Are you still with her? Where are you? Okay, I'm not far from there. I'm on my way," I say, as I blurt out my questions. I throw wads of cash on the table not even counting it but knowing it will be more than enough.

"What's happened?" Logan asks, following behind me.

"Some girl thinks Willow's been drugged. Where's The Nightingale?" I ask. I'd told the girl I wasn't far but it's because I wanted her to stay with Willow when in fact I have no clue how far away I am.

"It's a couple streets downtown. Come on. I've got my car," he says, grabbing my sleeve and directing me a street over to where his car is parked. We get in and he pulls out into traffic. It's busy here in the city with people out at bars and restaurants for a Saturday night. My knee bounces as we get stuck at a red light. "I should have answered her call," Logan says, more to himself than me.

"Was it her who called you earlier?"

"I didn't answer because I didn't want to wreck our catch up if I mentioned she was calling. If I'd known she was in trouble, I would have answered," he says, my blood boils but I tamper it. It's not his fault. He was trying to be a good friend to me. He didn't know. I say all these things to myself in my head to calm myself before he pulls onto another side street.

There's a line to get into the club but there's no way I'm waiting when she's in there somewhere unconscious. I storm past the security guards who try to stop me but Logan interjects and explains to them as I pull open the door and enter. He's still talking to them as I look behind and see one talking into his ear piece, probably calling for backup. I scan the humid room with sweaty people grinding on each other on the dance floor as the music pounds in my ears. I stride straight through the crowd, pushing past anyone in my way, not giving a damn. I get to the hallway and see the sign for the bathroom and push straight in.

"Hey that's the ladies one," one woman calls behind me, but I ignore her. A girl pops her dark burgundy pixie hair out of a stall and looks at me with wide eyes.

"Rose?" I ask, causing her to nod.

"Fucker who left who I shouldn't call?" she asks, and my brow raises as I stop in my tracks.

Another girl with bright blue hair pops out of the same stall and says, "It's what she has you saved under in her phone. No one else was answering so we thought it might be worth a try calling you." Her wide smile greets me as her piercings in both cheeks protrude. My lip twitches as I try not to smile at the thought of her nickname for me in her phone but as I step forward, my smile drops.

"Damn it Low," I hiss, as my heart cracks. I've tried so many times to warn her to be careful but she doesn't listen. I close my eyes to calm my thoughts as scenarios of what might have happened if these two girls weren't here to help her. "Do you know what happened?" I gaze at both of them from where I'm crouched in front of Willow who is slumped over, leaning against the sidewall of the cubicle. I'll worry about the sanitary problems of this situation later. The bathroom door banging against the wall has Rose popping her head back out.

"Sully?"

"I'm back here," I call to Logan, who stomps forward.

"Shit," Logan cusses, as he gets his first look at Willow.

"Back to what I was saying, do you ladies know what happened?"

"Some creepy guy had his arm around her, trying to drag her into the guys's bathroom. We intercepted them and pretended we knew her and he scampered away as soon as he thought we knew her," Rose rushes out.

"Was she conscious?" Logan asks, looking around me at Willow.

"Yeah she told us the code to her phone so we could unlock it but she faded fast afterwards," Smurfette says.

"We weren't sure what to do so we went through her call list and her contacts as no one was answering," Rose explains.

"You guys did good. Thank you so much for helping her," I say as I offer a genuine smile, grateful these two happened to come across her when they did.

Their cheeks blush as they look at each other after I give them the compliment.

"I'm Logan by the way and this is Sully," Logan introduces us.

"Ah yes Logan we tried you but you didn't answer. I'm Rose and this is Shonnie."

"What should we do?" Logan voices.

"I'll carry her to the car and we can take her to the hospital," I say, moving forward to hoist her into my arms. Her head flops against my chest.

"What are you two gonna do? You can come with us if you want to make sure she's okay," Logan suggests. They look at each other and Shonnie whips out her phone, holding it out and snapping pictures of both Logan and I before tapping away with her thumbs. She pockets her phone before smiling at us.

"What just happened?" I ask, confused.

"Oh I took your photos and sent it to my cousin so if something happens to us, she can take your pictures to the cops and you guys will be the main suspects," she rambles on, while Rose nods.

"Willow needs friends like you," I tell them, as Logan lets out a chuckle behind me.

"We make life interesting, that's for sure," Shonnie says.

"No. You prioritise safety. It's exactly what she needs," I tell them, glancing at Willow. Her shallow breaths are quiet and almost non-existent.

"Is there a back door out of here?" Logan asks, and I nod as it's a good idea. I don't want to drag Willow through the crowded club like this.

"Yeah there is. Come on, follow us." Rose leads the way out of the bathroom until we arrive at a random door. She opens it and a security guard stands on the other side.

"Tell your boss someone was in here spiking drinks tonight," I tell the guard, who eyes up Willow in my arms. He looks as if he wants to say something but I don't give him the chance, walking away with Willow while the rest follow me. Logan takes over the lead as he knows where the car is. I would have led us round in circles.

Finding the car, we pile in. Rose sits in the front with Logan while he drives and I cradle Willow in my arms while Shonnie sits next to me. There's a hospital close by so Logan heads in that direction as he dials Kate's number from his phone via the car's bluetooth.

"Babe?" her groggy voice sounds through the car when it connects.

"Hey babe, sorry did I wake you?"

"Yeah it's okay, I was resting and waiting to hear from you. Are you on the way?"

"There's been a change of plans. We are on the way to the hospital."

"Why? What happened?" The sound of banging drawers comes over the car speakers.

"Long story but we think Willow has been drugged so we are taking her to the hospital now."

"Babe?"

"Yeah?"

"Who is this 'we' you are talking about?"

"Me, the two girls who found her and Sully," he winces in the rear view mirror, as he says my name.

"Shit. She's gonna murder you. What hospital? I'm on my way."

"Parkinson Memorial. Ring me when you're there and I'll tell you where to find us."

"See you soon," she says.

133

"Damn it. She's pissed," he says, his eyes finding mine in the mirror again.

"Well I'm glad I'm getting such a warm welcome," I joke.

Sighing he says, "It's not that. We were the ones who picked up the pieces after you left and it was not a pretty sight. Now you are here and Kate will be worried she might go back to the same dark place again."

"I could leave before she wakes and no one will mention I was here?" I offer, but as the words spill from my mouth, they twist my guts. It's the exact opposite of what my heart wants to do. Now I've seen her like this, I want to make sure she's all right before I leave again. Will her seeing me and me leaving her make her go downhill again? Logan never mentioned what she was like after I left but I did avoid him for as long as I could. Glancing at the comatose girl in my arms, I wonder if I'll ever be able to fix the hurt I caused.

I tuck a stray hair behind her ear. It's longer than it was, hanging past her shoulders now with her bangs still sitting above her eyes. She must have her contacts in as her glasses aren't on her face. It makes me wish I'd told her I liked when she wore her glasses. Something about them made her more herself in those few moments she let me see her with them on.

"We're here," Logan's voice pulls me from my thoughts, as he's parked in an emergency bay for us to get out. The girls and I exit as Logan drives off to find a car park.

Walking through the automatic doors, the lady behind the waist high desk looks at us. One look at me carrying Willow and she lifts the phone receiver. People come running from all directions and organised chaos follows as one pushes a gurney forward and someone else helps me lay Willow on it.

"What happened?" someone asks, as my eyes stay on the unconscious girl, unaware of what's going on around her.

"We think she may have been drugged. She was at a club but said she didn't drink much. She pretty much passed out and hasn't woken up since," Rose explains, as I forget to talk with my thoughts running wild as I stare at the black haired girl. Another person arrives and they wheel her away through a pair of swinging doors.

134

The first lady behind the reception desk when we arrived, places a hand on my chest.

"Sorry," she says, when my eyes flick to hers, removing her hand from my chest. "You can't go through yet. They'll get her stable and once she's settled in a room, I'll be able to direct you. For now you'll need to take a seat out here." The sound of the automatic doors opening registers behind me before Logan's hand on my shoulder directs me to the hard, plastic red seats to wait. I rest my elbows on my bouncing knees as I keep watch on the swinging doors they pushed Willow through.

The receptionist comes back over with a clipboard and a form, holding it out to Rose. "Can you fill in your friend's details please?" Rose looks at Logan and I and Logan puts a hand in the air.

"I can fill the forms in Miss," he says, and she walks over and hands it to him before explaining what she needs, the more information he can provide the better. The scratching of the pen on paper distracts my thoughts for a minute. "Does she have any allergies?" he whispers to me.

"Not that I know of," I tell him, realising there's probably a lot I don't know about her but I do know she has my heart. I only wish I was worthy enough to deserve hers. Logan finishes filling out the form and walks to the desk and hands it over to the receptionist as a dishevelled Kate rushes into the waiting room.

"Where is she?" her frantic voice calls to Logan.

"They took her through not long ago so we don't know anything. They'll let us know when we can see her." He wraps her in his arms and she squeezes him back. Logan grasps her hand, leading her over to where he was seated next to me. I lift my head as she gets closer and the sharp sting of her palm slapping my cheek echoes in the room.

"That's for leaving her like you did, you son of a bitch," she hisses at me, before taking a seat on the other side of Logan.

"Oh em gee," Shonnie squeals.

"Sorry man," Logan whispers to me.

"I deserve it," I mutter back, as the ache in my cheek heats my skin.

"You deserve a lot more," Kate murmurs from the other side of him. "These girls better not be with you either," she says louder.

"Calm down Kate. These are the girls who found Willow and helped her," he explains, grabbing her hand and pulling her back into her seat before she can get back up in my face.

"Uh we can go if you want?" Rose says, wringing her hands next to me.

"No. If you wanna stay and see Willow is okay, we aren't going to stop you. I'm sure she'd be happy to thank you for helping her as well," I tell them.

"Yeah sorry. I'm sure Willow would love to thank you. Don't mind our drama, it's been a long time coming," Kate tells them.

"No worries. We'll stay. We love drama," Shonnie says, causing Kate to laugh.

"Well you're in the right place because there's sure to be more tonight if Sully is around," Kate replies.

Someone else rushes into the emergency room, blood dripping from their hand while the person with them helps to hold their makeshift bandage around it. The receptionist jumps into action again, picking up the phone and someone comes through the doors to take the injured man away before his friend joins us in the waiting room.

Kate hops up, choosing to sit next to Shonnie as the three girls chat away. I vaguely listen and hear how Kate and Rose take some of the same lectures and Shonnie says she recognises Willow from around campus. I drop my head into my hands, my foot tapping against the linoleum the longer time drags on.

"Anyone want coffee or anything? I'm gonna go find a vending machine," Logan informs us.

I shake my head as Shonnie and Rose say, "No thanks," in unison. Kate jumps up and links arms with Logan, resting her head on his shoulder as they walk off. I stand stretching my legs, walking back and forth, looking out the huge floor to ceiling windows at the darkened car park.

Logan and Kate return with their arms loaded full of treats but I eat nothing. All I can think about is her. Halfway through demolishing their snacks, a doctor in green scrubs pushes through the swinging doors and pulls off his matching cap.

"Willow Reynolds?" My heart stutters as I stand.

"Yes."

"Are you her family?"

"Yes."

"She's stable now. We've given her some fluids to help with the dehydration. She's asleep but when she wakes up, she may feel disorientated or even experience hallucinations. It was good you brought her in. The nurse is getting her situated in a room now so she'll come get you in a bit. We will keep her until tomorrow for monitoring when she will be free to leave but she may feel out of sorts for a few days."

"Thanks Doc," I say, extending my hand for him to shake. I run my hands through my hair as relief washes over me. Closing my eyes as I hold the back of my neck, I breathe in slowly and exhale.

"Are you gonna hang around to see her?" Logan whispers, so the girls don't hear. For a minute I forgot I'd left Willow and here I am ready to storm into her room to see if she's okay with my own eyes. I need to see if she is okay. I'm being selfish, wanting to see her especially if seeing me would set her back. "I'm sure it'll be okay," Logan adds, after I take too long to reply.

A few minutes later, an older lady walks through the same swinging doors and tells us to follow her. She said we can see her for a few minutes but we can't all stay. She takes us to level seven in the elevator before showing us to room twenty.

"She's still sleeping so let her rest. It's the best thing for her," the nurse tells us, before pushing open the door and sliding the blue curtains open.

My short breaths pick up speed as I stare at her small body in the hospital bed. A white sheet covers her and the hospital gown they've changed her into. A drip stands beside her bed connected to her hand. The beeping of the machines alerts us, letting us know she's okay.

Kate takes the seat beside her bed, while Logan pulls another from the wall over.

"You wanna sit?" he asks me, but I shake my head, my feet unable to move any closer.

"Do you think we should stay until she wakes up? We don't want to overwhelm her?" Rose says from where her and Shonnie are standing, right inside the door.

"How about I get your contact numbers and give it to Willow to get in touch? She might be out of sorts when she comes to," Kate suggests, as she pulls her phone from her bag, handing it over to Rose as she walks around the bed to her. Tapping away, she adds hers and Shonnie's numbers before handing it back.

"Please get her to contact us," Shonnie says.

"Do you girls need a ride somewhere?" Logan asks.

"Nah, we were gonna catch a taxi home from the club so we'll catch it from here instead."

"You sure?"

"Yeah, we'll be fine. Tell her we are glad she's okay. It was nice to meet you guys," Shonnie says, as they wave and leave the room.

"You should go too," Kate directs my way, without taking her eyes off Willow.

"Come on Babe, stop it," Logan says, defending me.

"Don't worry Logan, it's warranted," I sigh.

Ten minutes later I talk myself into leaving before she wakes but her eyes peel open. Blinking a few times, she shakes her head as she looks at me.

"Hey Willow, it's alright. I'm here," Kate soothes her, drawing her attention as she clutches her hand.

"What happened?" she croaks, her voice raspy.

"Your drink was spiked at the club. A couple girls found you and kept you safe. You're at the hospital now. The doc said you might experience hallucinations and be out of sorts for a few days," she explains.

"Spiked?" she says, her eyes close and open again with tears shimmering along her lash line. "Did anyone....anyone...." she stutters.

"NO!" I yell, heaving at the thought of someone hurting her.

"Is he a hallucination?" her voice chokes out at my outburst.

"Sadly no," Kate sighs. I hold my ground when all I want to do is touch her and pull her into my arms. The tears in her eyes pull at my soul, begging me to comfort her. I force my weight into my heels and stay put.

"Should we leave? Give you two a minute?" Logan asks, his eyes flicking back and forth between Willow and I. She closes her eyes before she opens them again. The tears have gone. A foreign expression appears on her face.

"Leave," she exhales. Logan and Kate both push back their chairs but her words stop them.

"Not you two. You. You leave," she says, as her eyes hold mine. My heart splinters but at the same time I want to puff out my chest at the pride which swirls through me at her standing firm with me and not letting me in easily. We stare at each other. My feet are locked and not able to move either way.

"Take care of yourself," I say, wanting her to keep the most important thing to me safe. Her. She doesn't realise I left her to protect her, not hurt her.

"You lost the right to worry about me the day you decided to leave without a word," she says, her voice not faltering.

"I'll always worry about you sweetheart," I say, which makes her jaw clench.

"LEAVE," she screams, both our chests rising and falling in the silence that follows.

Logan pushes his chair back and comes to stand beside me, placing a hand firmly on my shoulder.

"Come on man. She's been through a lot tonight," he whispers, so only I can hear. Regret washes over me as I stare at her. I use my index finger to swirl the anxiety ring on my thumb I haven't had to use in a while. Her eyes flicker to the movement causing one eye to twitch. My skin burns at the prospect of leaving her and Logan's grip becomes firmer on my shoulder.

"What was it you said? Not all guys are good, especially you. You proved it when you walked away so do me a favour and go back to wherever it was you ran off to," she states, causing my heart to flutter. My eyes burn with a foreign heat behind them and her eyes widen.

"You also told me you're not worth my tears but you know what, I am worth yours and you'll realise it too late. Now get the fuck out," she screams the last part, as my breath hitches. Tingling in my fingers is the sign I need for my feet to move. I commit her resigned face to memory as I turn and walk out the door, struggling to get my breaths under control.

"Give her time," Logan says, walking me out.

"Look after her."

"You know I will. Come on, I'll give you a lift to your hotel," he says, patting my back. I focus on inhaling and exhaling as our steps echo in the quiet corridor, taking me away from the one my heart wants but my brain still tells me I'm not worthy of.

Willow

I wake in the morning, lying in a sterile hospital bed. My brain is foggy from whatever was slipped into my drink. I blink against the light someone turned on and forgot to turn off.

"Sorry Sweetie. I didn't mean to wake you. I need to do your obs if it's okay with you?" the nurse in the light blue scrubs says, forcing me to direct my gaze to her. I catch sight of the empty chairs. She catches my gaze and adds, "Your friends popped out to get some coffee. They shouldn't be long."

"Thanks," I croak.

"Here, have some water," she says, walking to the pitcher at the side of my bed and filling one of the plastic cups. She holds it out for me so I can suck some of the cooling liquid through the straw.

"Thank you," I say again, my throat feeling less dry.

"It's no problem at all. Did you want me to get some water for your flowers as well?" she offers, making my brows scrunch in confusion.

"Flowers?"

"Yes. These here," she says, grabbing the bundle of sunflowers neatly arranged in white paper beside my bed. She lays them on my lap and I search for the card, but don't find one.

"Do you know who left them?" I ask, already knowing the answer.

"No, I didn't see who left them."

"Water would be great," I tell her, holding them out for her to take. I let her finish her job, taking my obs and recording it on the clipboard hanging on the end of my bed before she leaves. She returns a few minutes later with the flowers in a clear vase filled with water and places them on the small table beside my bed.

"Try to get some sleep," she tells me, patting my foot gently before leaving me alone. I turn on my side, facing my favourite flowers and release a sigh. I wish I could get past the hurt of him leaving me but some wounds cut so deep they never fully heal.

"Damn you Sully," I whisper, before closing my eyes and pushing thoughts of him out of my mind for good.

Chapter Twenty-two

FOUR YEARS LATER

Willow

"Let's go, lets go, lets go," Logan hollers, as he ushers me out of the apartment I share with him and Kate.

"Why do we have to leave so early?" I whine, cupping the thermos in both my hands, taking a sip. The hot hit of coffee hits my throat as he puts a hand on my shoulder.

"If we don't leave early, we will get stuck in traffic and I'll have to stop every five minutes for one of you ladies to go to the toilet." Logan's smile shines at me as I roll my eyes at him. He's annoying when he's right.

"Fine. I'm only being nice because you planned this birthday getaway for me and I really appreciate it," I tell him.

"I'm coming babe. You don't need to yell. You know my morning routine takes ages," Kate whines.

"It's exactly why I woke you half an hour earlier than Willow."

"Ugh you ratbag," she screeches, as she whacks him across the chest.

"Come on you two let's get going, shall we," I suggest, not wanting them to get side tracked, it's happened before.

"Yeah, let's go. I've taken your bags to the car already. Is there anything else you need?" Logan asks us. I run through a checklist in my head, ticking it off as I remember putting the items in my bag.

"I'm good," I say.

"Me too," Kate adds.

"Are you sure Milo will be okay?" I ask, worried about their cat.

"Yeah Mrs Thackett said she will pop in, feed him and check on him every day," Kate reminds me again.

"We are good to go, I reckon. Let's get out of here and get this show on the road," Logan says, pushing me out the door and pulling Kate behind him before he shuts the door and the lock clicks in place.

"Road trip," Kate squeals. The laughter bubbles out of all of us and I can't help the excitement that flows through me.

We arrive at our destination after two and a half hours of driving. Logan and Kate wanted to do something nice for me this year so they planned this whole trip as a surprise, springing it on me a few days ago. The last half hour of our drive has been nothing but acreage every which way you turn. I have asked them multiple times during the drive where we are going but they didn't crack and haven't given me the slightest clue so I'm completely in the dark. Logan assures me we are near our destination, and houses appear more frequently as a small town takes shape. Logan stops in front of a two storey house with a sign out the front declaring it Clara's Bed and Breakfast. I wonder what Clara's has in store for us.

Chapter Twenty-three

Willow

"Where's this surprise you are taking me to?" I ask the next morning, as I shovel a forkful of pancakes smeared with syrup into my mouth.

"It's about a thirty minute drive from here," Logan informs me. He ordered a big breakfast, consisting of scrambled eggs on toast, hash browns, breakfast sausage, bacon and half a tomato he has not so kindly pushed to the side of his plate in disgust. Kate couldn't decide what to eat but as soon as she heard me say pancakes she ordered the same.

The talk slows for a minute while we enjoy our food. The clanging of cutlery fills the air. We sit at one of the small tables they have set out for their guests. A young couple sits at one and an older couple with a toddler sit at another.

"So where are we going?" I blurt out, hoping to catch them off guard.

"We aren't telling you Willow so stop asking," Kate chastises me.

"You'll see soon enough," Logan says.

"What else have you got planned for this adventure of ours?" My eyes flicker back and forth between the two of them.

"We haven't thought past this stop. We thought we could play it by ear," Logan tells me, before he grabs his crispy bacon with his fingers and bites the end off.

"Do you think I'm too young to be having a mid-life crisis? I am, aren't I?" I rub my eyes before sliding my hands across my forehead.

"Hey. Your job was absolute crap so I don't blame you for quitting. Yes it would have been nice if you had something lined up but if you did, you probably wouldn't be here with us on this trip. This way you can take a breather and reset before job searching again." Kate's words calm the mini breakdown I could feel brewing inside.

Ever since quitting my job, I've felt a whirlwind of emotions wondering if it was a mistake or not. I hated the job from the first day and it never got any better so I am happy to be rid of it. In hindsight having more savings in my bank account would have been nice because Logan and Kate are covering the rent while I find my feet again. They have mentioned they don't mind as it's practice for the day they have their own place but I don't want to be a burden.

Finishing our meals Clara clears our empty dishes and chats to us about the meal. She asks about our plans for the day but Kate and Logan have their lips sealed so don't spill the beans. I never knew the pair of them were so good at keeping secrets, usually Kate tells me everything, and I mean everything.

Jumping in the car with a full stomach, I settle in for the ride as Logan drives us to our secret destination for the day. The blue skies above promise a beautiful day and I hope it's outside so we can enjoy the nice weather.

Cars line the dirt road Logan has turned into and he parks behind another car, before he turns the engine off.

"Happy birthday Willow," they both chime in sync. Laughing I lift my eyes to look out the window for any clues about our destination but can't see past all the cars. Slamming our doors shut as we get out, we weave through the cars to the front of the lot and my breath stutters.

The huge white sign with the pretty picture reads Willow's Sunflower Fields. I turn around and glance at Logan and Kate with my mouth wide open as their smiles spread across their faces.

"How? What? When?" I stutter, not able to get a full question out which makes them both laugh.

"You can thank Logan. He's the one who happened across it one day and thought it would be a perfect surprise for you. It's like it was made for you," she gushes. My eyes flicker to Logan and I catch his eyes widening before he plants a huge smile on his face again. My brows furrow at his expression but it's forgotten as Kate links her arm through mine and drags me towards the entrance. "Come on birthday girl, let's go explore."

Entering behind a crowd of other people, you can see it's a popular place and as Logan shows our electronic tickets on his phone and we walk through, I realise why.

"Oh my gosh," spills from my lips, as I take in the sight before us. My feet forget how to move and Kate has to tug me to the side as other patrons enter behind us.

"Look at this," Kate points to a huge plaque, which tells of the story of how this place came to be. There are over half a million sunflowers spanning the acreage in front of us. It says the owner had a dream of creating something so beautiful for his one lost love he let slip away. She loved sunflowers and it's his hope one day she'll come across this field and he'll be able to win her back.

"Logan, take notes. This is the type of grovelling you will need to do if you ever need to win me back," Kate turns to Logan, showing him the part about this being a gesture of love.

"I will never have to do something like this because I don't plan on losing you. Ever," he says into her ear, as he wraps his arms tightly around her waist from behind. I turn back to the sign, giving the lovebirds a minute. It would be nice to be here with someone I loved. I haven't had the greatest track record with relationships in the past and I've been single for over a year now. It doesn't usually bother me until romantic things like this happen and the thought crosses my mind how it would be nice to be able to share it with someone special.

I push the thought out of my mind as quickly as it occurred, ready to enjoy my birthday. Continuing to read the plaque, I find out they have a gift store, a maze through the sunflowers you can navigate, a helicopter ride you can partake in for an extra cost and a cocktail dinner set out in the middle of the field.

"This is the perfect present for my birthday. Thanks so much you two," I gush, turning to them and pulling them both into my arms for a three way hug.

"I'm glad you like it. Now should we get to work on this maze?" Logan suggests.

"Yes, let's do it," I say, bouncing on my tip toes. We walk towards the sign for the maze and follow other small groups of people. Most stop to look at the beautiful flowers towering over everyone. Phones and cameras flash in all directions as people find the perfect spot for their pictures and selfies. We continue on through the maze until we find an empty spot to take some photos. I pose with my hands in the air, a huge smile on my face being surrounded for miles by my favourite flowers. Kate and I want an action photo of us jumping in the air so Logan has to direct us and it takes a few attempts before we get one which looks amazing on his phone.

We carry on through the maze laughing, chatting and posing for photos along the way. I'm glad I thought to bring my huge white bucket hat as it's keeping the bright sun off my face. It turned out to be the perfect weather to explore a field of flowers.

When we find the end of the maze, we head over to the food stalls they have set up and order some hot chips and drinks. Taking a seat at a small wooden table with a red and white chequered table cloth, we enjoy our hot snack even though the weather calls for something cold.

"It looks like they've got ice creams for sale inside the gift shop if you ladies want one?" Logan asks, as he flattens his empty chip carton.

"Yes please," I say, craving something cold to cool me down.

"Me too," Kate adds.

"I'll be back in a tick," Logan says, before throwing his carton in the rubbish and walking off to the shop.

"Are you enjoying your birthday?" Kate asks, before she pops a chip in her mouth.

"It is honestly the best birthday I've ever had. I don't think I can say thank you enough."

"We know you've been through a hard time lately and wanted to do something to make you smile."

"Well the smile on my face won't be wiped off for a good year after this," I tell her.

"Good. You deserve some happiness."

"Thanks Kate."

"Here you two go," Logan calls from behind me as he hands over two pre-wrapped ice cream cones. Ripping open the wrapper ,I take a bite of the vanilla ice cream covered with peanuts and choc sauce. We enjoy the coolness of the smooth texture as the burning sun shines high in the sky.

"I've booked us in for dinner too," Logan informs us, before he slurps some of his ice cream that has dripped down the cone.

"Did you just organise that now?" I ask, between licks.

"No, I booked it online when I booked the tickets. You have to get in quick because the dinner slots fill up fast as the flowers only bloom for about three to four weeks," he explains.

"Aww they only last for a month? That's so sad."

"The farmer blooms them every year so they'll be back again this time next year," Logan tells me.

"No it's not that. The farmer only has four weeks out of the year for his one true love to magically come across his sunflower fields and fall back into his arms so they can live happily ever after. It's an unrealistic plan and quite sad, like finding a needle in a haystack."

"You never know, miracles do happen," Logan says, biting a chunk off his cone which has suddenly become interesting.

"What's the plan for the rest of the day? There's a bit of time to kill until dinner," Kate says, as she swipes Logan's hair off his forehead.

"We could head back to the bed and breakfast and hang for a bit before we get ready for dinner and come back out?" His raised brows glance between us.

"Are the tickets you bought good to get back in later?" I ask, hoping they haven't spent a ridiculous amount of money on me.

"Yeah I got all day passes for today so we can come and go as we please. I wasn't sure if you'd wanna hang out here all day until dinner or not. We can totally hang here if you'd prefer to spend time in the fields," he suggests.

"Hmm, it sounds like a nice plan. I'd love to chill and spend some time outside. It could help provide some insight into what the next step in my life should be."

"I don't mind that idea. We could go find a nice quiet part of the field, away from everyone and out of hearing distance," Kate says, waggling her eyebrows at Logan whose eyes light up when he catches on to what she's suggesting.

"Gross! Too much info guys," I screech, and roll my eyes as they laugh.

"How about we meet back here around five? We are seated for cocktails at five thirty," Logan tells me, as he stands and pulls Kate out of her seat.

"Yes, off you two love birds go," I tell them, smiling as they run off and head back into the maze. I pop the last bite of my cone in my mouth and push my chair back to dispose of our rubbish.

Walking into the gift shop, I peruse the paraphernalia around the aisles. Everything is sunflower themed. There's a wide range of clothes. They have t-shirts, hats, even a few pretty sundresses with sunflower prints on them. Since it's my birthday, I decide to splurge on myself. Why not? It's the one day of the year I should be able to celebrate myself with no worries so that's what I do. I scan the room and catch sight of some red baskets to hold all the goodies I plan on buying. It's not every day I'm let loose in my ideal store and I intend to make the most of it.

I grab a navy blue shirt with a sunflower print front and centre which ties around the waist. Holding it by the coat hanger I tell myself to stop overthinking and place it in the basket. Next I grab a tan wide brimmed sun hat that has a navy ribbon wrapped around the centre and a bright fake sunflower weaved into it. Scanning the aisles I keep moving, and my collection grows. A keychain, a canvas of a pretty painted sunflower and another one with a poem on it with the sunflowers in the background all make it into the basket. I grab a couple of assorted pens and a black notebook with sunflowers on the cover. I get carried away and grab some magnets for the fridge and some drink coasters, telling myself it's for the apartment as a whole and we are in desperate need of coasters. We are in fact not.

I think I'm finished making my way through the whole shop before I spot a section of stuffed toys I missed. In goes a stuffed sunflower. It's not as big as the real deal outside but it will make a perfect addition to the throw pillows on my bed, so will the cute bee with bee-utiful printed on the side. You can't have flowers without bees so it seems silly to get one without the other.

The air conditioning in the small shop has cooled my sun kissed skin and I'm not sure I want to leave and venture out into the heat again. Glancing around I find a clock above the entrance door telling me it's four o'clock. I've managed to waste the good part of two hours here. I guess my love for these flowers has consumed me.

Walking to the counter the phone rings and the girl behind the counter mouths "'sorry" as she answers it. While I wait, I scan the counter and grab a last minute battery operated sunflower fan before tossing it in the basket with my other purchases. Placing the basket full of my haul on the counter, I wait as she continues on the phone.

"Yes sir. I understand. Okay. Bye." I catch the tail end of her conversation before the call ends and she smiles at me. "Sorry about that," she says, as she grabs some cute brown paper bags printed with Willow's Sunflower Fields and an image of a single sunflower in the middle.

"Has the Willow from the love story ever been in here?" I ask, curious if they have already reconnected.

"No. My boss still waits for her to appear," she sighs.

"How long have the fields been running?"

"It's been a few years now, possibly four. I've worked here the last two summers since it's a seasonal gig," she tells me, as she extracts things from my basket and places them straight into the bags. "You like sunflowers?"

"Yeah," I laugh, before adding, "I've always had a special love for them. My grandpa used to grow them every summer and they were the prettiest thing I had ever seen. I was little when he did it and I would always be in awe of these huge flowers towering over me. I guess a huge part of me loves them because of him," I tell her, reliving the moments of my grandpa and I sitting under the little patch he had in his garden.

Lost in my thoughts I nearly miss when she says, "All done. I hope you enjoy it all."

"Thank you. What do I owe you?" I rummage around in my bag for my wallet.

"The cost is covered today. Happy birthday," she says, smiling a friendly smile at me as my cheeks heat.

"He covered it all?" I ask, flushed he and Kate knew I would come shopping in here and organised this behind my back.

"Yes, it's all covered. You don't need to pay for anything. I hope you enjoy the rest of your birthday."

"Thank you so much," I gush, as I take the bags in my hands and a smile appears on my lips. I still have time before we need to meet and I want to spend some time under the flowers like I used to with my grandpa. Carrying my huge haul into the maze, I find a quiet spot and creep between a few of the plants to get some shade from the hot sun.

Carefully placing my bags beside me on the dirt, I rummage through to find one of my pens and the black notebook I bought. I flip to the first page and decide I don't want to ruin the first page so I flip to the next page. At the top I write GOALS. Tapping my pen against the paper, I urge something to come to my mind to help lead me in the right direction. I don't even know what I want out of life these days. I know I don't want a job in an accounting office, slaving away like everyone else in there. Some people may enjoy that particular type of work but I'm glad I figured out it's not for me after a year instead of a lifetime.

I wish I had a business degree so I could start my own business much like the man who planted this flower field. He had a dream and went for it. All I need now is to figure out what I'm passionate about and get to it. I should write what I don't want instead, it might be easier.

Flipping to the next page I write in big bold letters, not an office job. Next comes not a regular nine to five job. I want to work outdoors. Work life balance. Passion. I write until the list has filled from the top to the bottom of the page. At least I know what I don't want. Lastly, I write I want a man to share my life with. Unfortunately a relationship seems to be harder for me these days than it is to get a good job. I don't know why it is so hard to find a good man. Where are they all hiding? I love seeing what Kate and Logan have built over the years. They've had their ups and downs but through it all, their love has survived and become stronger. I should look for a new apartment as well as a new job so they can have their own space.

I flick my wrist to check my watch and see I've let time slip away from me again. Packing my pen and book away, I stand and wipe my hands on my butt to clear the dirt away. Now I'll have to go to dinner with grubby shorts. Picking up my bags I follow the path back the way I came so I don't get lost in the maze. The air is cooler as the sun has lowered with the evening beginning to settle in.

I exit the maze and catch sight of Logan and Kate sitting at the same table we were at earlier.

"Hey," Kate calls out. "How was the rest of your day?"

"It was so good. Thank you for the gifts. You guys shouldn't have."

"What?" Kate asks, but she is interrupted by Logan.

"It was our pleasure. We are glad you've enjoyed your day. Do you want me to stow your things in the car before dinner?" he asks.

"Yes, that would be amazing. Thanks," I tell him, holding the bags out for him to take from my fingers.

"I'll be back in two ticks," he says, before planting a kiss on the top of Kate's head.

"Do you want to come look at some of the dresses with me for dinner? My shorts are dirty and I'm a bit of a mess from being in the sun all day."

"Yesss. Sounds like a great idea. I'm a mess too but it's because getting down and dirty in a sunflower field is what we did. Literally," she winks at me. My cheeks heat at the information.

"Come on you rebel," I tell her.

Scanning through the dresses in the gift shop, I pick out a white one with huge sunflowers on the front which ties around my waist with a pretty bow. Kate chooses a black one similar to the cover of my notebook.

"Let me get these," Kate says, pulling the dress from my grasp and placing it on the counter with hers.

"No. You've already done so much for me today."

"It's nothing. You deserve it," she tells me, tapping her card against the machine before I can protest further.

I take the bag with our garments and we walk to the toilets to get changed. She hands me mine and I go into the cubicle, strip off my dirty clothes and replace it with the pristine dress. I smile looking at the dress which falls above my knees. Walking out of the stall, I meet Kate who looks as pretty as ever in her dress.

"I'm so borrowing yours some time," I tell her, loving the way hers looks against her skin.

"Put your clothes in the bag. I'm sure Logan won't mind carrying it for us. He said we could drink since he's gonna drive us back to the bed and breakfast." She leads the way out of the bathroom and we meet Logan back by the table where he's waiting for us.

"Well don't you two look gorgeous," he greets us, as we arrive. Kate does a spin for him before falling into his arms and giving him a quick peck.

"Could you carry our clothes for us please?" she asks him, and he takes the bag without question. We sit at the table and wait for the time to hit five thirty. A guy comes over to us dressed in a white shirt and black slacks.

"Party for Logan Jacobs?"

"That's us," Logan replies, and we all stand.

"Right this way. I'm Phil. I'll be your server for this evening." He leads the way into another row of sunflowers, away from the path we took this morning for the maze. No other people follow us and it's at this point I realise the entrance to the fields which has been constantly buzzing with activity all day is now quiet.

"Have the other diners already gone through?" I ask.

"No, you are the sole reservation for tonight," Phil says over his shoulder, as we follow him.

"More cocktails for us," Kate says, knocking my arm with hers.

"Not too many please babe. I don't want you guys spewing on the drive back," Logan whines.

"If I get too wild you can cut me off okay?" she tells him, causing him to laugh. She has him so wrapped around her finger, he'd let her get away with murder so I doubt he'd stop her drinking too many cocktails if that's what she wanted to do.

"Here we are," Phil says, as he gestures to the long table with the white tablecloth and about twenty chairs seated around it.

"It must be a quiet night if it's just us," I whisper to Kate, and she nods in agreement.

"Cocktails are to the side here at the bar. We have some punch but if you'd like something specific, Stanley here will be more than happy to accommodate you. There's no extra cost for the alcohol either. Order whatever you'd like. I'll let you settle in and I'll be back in an hour to take your dinner orders," Phil tells us.

"Thank you," we say in unison, and Phil leaves and walks back the way we came.

"Let's get this party started," Kate squeals, her mood infectious as a smile spreads on both mine and Logan's face. Logan asks Stanley for some water while Kate and I have a glass of punch each which is super fruity, making it hard to distinguish exactly how much alcohol is in the beverage. Soft music sounds around us and Kate in her element sways to the beat as if she's had about ten glasses of punch and isn't on her first drink. She grabs my free hand making me stay and dance with her.

We spend the next hour avoiding more of the punch, and instead enjoying tasty drinks from the cocktail menu with funny names. I can't say I have ever tasted a slippery nipple or sex on the beach before. Logan sticks to his word and sits with his water while we dance and laugh. Phil returns on time, handing us menus and waits patiently as we look over the options. I settle on the salmon, Logan orders the steak and Kate orders the chicken. Since we are the only ones dining, we ask if they can bring out our seafood platter with the mains for us to share.

We continue to drink our share of cocktails as we wait for our food to arrive. The string lights hanging around the canopy above shine on us as the sun sets. The ambiance sets in and I sigh as this would be the perfect setting for a date. Kate sits on Logan's lap as he whispers into her ear. Her giggles drift away in the wind. I take a seat opposite them, smiling at their shared happiness and trying not to let gloom set in at the jealousy my heart feels. I am absolutely over the moon for my best friends but it sucks to be the third wheel all the time especially on a lovely night like tonight.

"I've had the best day guys. I know I've said it all day but thank you again," I stutter out, the alcohol finally hitting me and making me giddy.

"We're glad you've had a great day," Logan says, squeezing Kate to him as she rests her head atop his.

"Here are your meals," Phil interrupts us. Another server joins him in delivering our plates to the table. They look like meals from a five star restaurant so I'm thoroughly impressed. Cutting into the salmon, I take a mouthful of the melt in the mouth flesh. Delicious. The other meals must be just as good as conversation stops as we enjoy our food.

"This is so good," Kate murmurs around a mouthful of chicken.

"Mmmmm," Logan moans in agreement.

We clean our plates and Phil and the other server take them away. Kate grabs us a new cocktail each. I sip the orange liquid through the paper straw as I sit facing the two of them. I sit with my back to the entrance of our little sanctuary when out of nowhere, Logan grasps my hand. My hazy eyes fall to him as his brows scrunch together. I press my thumb against his forehead, wanting to smooth out the furrow.

"Why so serious?" I ask, making Kate's tipsy laughter grow in sound as mine adds to it.

"You know I love you right?" Logan asks. Now my own brows furrow.

"Yeah?"

"And I only want you to be happy?"

"Yeah?"

"And I wouldn't do anything to hurt you?"

155

"I know that. What's this about? You're not making much sense Logan."

"Just remember all of that in the next thirty seconds. Everything I've ever done is out of love," he says, squeezing my hand in a death grip.

"Wha..."

"Happy birthday to you," a lone voice sings from behind me, as Logan's grip on my hand tightens. Kate's face drops and I'm fascinated as it morphs into her stone cold resting bitch face. A hiccup erupts unexpectedly out of me as the singing continues. I don't dare turn around, stuck in a trance, watching Kate as her jaw clenches. Logan tries to grab her hand resting on the table but she smacks his hand away.

"Don't you dare," she threatens him, causing my breathing to increase. The singing gets closer.

"Happy birthday dear sweetheart," he sings, and as Kate glances at me my eyes widen and draw in a deep breath. "Happy birthday to you," he finishes, before placing the chocolate fondant covered cake with two bright burning candles on the table. The flame on each candle flickers, waiting to be blown out and for me to make a wish. I stare at the two flames as they blur before my eyes.

"Willow, make a wish," Logan's voice says.

"Don't tell her what to do. You've done enough, don't you think?" Kate hisses. I move on autopilot, lean forward and blow out the candles. No clapping follows, only dead silence.

I push back my chair, stand and my eyes flick to Kate.

"I need...." my voice trails off, not knowing what I need other than to run. My chair hits the dirt with a thud as my legs and arms work to remove me from the situation. My heart senses a threat and my fight or flight mode sets in. It chooses flight. My breaths and sandals hitting the dirt are the only sounds as I race along the path. It's pitch black now, surrounded by the flowers I love. A few lanterns light the way so I follow those. My ears prick at the sound of a second set of feet speeding towards me. I push myself to move faster, panting as I make my escape.

"Aahh," I react, as thick arms wrap around my waist and pull me against his solid chest.

"Please Low, stop for a second," his husky voice whispers in my ear. The sound of our exertion fills the silence as he pins my back to him. My feet dangle off the ground due to our differences in height so I'm at his mercy. From his hold around me, I can tell his arms are thicker than I remember. His rough exhale tickles the skin of my neck as he holds me effortlessly. My whole body remains stiff in his embrace as he moulds around me. "Please if I put you down, can you not run away?" he pleads. I nod, even though he can't see me as I fear words will fail me if I try to speak.

His hold on me stays firm until my feet hit the ground before he releases me. I remain facing away from him, not yet ready to see his face.

"Low, please look at me," he says, his voice deeper than I remember. Many things have changed but my heart still hurts the exact same way it did when I realised he left me all those years ago. With my head hanging low, I shuffle my feet around until my eyes land on his loafers. Loafers? When did he become a loafer man? A giggle at the thought bubbles out of me, causing me to hiccup.

"Something funny?" he asks, a hint of a smile in his voice. I continue staring at the brown shoes with the frilly leather, holding in my laugh this time. He's not wearing socks either, which makes me think he's changed in more ways than one. His loafer covered feet scoot forward and his familiar move of his fist under my chin has me sighing as he raises my eyes to his. The hazel eyes I stared into so long ago stare back at me. His wavy hair is still long as it hangs past his shoulders. Stubble across his sharp jaw is new but makes him look more masculine. I was right about his body. It looks as if he's spent the good part of the last four years at the gym or on steroids. He's taller too as my neck has to crane back to meet his eyes.

His hand moves from under my chin, before he grasps a lock of hair and slides his fingers through the length I now wear half way down my back. Rubbing the ends together with his fingers, an entranced look shows on his face.

"You wear loafers now?" my drunken brain blurts, snapping his eyes to mine as he drops my hair.

"I guess I do, yeah," he says, as he shoves his hands into his pockets.

"What are you doing here?" I demand, as my hands fly to my hips. His eyes drop to the dirt for a second before they raise to mine again.

"Have you not figured it out yet?"

"Figured out what?" I huff, throwing my hands in the air. His hand raises, moving slowly around as he gestures to the sunflowers. Sunflowers. The alcohol has slowed my train of thought and I can't connect the dots.

"Can you spit it out? I'm too drunk for this," I admit.

"I did all of this for you. I'm the owner Low," he says, holding eye contact with me as my heart gallops and my chest heaves. My flight sensor reactivates and I'm off running, faster than before in the hopes I can out run his freakishly long muscular legs. At the entry point I make a dash to the right where the toilets are situated. I manage to push into the women's and lock myself in a cubicle, breathing deeply as I rest my head against the door.

"Willow," his voice bellows. I jump at the sound. I close my eyes to focus on my breaths and slow them. My thoughts run wild, making it hard to control my breathing. He grew a field of sunflowers for me. A field. Of sunflowers. For me. Who is crazy enough to do that? He is obviously, but a whole dang field? I don't even know what that entails or why he came up with this outrageous plan. It said the owner was trying to win back his lost love's heart. It can't be right. He left me. He chose to leave me. He didn't choose me.

"Willow, open the door please. You're hyperventilating and I will break the door down if I need to. It's no skin off my nose," his shaky voice shouts, from the other side of the door. I twist the lock and pull the door open as my hurried breaths puff in the room. "Sweetheart, slow them down," he pleads, but my eyes scrunch up at the use of sweetheart which makes it worse. "Shit. Sorry. Willow. Please Willow. In, five, four, three, two, one. Out, five four three, two, one," he instructs, and with my eyes still tightly shut I follow his commands. It takes a while for my breaths to slow before the rough skin of his hand grabs my forearm. I pull it back out of his grip and my eyes flash open.

"Don't," I demand. Staggering around him, I turn the tap on at one of the basins. Cupping my hands I fill them with cold water, and splash my face. I repeat the process a few times until the shock of the cool liquid calms me more.

"Can we talk please?" his voice says, from right behind me.

"Can you stop creeping into my space?" I yell, because the closer he is the more unsettled I become.

"Willow?" Kate calls, rushing into the bathroom. Her eyes flick between us as she comes to stand next to me. Logan arrives a second after her. I notice his eyes stay on Sully as they have a private conversation. "You okay?" she asks.

"Yeah. I'm ready to go," I tell her.

"Lets go."

"Willow please talk to me," Sully pleads again.

I ignore him and look past him to Kate, before saying, "I need to pee before we go."

"Logan, if you know what's good for you, you'll remove your friend and let us pee in peace," Kate snaps at her boyfriend. I walk to a stall and lock the door again, not wanting to look at him anymore.

"Come on. We can wait outside," Logan says, as their footsteps leave and the door bangs closed behind them.

"They're gone babe. We're alone," Kate tells me. I breathe a sigh of relief. The alcohol was ready to burst my bladder for holding it in as long as I did so I take care of business then wash my hands and wait for Kate.

"Did you know?" I ask, meeting her gaze in the mirror.

"No way. I'm as shocked as you are. I'll be giving Logan a piece of my mind when we are alone," she huffs, as she roughly washes her hands, causing water to spray everywhere.

"I don't want you guys fighting because of me," I sigh, pulling a paper towel out of the dispenser as she does the same.

"It's not because of you babe. It's because he's an idiot who did something behind my back and purposely hid it from me because he knew it was gonna blow up like it has."

"Don't be mad for too long," I tell her, throwing my rumpled paper towel in the black lined bin. She follows suit and steps towards me to pull me in for a hug. I close my eyes, clinging to her as my body sags in her embrace.

"How are you feeling?" she says, holding me as tightly as I hold her.

"I don't know how I feel. I'm overwhelmed, I didn't think I was ever gonna see him again and I had accepted it. He left me," I stutter the last line. The hurt is still evident in my voice.

"I wanna kick him in the balls," she admits, making me burst out laughing as we pull apart.

"It would be well deserved, that's for sure," I tell her.

"What do you wanna do? Do you wanna talk to him or head back to the bed and breakfast?"

"I can't even think properly at the moment, he's setting off my anxiety so bad and if you add alcohol into the equation, it's probably best if we go. I can't deal with him right now," I say, my head dropping. She pulls me in for another hug as I rest my forehead on her shoulder.

"It's fine. Whatever you wanna do. Come on. I'll talk so you don't have to." She grabs hold of my hand and drags me out of the toilets. Outside we see Logan and Sully talking, both throwing their hands in the air. They catch sight of us walking out of the restroom and their conversation ceases. Sully takes a step forward but Logan's hand stretches out, grabbing his forearm and holding him back. Our slow staggered steps draw us closer to them and Kate's grip tightens as we near them.

"We are going to the car and we are leaving. Willow is not in the right state to talk to you tonight," Kate states, dragging me forward and not stopping. I keep my eyes focused on the ground as we walk past until Kate sighs. "Looks like Logan is talking to him again."

We lean our backs against the car. It sits in the empty car park with a few other cars. The air is cooler too as night has set in and the stars have filled the sky. I turn my eyes upwards and gaze in awe at how many white twinkly stars shine above us. There's so many out here compared to in the city. It's a magnificent sight to behold.

"It's beautiful," I say out loud. In my periphery, I see the movement of Kate's head leaning back and we both stand there with our eyes to the sky.

The sound of approaching feet has me tearing my gaze away from the stars to see who is coming. Logan shrugs his shoulders at me as he pulls his keys out of his pocket. Sully stands back at the entrance under the Willow's Sunflower Fields sign and my breath hitches as it further drives home the point he did all this for me. I just don't understand why.

Chapter Twenty-four

Willow

Stretching my arms above my head, a yawn takes over me as my muscles loosen up. A slight pounding behind my eyes from all the cocktails brings back memories of last night. I was totally caught off guard when Sully showed up and declared he was the owner of the sunflower fields. Flinging the blanket off, I stomp over to my bag which I hadn't unpacked and rummage through until I find my toiletry bag. The green box with paracetamol in it is right at the bottom, luckily it is something I never leave the house without. I quickly toss the white pills into my mouth and swallow them with a large glass of water.

A light knock at the door draws my attention so I toss the pill bottle on my bed and shuffle towards the door. Turning the lock, I open it and am not surprised to find Kate on my doorstep.

"My head is killing me. How's yours?" she whines, as she traipses in and throws herself on my bed. I sit on the bed and lean against the headboard.

"I've got paracetamol if you need it," I tell her, closing my eyes.

"Remind me never to mix cocktails again." Her words come out muffled as her face is buried in my blanket.

"How are you and Logan?" I ask. Her head flings to the side so she can see me and leans her hand on her palm.

"I'm still mad at him for going behind our backs," she huffs.

"Don't be too hard on him. He was trying to help his best friend," I sigh, remembering what he told us last night on the car ride home. Sully had enlisted his help in getting me out to the field for my birthday. He told Logan how he'd been growing it for years in the hope I would come across it on my own but he felt like his efforts were hopeless and fate needed a push in the right direction. Logan, ever the romantic, jumped at the chance to help.

"Well he still should have asked for my opinion before doing something as idiotic as this. Have you decided if you want to see Sully?"

"I don't know. What's it going to achieve? I closed the book on us a long time ago. He's only got himself to blame."

A knock on the door has us looking at each other.

"Is it Logan?" I whisper, hoping it is him.

"He said he was gonna have a shower. I told him I wasn't gonna be long in your room but he might have come looking for us so we can eat breakfast together," she says, as she shrugs her shoulders at me.

I slide off the bed, walk to the door and fling it open. My stomach drops, it's not Logan. I get my first proper look at the older version of the boy I was in love with. His hair is tied back at the nape of his neck, tan skin glows under his white short sleeved button shirt which squeezes tight around his muscular arms. He must spend a lot of time in the gym.

"Willow, can we please talk?" he asks, as his dejected eyes look at me. I stare back for a few seconds before I make up my mind.

Turning my head towards the bed I call out, "Kate, go find Logan and I'll meet you guys in the dining room for breakfast shortly."

"Yeah sure," she says, as she walks to me. She grasps my hand and gives it a squeeze before she passes. I catch the glare she gives Sully as she exits. I turn, walk into the room and let him follow. Hearing the door close, I turn around to face him with my arms folded. It's quiet for a beat and I wait but he doesn't speak a word.

"Talk."

"Could we sit or something?" he asks, as he fidgets with his fingers. I zone in on the movement and notice his old anxiety ring from when we were at school and how he spins it around now. I wonder if

163

he realises he's doing it. Letting out a breath, I walk over to the love seat facing the fireplace and sit at one end, crossing my legs under me. He sits at the other end but his thick legs need a lot more space than I do. I chew on the corner of my lower lip while I wait for him to talk.

"Damn it, this is harder than I thought it would be," he mumbles.

"Why don't you start from the beginning, it might help."

"Beginning okay," he says, drawing a deep breath in. "You know back at school how things were with my old man?" he asks, and my stomach drops at the memory of Sully with a bruise on his face or body every other week. I nod, as my throat feels tight all of a sudden. "Well with all the abuse I suffered, I felt I wasn't worthy of love. Like I wasn't good enough for anyone. He ingrained the thought into me every time he hit me. After a while the punches weren't what were hurting me, it was his words he spewed out doing all the damage. I didn't realise they were having such a big impact on me until a few years ago."

"Okay," I say, not entirely sure where he's going with this.

"When I left you before graduation, my dad had beaten me the day before pretty badly and I honestly thought you were better off without me. I didn't think I deserved to be shit on your shoe with the way I was feeling about myself. When I was with you, I felt like I could become something, be better you know? But the day he broke me, I felt you deserved someone better and who had more to offer than me," he explains, his eyes cast down on his fidgeting hands rather than meeting my eyes.

"You didn't have to leave me without a word. I would've helped you," I whisper, not even sure why I say it. My eyes lock with him and his shimmer back at me.

"Leaving you will always be the biggest mistake of my life," he confesses, and my heart beats faster in my chest. "I'm trying to right the mistake I made, Low. I'm sorry you had to figure out I was the guy from the dark room at the party how you did but I've always remembered what you said about the guy of your dreams making an effort. I've held onto that and it took off on this crazy flight path and inspired the sunflower fields," he says, as his cheeks redden with his admission.

"You grew millions of sunflowers to win me back?" I huff, laughing while shaking my head before I stand, needing some distance between us.

"Yes. Why is it so hard to believe?" He stands too.

"You expect me to believe you've been pining after me all these years and making plans for this big gesture?" I huff, crossing my arms over my chest.

"Yes, I did it all for you," he says.

"Have you ever heard of something as simple as a damn phone call? You could have texted or called or even come to see me one time in the last five years instead of focusing on growing some stupid flowers in some big grand gesture which is frankly crazy when you think about it." My outburst has me drawing in breaths to calm the fire heating my skin.

"I saw you the day in the hospital and you screamed at me to get out. I didn't think you'd take too kindly to me trying to contact you again," he admits.

"You didn't even try Sully. You know what, now it's too late," I tell him, releasing a sigh. His eyes flick back and forth between mine, searching for the truth in my words.

"It's not too late. Please give me a chance to prove to you I've changed," he begs.

I close my eyes before replying, "Changed? I never wanted you to change. I wanted you as you were, flaws and all. I only wanted you to want me enough in return," I stutter, as my eyes water.

"Damn it Low. That's the problem. You should have wanted more instead of settling. I wanted more for you than what I could offer you. Why can't you see that? You deserved so much more. Why couldn't you see you deserved the world and you still do. Wanting you was never the problem. Can't you see I did want you? I wanted more for you at the same time and that was the part of me which won out in the end," he says, as his own voice cracks.

"It was my decision to make. Not yours."

"You would have chosen wrong, damn it," he yells at me, as his chest heaves.

"I would have chosen us," I scream back.

165

"Choosing us would have been the wrong decision. Why can't you see I was putting you first because I knew you would never do it."

"Choosing us would never have been the wrong decision."

"Well I disagree," he grunts. We stand and stare at each other for a moment before I cross my arms over my chest.

"I don't know what you want but there's too much hurt to wade through," I tell him.

"I want you, damn it," he yells, causing a tear to tumble over my lash line.

"Sometimes wanting someone isn't enough. There's too much history for us to get past Sully."

"Please. Give me a chance to prove it to you."

"Prove what?" I yell.

"How much I love you," he yells in return. My heart thunders in my chest at his confession after all this time. He never said the words before but it is what we felt, right? My heart wants to run into his arms but my feet hold me still. The hurt I felt when he left me is still evident as if the pain was caused yesterday. The pain and hurt regretfully forces the next words out of my mouth.

"Love sadly isn't enough sometimes," I say softly. We both face off against the other, chests heaving as we breathe.

"That's it?" he asks.

"That's it," I tell him, as my heart hammers away. He watches for a moment before his shoulders sag in defeat. Walking to the door he stops with his hand on the handle. He doesn't move for a minute before he turns and walks back to me. He stops right in front of me before bending and pressing a soft kiss to the edge of my mouth like he did all those years ago, the first time I met him in the dark.

Whispering in my ear he says, "Sorry I was such a disappointment," before he swiftly walks from the room, closing the door behind him. My legs give way and I drop to the carpeted floor, rocking back and forth, trying to digest what just happened. If what I said was true and love isn't enough, why is my heart breaking at the thought of him walking out of my life again?

Kate finds me later, curled in a ball, rocking back and forth trying to soothe my breaking heart.

"Aww babe," she sighs, as she sits on the floor beside me before she pulls me in for a hug. I release all the hurt and sadness I've kept inside over the years. I've pushed those emotions away not wanting to deal with it. Logan stopped mentioning Sully years ago after the last time I sent him away from the hospital. He knew I didn't want to hear about him anymore. I learnt to ignore the part of me wanting answers and I trained myself to move on without any closure.

I never knew his dad beat him up the day before he left. It makes me ache for the boy he was and what's worse; he had to go through it alone. I don't know where he went or what happened. Do I want to know? The curious part of me does but the hurt part doesn't know if I should open old wounds again. It was hard enough trying to gain closure without answers before.

"Do you want to talk about it?" Kate asks, as my sniffles quieten.

"I don't know how to feel. He says he wants me back but it's been five years and he waltzes back in with a sunflower field like it's the sanest idea in the world for someone to plant a bazillion flowers for another person," I huff.

"It was romantic," Kate swoons. I push out of her hug with raised brows as she scrunches her lips to the side. "What? It was. Don't look at me like that. You know it was romantic as all hell. It's a shame it was Sully who did it," she admits, rolling her eyes.

"Do you not find it hard to hold a grudge against your boyfriend's best friend?" I ask, tilting my head to the side.

"Not really. The grudge is because of what he did to you, not because of what he did to Logan. It's harder on Logan as he doesn't discuss him with me now because he knows I don't want to hear it," she says.

"You should ease up on the grudge. I don't want what he did to me affecting your relationship with Logan. It's in the past anyway," I say, standing and dusting myself off. She follows suit.

"If it's in the past, why were you bawling your eyes out for the last half hour?" she asks, as her brow raises at me.

"Call it residual emotions I had to release," I say, turning my back on her.

"Did you guys hash it out?" she asks, as she follows me to my bed.

"Not really. I told him there was no point in trying to win me back, the past is in the past and nothing can change that."

"You're happy with the decision you made? Because it didn't look like it when I walked in here. Just saying babe."

"Residual emotions remember. I gotta shake them off and I'll be back to my normal self who is in the middle of a midlife crisis," I tell her, forcing a fake cheesy smile on my face which makes her laugh.

"You're a dork," she chuckles.

"And you love me regardless."

"You know it. Now get your cute butt packed because Logan said we are leaving," she informs me.

"What? Already? I didn't even get to unpack," I whine.

"Yeah, since his plan of you and Sully reuniting didn't play out how he thought it would, he thinks it's best if we head onto stage two of your birthday celebration in hopes you will forget about this blunder and enjoy the rest of the time we have left."

"Do you know what we are doing?" She pretends to zip her lips and throws away the fake key.

"I'm not telling. Now hurry up because he wants to get a wriggle on since it's a couple hours of driving before we reach our next destination."

"Okay. I'll shower and be done in twenty minutes," I tell her, walking back to the bed.

"See you soon," she says, closing the door behind her as she leaves. Releasing a sigh, I walk to my still packed suitcase and pull out a pretty red sundress to wear. I pack everything else I had taken out but it isn't much so it doesn't take me long. In less than twenty minutes I'm showered, changed and standing outside Logan and Kate's door, ready to go.

"Hey," Logan greets me, after I knock on their door.

"Hey yourself," I say, dragging my suitcase inside.

"I'm sorry, okay? I thought I was being helpful trying to get you two back together but it was obviously the wrong thing to do. I've made a complete mess of your birthday. Can you ever forgive me?" he pleads, his hands pressed together in prayer.

"Of course you're forgiven. No more stupid stunts without consulting me first, yeah?"

"I promise. Cross my heart," he says, as he crosses his heart with his index finger. I open my arms for a hug which he steps into. "I really am sorry Willow," he says, softer.

"I know."

"Come on you two, enough of being downers. We are back in celebration mode and we are on to phase two of celebrating Willow," Kate says, in an enthusiastic voice that makes me laugh.

"Let's get this show on the road," I say, pulling my suitcase with me out the door as they follow with their own. Returning our keys and making sure the bill is settled, we pack the car and with Logan in the driver's seat, we begin the journey to our unknown destination.

"How's it looking?" I ask, as I take a drink of water from my bottle.

"It's safe to say smoke coming from the engine is not a great sign," Logan says, waving his hand in front of his face to clear the smoke he mentioned, which is in fact coming from the engine after he popped the bonnet.

"Any idea what it could be?" Kate asks, taking a drink of her own water. The midday sun shining on us is harsh and with the car out of commission, we are sitting ducks here on this stretch of highway with nothing around us for miles. We have been driving for about an hour since we left the bed and breakfast. We passed the sunflower fields and it was close to the last time we were around civilisation before it turned into a long stretch of dirt road. I still have no idea where we are going.

Logan turns to me, wincing like what he is about to say is going to hurt.

"We are gonna have to call Sully."

"Ugh, really? What about a tow truck?" Kate whines.

"I don't think a tow truck is gonna do much. It will take us back the way we came and we'll be stuck waiting on a mechanic to fix it. I wanna carry on with your birthday since yesterday was a complete mess," Logan says.

"It wasn't a complete mess. I enjoyed myself," I tell him, meaning it. I did have a great day, until my cake was brought out. He offers me a small smile.

"Well if that's the case, can I please ring Sully? I know he's not your favourite person but before everything, we were all good friends. Couldn't you go back to being friends at least?" he asks.

"We weren't ever friends, you know? We fought. A lot," I remind him.

"You know what I mean. We were close at least."

"Yeah I guess. I'll try for you," I tell him, putting myself in his shoes. It must be hard having to split his time with his best friend, his girlfriend and me because we don't see eye to eye.

"Thanks Willow. Would it be okay if I asked him if he wanted to join us? He's driving out this way and he's going to have to drive us to our destination, hours out of his way. It makes more sense if he stays," he justifies. I squint my eyes at him, wondering if this is another tactic to get Sully and I back together.

"It's not like that. I promise," he assures me, so I nod.

"Do I get a say?" Kate butts in.

"Sweetie please? For me?" Logan pleads, as he slings his arms around her waist before he pulls her close and nibbles her neck, making her giggle.

"Fine but you owe me big time," she tells him.

"You got it," he agrees. He kisses her on the cheek before pulling his phone from his pocket. "Hey Sully," he greets him, and walks away out of ear shot so we can't hear any more of the conversation.

"Are you okay with this?" Kate asks, as we both watch Logan, walking back and forth while he talks on the phone.

"Yeah. I shouldn't have put you and Logan in the middle of all my drama with Sully so for everyone's sake, we should try to move on as friends or at least as people who can get along for their friends' sake," I tell her. She throws an arm over my shoulder and I lower my head to rest on her shoulder.

A few minutes later Logan walks back to us, a wide smile shining at us.

"He'll be on his way soon. He's gotta run through things with his manager since he's leaving him in charge and he's ringing his friend who is a mechanic in town. He'll get him to organise a tow truck and have the car taken to his garage so his friend can work on it while we are doing what we are doing. The car should be ready by the time we are done," he says, as happy vibes waft off him.

"How long is this so-called celebration of Willow gonna take?" I ask.

"About a week. Hopefully you can figure out what you want to do with your life going forward without the hustle and bustle of the big city. I'm hoping it'll help clear your mind," he tells me. I take another sip of water and let his words sink in. I hadn't considered what I was going to do when I returned. Hopefully this week will give me enough clarity to know where the hell I'm going.

We sit in the car to protect ourselves the best we can from the sun. The hot wind doesn't help cool us down but at least our faces aren't going to get too sunburnt. It isn't until an hour later, a blue double cab truck comes barrelling along the highway towards us. Sully stops right next to us and gets out. He offers me a small smile which I return, wanting to be cordial so the rest of the trip is a happy one.

"Chewy wasn't far behind me so by the time we get your stuff into mine, he'll probably be here. Grab everything you need," Sully says. Logan helps him unload all our bags and stuff from the boot into his truck bed. I grab my small backpack and bottle and move to stand next to Sully's car with Kate.

"We can sit in the back," Kate whispers to me, and I nod in thanks. Like Sully said, it isn't long before his friend Chewy arrives and pulls the tow truck in front of Logan's car. He hands over the keys and the guys chat as Kate and I wait. Sully glances towards us and comes over. He turns his car back on and turns the air con on high.

"Hop in and cool down," he tells Kate and I. We don't need to be told twice as the heat from the sun is burning us, the longer we stand out in the open. We settle in the back, the cold air hitting us and we both sigh in relief before giggling. We watch as the guys help Chewy get Logan's car loaded on the tow truck. We even wait for him to do a u-turn and head back the way he came before the guys hop in the car. Sully sits behind the wheel and Logan sits in the passenger seat. Sully doesn't ask for directions so I'm guessing Logan filled him in on where we are going.

"Did Chewy say how long he thinks it'll take to have the car back up and running?" Kate asks from beside me.

"Probably about a week. He needs to see if he's got all the parts when he checks it over," Logan replies to her.

"Will you let me know where we are going yet?" I ask, hoping to catch them off guard.

"No," Kate and Logan respond, making me groan. A tiny chuckle comes from Sully as he drives, otherwise he's quiet. I rest my head on the window as there's not much to look at and close my eyes instead. My head throbs as the paracetamol from this morning wears off. Closing my eyes I zone in on the rumble of Sully's engine and let it lull me to sleep.

"Wakey wakey sleepyhead," Kate says, as she shakes my shoulder to gently wake me.

"Are we here?" I ask, as I blink my eyes to adjust to the sunlight again and take in the lush trees surrounding us. We've driven right into a campsite.

"Camping?" I squeal, which has them all laughing at my expression.

"Well you mentioned last year you've never been so I thought it might be fun. This part of the trip was my idea," Kate says, pushing her shoulder against mine.

"I gotta go see the camp manager and find out where we can set up," Logan says, sliding out of the car.

"I'll come with you babe," Kate tells him, quickly exiting the car as well, leaving me and Sully alone. Kate and Logan walk off hand in hand towards a block building to the side of some trees.

"I'm sorry if I'm crashing your birthday. I know you probably aren't thrilled to have me here," Sully says.

"It's fine Sully. Logan reminded me how we were once friends and I don't want you to have to avoid him for my sake anymore so how about we put the past behind us, call a truce and try to move forward as friends?" I suggest.

"Friends? Okay, I can do that," he says quietly, holding out his hand. I grasp his hand before he shakes mine. He hangs on longer than is normal so I tug my hand back so he knows to release it. Logan and Kate come back laughing a few minutes later, both hopping back into their seats.

"We are over in section G," Logan says, as he directs Sully. He holds a paper map he must have gotten from the camp manager.

"How big is this place?" I ask, shocked they need a map to give us directions.

"Not too big but it's easier to hand out maps to save them from being asked the same questions time and time again," he explains. "There we are," he says, as he points to a patch of unoccupied grass where there is enough space for us to park the car as well as erect our tents. "The toilets and showers are in the block straight ahead too." He points to the forest green brick building straight ahead of us in the distance. We all exit the car as he turns the ignition off, stretching our limbs out after the long hot ride. Being hungover didn't help either.

"So what's there to do around here?" I ask, wondering why we came out all this way.

"To be straight with you, not a lot. We thought it would be a good place for you to relax and unwind and see what the next step to take would be without all the distractions of city life getting in the way," Kate tells me, as she pulls me in for a hug.

"Yeah I guess it will clear my mind being out here," I agree, until I catch sight of Sully and Logan laughing at the front of the truck. My mind won't be as clear as I'd like it to be with someone else filling in the space.

"Come on. How about we go for a walk and let these two unpack?" Kate suggests. I nod and she calls out to Logan letting him know we'll be back soon. Sully's gaze flits to me but I avert my eyes and focus on Kate. I follow her away from the truck as she leads me to the toilet building Logan pointed out. We decide to make a toilet stop and it allows us to check them out as well. I've never been camping but I'd think as far as toilets go, these are pretty decent. The showers aren't too bad either. I'm glad this isn't a super authentic camping trip and there are no long drops in my future.

Next we find another building which holds a small kitchen which some of the other guests tell us we can use if we need. We carry on doing a wide lap of the complex. There's a washer and dryer tucked away in one corner and even a ping pong table. We find a couple of picnic benches as well as some barbecues. I'm guessing those are what most people use to cook their meals. Speaking of food, my stomach rumbles causing Kate to look at it before she meets my eyes.

"I am pretty hungry too now your stomach mentions it," she cackles.

"We don't even have food," I remind her.

"When I found this place, Logan said there was a supermarket not too far away. We'll have to go do a food run." Following her around, she walks through some bushes and stops in her tracks. Beautiful blue green water greets us as it washes against the sandy beach. A couple of people are out on kayaks and you can hear their laughter from where we stand on the shore. A small hut sits to the side offering more kayaks for people to take out.

"This looks like fun. We'll have to go out sometime," I tell her.

"Yeah it's so pretty. I do hope you find some answers while you're here."

"Thanks Kate for all of this. I'm really grateful," I tell her, wrapping my arms around her waist in a side hug.

"Good. You deserve it," she tells me, lowering her arm over my shoulders. "Should we go for a swim while we send those two off to get supplies?"

"I didn't bring a swimsuit."

"That's where you're wrong. I packed some extra clothes for you in a separate bag as I knew you'd need some more things," she tells me, smiling.

"You've thought of everything," I tell her, releasing her as we turn around to head back to find the guys.

"Pretty much," she says, winking at me. It doesn't take us long before we find the guys standing around the truck, unpacking things. They've managed to get one tent up in the time we were gone. Logan's head pops up from stomping a peg into the ground as he hears us approach. The wince on his face doesn't look promising.

"Great work guys," Kate says, smiling at him but I slow my steps, anxious about what he might say.

"We have a problem," Logan states, his eyes flashing to mine.

"What kind of problem?" Kate asks, crossing her arms over her chest.

"We only have two tents. Would you mind if Sully shared a tent with you Willow?" His wince deepens as my brows pull together.

"I…"

"How about you guys look for an inflatable mattress while you go get food supplies so Sully can sleep in his truck bed," Kate suggests. Logan rolls his eyes at her but it's Sully's voice which catches my attention.

"That's a great idea. How about we head out now and have a look?" Sully says, directing his eyes to Logan.

"Okay. Give me a minute and we can go. We can assemble the other tent when we get back."

"Great. All sorted. Willow and I are gonna go for a swim so we'll be there if we aren't back when you are," Kate says, walking over to Logan and giving him a quick peck. She grabs the black duffle bag from the ground and throws it at me. "Your suit is in there," she tells me, as I catch it with an oof.

"Thanks."

"Let's go change in the bathrooms," she suggests, slinging her bag over her shoulder. "Sorry, I guess I didn't think of everything but in my defence he wasn't supposed to be here," she whispers to me, so the guys can't hear.

"It's okay. Let's hope they find a mattress," I say, as we get to the changing sheds.

"If they don't, I can jump in with you, and Sully and Logan can share," she suggests, dropping her bag and unzipping it. I rummage through mine, finding the swimsuit she packed. It's my black bikini. With Sully being around, I wish she had packed my one piece instead.

"Don't be silly. I'm not gonna have you two sleeping separately because of Sully and I. If it comes to it, I'm sure we can be civil and share a tent," I tell her, walking into the toilet stall to get changed. She mumbles something I don't catch but my mind is occupied with thoughts of Sully having to share a tent with me. I'm more worried about the fact my heart sank at the thought of him not sharing with me.

"Shoot, the towels are in the other bag," Kate calls out. I unlock my stall to see her standing in front of the mirror, examining herself in her red bikini.

"You ready?" I ask, hoping the guys have already left.

"Let's go," she says, as she hoists her bag over her shoulder. I follow behind her as we head back to the truck which is still there. I gulp, hoping Sully isn't around as I would be self conscious in my bikini in front of him. I'm not as skinny as I was in high school having filled out the last few years. I love my new curves but it's still nerve wracking having the guy you used to be in love with see you half naked.

They aren't at the truck so Kate fishes two towels out of another bag for us, and hands me one. I shake it out and quickly fling it around me before Logan's voice sounds out.

"We are off babe. We'll be back soon," he says, as he walks from the bathrooms with Sully by his side. Kate walks to him and gives him a lingering hug. My eyes roam to Sully but he averts my gaze, no indication he saw me in my bikini before I covered myself.

"See you guys soon," Kate says, walking towards me. Sully's eyes lift to mine and he gives me a slight head nod, which I return before following after Kate.

Chapter Twenty-five

Sully

"I don't think me coming along was a good idea man," I tell Logan, as he slides into the passenger seat. I reverse my truck, catching sight of Willow walking towards the beach, her towel wrapped tightly around her as if she's scared I can see right through it. Heat warms my skin thinking about the glance I did catch before she covered herself with the towel. She's always been a beautiful girl but now she is all woman, having filled out with luscious curves I want to grab. I have to remember to restrain myself as she isn't mine to touch anymore.

"It'll be fine bro. If we can't find a mattress, you can always share with me and Kate can share with Willow," Logan suggests.

"No way. I'm not having you give up sleeping with your girl for me. I'll sleep in the back of the truck with or without a mattress, it'll be fine," I tell him, as we peel out of the camping complex and head to the supermarket and a few rows of shops they have nearby.

"Well let's find you a mattress," he says, as I pull into a parking spot. We exit the truck and head into the department store. We manage to find a double inflatable mattress. They have tents but are all sold out so the mattress will have to do. We take the mattress back to the truck then we head to the supermarket, grabbing a trolley to hold all our items.

"Do you think the girls will wanna go fishing one day?" I ask, thinking we could have fish for dinner if we caught anything.

"I reckon they would. We are trying to make this trip as relaxing as possible for Willow so a day spent clearing her head might be exactly what she needs," he says, as he throws some peanut butter into the trolley. I grab some tinned baked beans and spaghetti while he grabs tuna.

"What's she needing to clear her head about? You sure me being here isn't making things worse?" I ask, pushing the trolley in search of some bread.

"It's not my place to say and I don't know how she'd feel about me sharing but she's trying to sort out which direction she wants her life to go in," he says. We grab some eggs, sausages and tomato sauce for us to cook today. There's a refrigerator at the campsite but we aren't sure how secure it may be. We try to grab food we can store or eat now if possible. "And no I don't think you being here is making things worse. She said she'd work on being friends with you so I'm hoping if nothing else, you guys can at least agree on that."

"Me too," I tell him, unloading our supplies onto the checkout counter. We pay for them and head back to the camp ground after loading the truck with our bags.

Driving into the same spot as before, there's no sight of the girls so we chuck the bags from the grocery store into the first tent and begin setting up the other. It doesn't take us long as we work silently to get it done. The tents are identical so we already know what to do from putting together the first one. Once it's secured into the ground, I use the car pump to blow air into the mattress.

Chucking it into the bed of the truck it fits perfectly so I have no doubt I will get a decent sleep under the stars. I have my sleeping bag to keep me warm.

"Do you want to go find the girls while I throw the eggs and sausages on the barbeque if it's free?" Logan suggests.

"Sure," I tell him. I walk off in the direction of the beach, wondering about how the last few days of my life have played out and I've ended up here. I let the girl of my dreams slip through my fingers. I pushed her away because I was a stubborn asshole and I couldn't wade through my own self loathing thoughts to realise the harm I was causing us both when I walked away. It was the most painful thing I've ever done and I had to force myself every day not to run back and fall at her feet and ask for her forgiveness. I saw her lying in the hospital bed after she'd been drugged and I knew deep in my bones I'd made the wrong choice. Letting my dad's abusive words feed into my insecurities of not being enough was what drove me to leave her.

I realised at that moment I would never love another girl like I loved her. I don't know what it was about her which kept calling me back. We fought and made up and we pushed each other. I wasn't afraid to call her out and she wasn't afraid to do the same to me. When it mattered, I knew I could rely on her. I wish she could say the same about me but I broke her trust so badly, I don't think I can repair it.

Walking to the edge of the sand, I sit on the small grassy bank as I catch sight of Kate and Willow. They both float with their bodies above the water, eyes closed enjoying their time relaxing. They look serene and I know Logan wants Willow to clear her head so I'll give them some more time to relax. It'll take Logan a while to get everything cooked anyway.

Back to mulling over my thoughts I guess. Since the day she sent me away from the hospital, I started going to see a counsellor. Someone who was helping me overcome the abuse I'd faced at the hands of my father. I would never see my mother or father again and I was alright with the decision. They were nothing to me and had never been anything except the people who gave birth to me. I've learnt it's okay to let go of people, especially family if they are hurting you. Abuse is never okay and what happened to me was not right. I can't go back in time to change what occurred but I can work to get help to deal with the trauma they've caused to help myself live a better life.

I've also learnt what I was doing when Willow first came into my life was not living. It was surviving. I've never known what a normal life was like. I've always been stuck in survival mode. My therapist is helping but some days I'm unsure if I'll ever fully overcome the trauma I suffered. It's ingrained in me and because of it, it's shaped who I am. I always question whether I'd be a different person if my life had been easier but it's something I will never know the answer to. I really hate what if questions. They just mess with my head.

It was a few years ago when I thought of my crazy idea to plant a whole field of sunflowers for Willow. I knew how much she loved the tall beautiful flowers and so I thought if I did this amazing and crazy gesture, she would float back into my life and into my arms. Boy was I wrong. I don't know how I thought it could possibly work.

Looking out at the water where the girl who got away floats, I realise she's changed. She's not the same girl anymore. I'm trying to convince the girl she was to realise she still loves me but I need another approach and I need the woman she is now to realise she could love the man I've become.

Coming to a resolution, I decide I'll try to be her friend. If nothing else comes from it, at least I will have her back in my life in some form. Being her friend would be a blessing because it will take a miracle for her to fully trust me again.

Thinking it's been long enough for Logan to have cooked our lunch, I stand and walk to the edge of the water.

Cupping my hands around my mouth I yell out, "Willow. Kate," before dropping my hands to my sides as their peaceful moment breaks. They flounder for a minute as their legs drop into the water and their heads search for me. I wave as they look my way and they doggy paddle their way back to shore, taking their time.

Once they can touch the sea bed easily, they walk their way in. Their easy smiles with each other tugs on my heart as I wish Willow smiled easily around me like she used to. The closer they get, the lower the water becomes and I gulp as water drips off Willow's skin as her bikini clad body rises out of the water.

They get within hearing distance so I say loud enough, "Logan's cooking lunch so he sent me to find you."

"Great, we are starving," Kate says, as she sends a smile my way. Feeding her could be a way to break down the walls of her fortress. My eyes flick back to Willow as I discreetly devour her body with my eyes. I have to force my feet to stay planted. I shove my hands into my shorts pockets to keep me from wiping a stray drop of water off her skin. They walk over to their towels and I internally whimper as Willow wraps hers around her, taking her body from my view. I need to put some distance between us so I walk in the direction of the barbecue knowing they are following not far behind.

I may act like the same cold, distant boy I once was but if I talk, it would probably be gibberish or else I'd blurt out my undying love for this girl. I don't want either of those things to happen right now, because it would most likely scare her and ruin any progress I have made. Although it was only this morning she was saying she couldn't move past our history so I'm not sure if I've made any progress at all.

We find Logan zipping back and forth over the grill as he tends to the eggs and sausages. Kate waltzes over to him, throws her arms around his neck from behind and kisses his cheek.

"Hey babe, how was your swim?" he asks, smiling at her before continuing on with his cooking.

"It was so good. We are gonna eat and head back out if you guys wanna join us?"

"Sounds like a good plan."

"Do you need me to do anything?" I ask Logan, wanting to distract myself from the thoughts I'm having of Willow. She takes a seat at the closest picnic table while Kate joins her and sits opposite her.

"I forgot the bread. If you wouldn't mind going and grabbing a loaf from the tent. Grab some of the drinks too."

"Sure thing, won't be long," I tell him, turning and heading back to our camping area. It's good to have my feet moving away from her so at least I can regain my composure before I see her again. I unzip Logan's tent and grab the bread and grab one of the ten packs of drink cans we got. I have an esky in the back of my truck I always have with me so I grab it and empty the cans into it. I make a detour towards a group of guys who are sitting around on camping chairs drinking some beers.

"Hey you guys wouldn't have some spare ice I could have, would ya?" I ask, as they look at me when I get closer.

"Ollie did you use all the ice?" one guy asks, calling out to someone. A guy steps out of his tent.

"Nah, I had a spare bag we couldn't fit in. Hold up," he tells me, as he steps around some of the guy's chairs and locates a bag of ice sitting on the grass. "Here you go," he tells me, holding it out as he walks towards me.

"Thanks guys, I really appreciate it," I tell them.

"No worries man. It was gonna go to waste anyway," the first guy tells me.

"Cheers," I say, after I tip the melted ice into my esky covering the drinks and walk away from the group.

"You're welcome," someone says, as I leave.

Arriving back to Logan and the girls, I place the esky by the table.

"I put ice in there but they should be cold in a minute I reckon," I tell the girls.

"Thanks Sully," Willow says, pinching my heart.

"No problem," I tell her, giving her a smile which she returns. I place the bread on the table too and head to Logan. He's finished with the sausages so I take the tray he's placed them on and put it on the table in front of the girls along with the tomato sauce. He joins us a minute later with the eggs before he sits next to Kate, leaving an available spot next to Willow. Taking a deep breath I walk behind her and lift my leg over the picnic bench and sit beside her. With my legs spread wide under the table, my thigh rests against hers. I pretend it doesn't affect me but it does. I don't dare move as I want this small connection for as long as I can.

I'm attuned to her but I notice no reaction at all from my leg touching hers, I obviously don't affect her as she does me. The thought makes my heart sink and I realise the ship could have truly sailed with her and I've messed it up so bad she no longer feels anything for me anymore.

We forgot to buy any paper plates at the supermarket so everyone grabs slices of bread and grabs sausage or eggs to make a sandwich. It's quiet while we eat. Everyone is hungry since our last meals were this morning. Willow opens the esky and pulls out cans of drink for everyone.

"Do you want one Sully?" she asks, as she's bent over the cooler.

"Yes please." She grabs one and places it in front of me before she grabs her own. I pop the tab and take a gulp of the already cold fizz. We finish off the food quickly.

"Come on, let's go back to the water. It's so nice out there babe," Kate says, turning to Logan.

"Why don't you and Willow head back and we will clean up and meet you out there?"

"Okay. Come on Willow," she says, pulling her to her feet and dragging her away as her giggling disappears with them.

"Are you doing alright?" Logan asks. His voice pulls my eyes to him from where I didn't even realise I was watching Kate and Willow walk away. My eyes automatically follow her.

"Yeah, I'm good man. It is what it is," I sigh, lifting the can to my lips and draining it.

"So what's the plan now?" he asks, as his cheeky grin grows and he rubs his hands together.

"No plan. I've missed my chance with her." I stand gathering everyone's empty cans, and throw them in the recycling bin next to the barbeque.

"No way. There's always hope," Logan tells me. With my back to him, he can't see my visible wince at his words. Hope. I've always hated hoping. Something about Willow always stirred the feeling inside me though. She made me hope for a lot of things and it made me angry because I didn't want her tying her future to someone like me who couldn't offer her anything. Even my smiles were hard to come by. Releasing a sigh, I turn to Logan.

"Let's go have a swim, yeah?"

He searches my face before saying, "Sweet man. Umm are you gonna leave your shirt on?"

"Yeah she's had enough of my crazy ass for one day, don't you think?" My words make him laugh before he pats me on the back and we follow the trail the girls took. At the beachfront, we see the girls already walking back into the water. Logan pulls his shirt over his head, dropping it on the grass and throwing his phone on top of it. I grab my phone and throw it next to his. My t-shirt stays on and safely covers my body as I wade into the water.

Willow

184

As Kate and I wade to chest height in the water, I push off the silky sand underneath my feet and resume my floating position I had before lunch. The water covers my ears so the sound of talking is muffled. I peer my eyes around without lifting it and catch sight of Sully's man bun in my peripheral. I close my eyes, block out the world and try my hardest to block out any and all thoughts which cross my mind. I can't make out the words they are saying but the three of them talk around me as I'm content to float and relax.

The warmth from the sun warms the top of me while I remain cool from the water. I'll probably spend the majority of this trip out on the water, working on figuring out what the hell I'm supposed to do next.

My foot comes into contact with something causing me to panic and my feet drop under me.

"Sorry, it's just me," Sully says, as he grabs my arm to calm me.

"Ugh I thought it was a fish," I confess, causing our group to laugh. I can't help being entranced by the easy smile shining on Sully's face. It's such a contrast to the boy I used to know. His devilish grin holds my attention longer than it should.

His eyes shift to my lips before finding my eyes again and I realise he's still got a hold of my arm under the water. I give it a gentle tug, causing the smile to drop off his face as he releases me and regret fills me as the smile disappears.

"Sorry," he mouths, so the others can't hear. I offer a tentative smile so he knows it's okay and continue wading in the water. I must have drifted a bit further out as I can't touch the ground where I am now. Logan and Sully touch it easily and Kate bobs up and down as if she's jumping, bouncing to keep her head above it.

Easy chatter fills the air as we laugh at Logan's story about a customer he had at his hardware store this week. He's the manager of the local store and one day he's hoping to be able to open his own.

Every time Sully laughs, I can't stop my gaze from shifting to him, wanting to catch the sight. Being deprived of his smiles so many times when he was younger, it makes me want to see it even more now. I guess my eyes don't believe it's him laughing as my brain can't comprehend it.

I do notice he still wears his t-shirt in the water, even though the weight of it must be pulling him down. It drags me back to the day he let me see and feel his scars and I can't help but wonder what they look like now. His body is bigger and more muscular so I wonder if they're still as pronounced as they once were.

"I'm ready to head in," Kate says, directing her words to Logan.

"I'll join you," Logan says. "You guys gonna come?"

"Nah I might stay out a little longer," I tell them.

"I'll stay with her. Can you take my phone back to the camp?" Sully says. Logan nods at him. Kate looks to me for confirmation, making sure it's fine to leave me with Sully and I give her a slight nod. We watch as Logan and Kate make their way back to shore.

"I'm gonna go back to my floating, if that's alright with you?"

"Go ahead," Sully tells me. My ears muffle all sound again but I'm content, closing my eyes and letting myself drift. If we weren't in the water I could easily fall asleep. I wonder if it's possible to fall asleep while floating?

I have no concept of time but I'm happy to stay out here as long as I can. Muffled talking pulls my attention but I keep my eyes closed. A hard tug on my ankle has me flailing in the water before thick hands pull me into a hard chest. My limbs automatically wrap around the waist, saving myself from being pulled under the water.

"Watch where you're going!" Sully's yelling grabs my attention. I push my soaked hair out of my face to follow his line of sight. A guy in a kayak paddles past where I was floating moments ago.

"Sorry man, didn't see her," the guy winces, lifting a hand in apology.

"Be more careful next time," Sully grunts, as his hands hold on to my thighs. They slide higher up my legs until his hands are inches away from my butt. His face is watching the guy while he paddles away.

"Umm Sully?" I softly say. He turns my way as his hands squeeze before his eyes widen.

"Shit sorry," he winces, as he releases me. I unwrap myself from him while my cheeks burn.

"It's okay," I tell him.

"Must have been muscle memory," he says, scratching the back of his head and I can't help but laugh which has him joining in.

"Thanks for saving me," I tell him, when our laughter quietens.

"Anytime. You know that," he says, staring into my eyes as he moves his arms back and forth in the water.

The silence lingers before I say, "Should we head back in?"

"Umm give those two a little longer," he says, a cheeky grin spreading on his face.

"Those two. Seriously can't take them anywhere," I chuckle.

"We could go get some alcohol? I saw a liquor store when we went to the shops," Sully suggests.

"Yeah okay. Let's do it." He smiles at my response and we wade back to shore.

I grab my towel once we get back to the sand and wrap it tightly around myself. We walk back to the tents and luckily after the guys erected my tent, they thought to put my bags in there. I grab one of my bags I know has my clothes, a towel and toiletries in it and head to the showers.

Once I'm finished I find Sully leaning on the back of his truck, sunnies on and his thick arms crossed. He still makes my heart thump wildly. He gives me a small nod of his head so I drop my bag in my tent and jump in the passenger seat.

"At least the tent wasn't shaking," Sully jokes, and we both break out in laughter as the tension between us dissolves.

As he drives along the road to the small row of shops, it's silent. The tension returned as soon as the joke was over. His fingers tap on the steering wheel along to the beat of the song playing softly from the radio.

"Since we are rekindling our friendship, is it alright for me to ask what you've been doing with yourself for the last few years?" he asks, pulling into a parking spot right outside the liquor store. We unbuckle and hop out before I answer.

"Well I finished my accounting degree and I was working as a junior accountant at this firm but I realised pretty early on I don't like working in an office. I love accounting but the office environment was toxic and draining so after a year I quit," I explain, as we enter the store. The coolness from the air conditioning battles with the heat outside.

"It's good you realised early on it's not what you want to do. Many people stay in jobs they hate for years before they work up the courage to leave, and still some never leave. I'm proud of you," he says, smiling at me. My cheeks redden under his gaze.

"Thanks. I've been thinking that I'm having a mid-life crisis."

"Nah. You know what you don't want to be doing and now you can go after what it is you really want to do."

Releasing a puff of breath I say, "If only it was that easy. I have no idea what I want to do now and doing nothing doesn't pay the bills."

"I'm sure it'll come to you. Don't be so hard on yourself in the meantime."

"Thanks Sully." Now it's time for his cheeks to redden.

"Do you know what you want to drink? I'll probably grab a couple of cases of beer for us guys," he says, pointing to the freezer area.

"I'll be over here by the wine," I tell him, pointing to the shelf with all the wines set out along it.

"Be back soon," he says, before walking off and opening the freezer door. I scan the selection of white wines. There's a sign saying there's a discount if I buy six bottles. A presence behind me makes me crane my neck to the side. Sully stands there holding two large twenty four packs of beer as if it weighs nothing.

"What are you thinking so hard about?" he asks. The hint of a smile on his face, distracts me from ogling his arms.

"Do you think six bottles of wine is too much?" I ask, pointing to the green tag with the sale sign on it.

"For you and Kate right?"

"Yeah."

"Nah it's fine. If you don't drink it, you guys can take it home with you," he says, walking over to the counter with his boxes.

"Hey man," he says to the cashier, before walking back over to me. "Which ones do you want?" he directs at me.

I grab two moscatos and my hands are full. Sully pulls them out of my hands, sending warmth through me. I grab another moscato which he automatically takes. I scan the bottles grabbing three of Kate's favourite chardonnays. Sully again takes one of the bottles, holding four in his hands while I hold two. We place them on the counter as well. The cashier scans all our items and Sully pulls out his card and taps it to pay before I can even offer to pay for the wines.

"I can pay for mine," I tell him, but his stone face I remember from long ago looks at me.

"My shout okay?" I nod. "Mate, have you got a box for the wine?" he asks the cashier.

"Yeah sure. Hold on," he tells us, scrounging around under the counter before popping back with an empty box. He carefully places the six bottles in there.

"Thanks man," Sully says, before turning to me.

"Will you be okay with this?" he says, holding out the box for me.

"Yeah," I tell him, holding my arms out for him to pass me the box. I take the weight and walk out to the truck with him close behind with the two cases of beer. He places the beer over the side of the truck in the open bed where there's a gap between the truck and the mattress.

"Do you want to hold the wine on your lap?"

"Yeah it's probably best," I tell him.

"Oh I'll grab some cups unless you guys are gonna chug from the bottle?" he says, a wide smile shining at me.

"Cups would be great," I say, laughing. He unlocks the truck for me to hop in as he heads back into the store, returning a minute later with a packet of red party cups and ice. He throws the ice in the back, jumps into the driver's seat, hands me the cups and turns the car on. "They've had plenty of time to finish right?" I ask, my face heating.

"Unless they've gone for round two or three," he says, making my face even hotter at the thought of Sully going for rounds two and three. I keep my eyes facing forward not wanting to lock eyes with him after his statement. The silence stretches as we travel along the road back to camp. Pulling into our spot I'm glad to see Kate and Logan seated outside on camping chairs, both looking freshly showered after their swim and extra curricular activities.

"Where'd you two go?" Logan calls, looking between us.

"Supplies," Sully says, walking around the back of the truck and pulling the two boxes of beer out. Logan's eyes light up when he sees it.

"Yes. A cold beer would go down nicely," he says, taking one of the boxes from Sully. "I'll put this one in the tent for tomorrow."

Sully walks over to the esky, rips open the beer box and places the beers carefully inside.

"Pass me some of the wine Willow." I walk over to him, pulling two bottles out one at a time and he places them in along with the rest of the cans. I take the box with the remaining wine bottles and place it in my tent while he heads to the back of the truck to get the ice. He walks over to a footpath off to the side of our grassy area and throws it to the ground to break it apart. He does it a second time to make sure it's fully broken up and rips the plastic bag open. The ice sprinkles on top of the alcohol as he empties the bag. Closing the lid he scrunches the bag in his hands before walking over to the bin and putting the rubbish inside.

"Is your hangover gone?" Kate asks me, handing me her chair as she grabs another one from the ground and shakes it out of its bag.

"Yeah the swim worked it out of my system. Doubt I'll drink much tonight," I say, which has her nodding as she flings her chair out and sits.

"Yeah same."

"Do you know what you are gonna do about work yet Willow?" Logan asks, taking one of the other seats.

"Nah not yet. I still don't know what I want to do," I say.

"You could work for me?" Sully's voice suggests, as he comes back from the rubbish bin and all eyes flick to him.

"What?" I ask.

"You need a job. I need a new accountant. Win win," he states, like it's the most normal thing in the world offering his ex a job.

"You don't think it would be weird?" I ask.

"Not unless we make it weird. We're trying to be friends right? Friends offer other friends jobs. Plus you would get to see the sunflower fields whenever you wanted," he bargains.

"It would be your dream job," Logan's voice pipes in from beside me.

"Can I think about it?" I ask.

"Sure. Offer is there as long as you need," he says, taking his own seat and pulling a beer out of the esky before throwing it to Logan and grabbing his own.

"Thanks Sully," I say, giving him a small smile which he returns. "How did you start the sunflower field business anyway?" I ask, as curiosity gets the best of me.

"My grandparents passed away within a month of each other in my first year of university. They left me their house so I sold it and opened the business. Had to make use of my business degree somehow," he says, before taking a sip of his beer.

"Sorry about your grandparents," I tell him, remembering back to when my grandpa passed and it was Sully who consoled me. He stares at me as he tilts his head to the side and I wonder if he's reliving the memory too. It's also the memory of my first kiss but I always try to forget that part.

"Thanks," he says, and I give him a small smile before turning away. Logan directs the conversation away from Sully, saving him from having to add anything further. It does make me wonder what he's been doing in the years he's been missing from my life but I stay silent not asking the questions I desperately want the answers to.

Kate and I wait a while before opening our wine and we drink one bottle. We all laugh and tell stories before we call it a night. My thoughts are distracted anyway wondering about the possibility of working closely with Sully and if my heart could handle it.

Chapter Twenty-six

Sully

Stretching my arms above my head, the sun shines brightly above me. It wasn't too bad sleeping out in the open air. It was warm enough in my sleeping bag, I didn't even realise I was under the elements. The beers I drank last night probably helped knock me out as well. Lifting my head there are a few sleepy eyed people heading to the bathrooms and such. I roll over and close my eyes again because it's still early but I doubt I'll get back to sleep now, especially with the sun already heating up. It isn't long until the rustling of Logan's tent grabs my attention and Logan emerges followed by a bushy haired Kate.

"Hey," they both croak at me, when they see I'm awake. They both wander off to the bathrooms and I decide it's probably time to leave my warm cocoon. We'll need to think of breakfast anyway so will need to get supplies.

Hopping out of my sleeping bag, I grab my discarded t-shirt and slide it back over my head. I put my sleeping bag out of the way as we'll need the truck to get the food. I pop it in the backseat and grab my toiletries before heading to the bathrooms myself. Placing my small grey bag by the sink, I relieve myself, brush my teeth and wash my face as I meet Logan who is doing the same.

"Kate and I might go grab some breakfast. We were thinking we could all grab kayaks and go out on the water later," he says, waiting for me to finish.

"Sounds great," I reply, placing my things back in my bag and zipping it up.

"Things between you and Willow are looking better," he says, as we slow our steps on our way back to our camp.

"Yeah, deciding to be friends was a good idea. I can't force her to want to be with me. I was dumb to let her go in the first place," I sigh.

He pats me on the back saying, "I'm sorry man. I know how much you love her."

"Yeah well apparently love isn't enough sometimes," I tell him, as we get back to our camp, right at the moment Willow steps out of her tent. Her eyes find mine as her lips twist to the side. From the look on her face, I know she heard the tail end of the conversation.

"Morning," Logan cheerily greets her.

"Morning," she replies, before walking past us and heading to the bathroom herself with her own toiletry bag.

"She heard us, didn't she?" Logan asks, when she's disappeared behind the building, well out of ear shot.

"Definitely," I tell him, sighing.

"Shake it off man. You're on holiday. Enjoy it," he says, trying to keep me uplifted.

"I'm good," I tell him, as Kate arrives back.

"Come on babe, let's do a food run," he tells her, and she nods as she tosses her things into their tent. I pass Logan the keys and they hop in the truck driving away as Willow arrives back.

"They've gone to get breakfast," I fill her in. She nods, turning to walk into her tent before stopping and turning back.

"Are we okay Sully? Like with us trying to be friends?" she asks, with her eyes to the ground. I gently release a breath before taking a step closer. The last thing I want to do is make her uncomfortable. Old habits die hard and I find my knuckles lifting her chin so I can see those beautiful eyes of her. She's got her glasses on today. The frames aren't like the ones she used to wear in high school, they are still black just thinner frames. I love the way her eyes look behind them. Big, bright and beautiful.

"We are good Low. If being your friend again is all I ever get, so be it. I will be eternally grateful for a second chance, so thank you," I tell her, and I can't help but slide my knuckle forward, savouring the feel of her skin before I release her.

"Okay," she breathes, rooted to the spot. It takes her a minute before she visibly shakes her head and turns back to her tent, crouching before she walks in. I take a seat in one of the camping chairs, leaning my head back, eyes closed and enjoying the morning sun on my face. A few minutes later her tent rustles before she sits in the chair beside me. I peek at her out of one eye and she's in the same position as me. Head resting back, eyes closed and facing the sun.

"Did you know the young sunflowers track the sun? They follow it across the sky until it sets and during the night they slowly move back to face the east so they are ready to do it again the next day," I tell her, watching as she remains with her eyes closed but a smile grows.

"I always thought it was all sunflowers who did that."

"No, only the young ones until they mature enough and then they stop doing it," I explain.

"It's cool they do that," she says, her smile growing.

"I don't blame them, the sun is beautiful," I say, my eyes and words solely focussed on her. She opens her eyes and turns her head my way. Her eyes widen, noticing my eyes on her and I wonder if she got the hidden meaning behind my words. I give nothing away, turning my face back to the sun as I close my eyes but not before the pink tinge covers her cheeks.

The sound of the truck pulls our attention towards it and I stand to go help them with the food.

"We grabbed pancake supplies," Kate calls out the open window. They both jump out and we all head over to the barbeque area to make pancakes.

"Willow, are you keen to hit the kayaks today?" Logan asks her, as he pours the pancake mix on the grill.

"Yeah it sounds like fun," she says, smiling at him while the three of us sit at the same picnic table as yesterday while we wait for Logan to cook. He's become our designated chef.

After we've filled our bellies, we sit around our campsite a bit talking while we let our food digest. Everyone is in a relaxed holiday mood today, the alcohol consumed last night probably contributed to it.

"Come on lazy butts, let's head out on the water," Logan directs, jumping up from his chair. The rest of us slowly move and the girls grab their swimsuits and head to the bathrooms to change. I grab some board shorts and pull off the shorts I'm wearing and change right in the middle of the campground. It doesn't bother me as I'm wearing briefs. I change my t-shirt for a fitted singlet as well while the girls aren't around to see.

"You got sunscreen?" I call out to Logan, who is changing in his tent. His head pops out as he throws the blue spray bottle out to me and I catch it, fumbling a bit. I spray some of the white cream into my hand, place the bottle on the ground and rub it all over my arms. I repeat it, rubbing it into my face and neck before tying my hair into a low bun at the base of my neck. Logan comes out of his tent and grabs the sunscreen and covers himself in it too. I finish off doing my legs before the girls arrive back.

"Can you put some on my back babe?" Kate asks Logan.

"Do you want me to do yours Willow?" I ask, and she offers a small smile before nodding and turning around, giving me her back. Logan throws me the bottle and again I spray it into my hands. She sweeps her thick black hair into a high ponytail, securing it with a hair tie. I massage her shoulders, rubbing the lotion in and her head flops forward as I move my hands around her neck. I lose myself for a minute forgetting I'm supposed to be applying sunscreen and not giving her a massage.

It's not until Kate says, "Ahem," and I see her raised eyebrow and smiling face that I snap out of it. Willow's head pops up as I stop.

"Aww why did you have to stop him? I was enjoying the free massage," Willow whines, causing us all to laugh.

"Hurry up you two," Logan tells us, as he pops back into his tent for something. I lean over the side of Willow away from Kate and whisper in her ear.

"I can give you a proper massage sometime if you want?" Her head nods, making my heart sing. I make quick work of applying the sunscreen to the rest of her back and can't help my hands when they linger at the curve of her lower back. "All done," I tell her. She smiles over her shoulder as I hand her the bottle. I walk over to my truck to grab a towel and sunglasses so I don't stare at her while she rubs the sunscreen into the rest of her body.

She makes quick work of it and we walk as a group to the beach. The camp manager said anyone who stays at the camp can use the kayaks so we each grab one and drag them to the water. Logan helps Kate in and gives her a push off so I do the same with Willow as she lays her oar across her body. I push her as far as I can and she paddles as she floats to a deeper patch of water. Logan and I have to walk ourselves into the water before we can hop in and use our paddles. The bright sun is high above us now. A few clouds splatter the sky but apart from that it's looking like a nice day to be out on the water.

We paddle around getting used to the oars. The kayak isn't as big as I'd like but I can sit without being too uncomfortable. Once we hit further out on the water where there aren't any swimmers, I rest the oar on my lap and float instead of working by paddling. Willow's laughter reaches my ears, causing me to turn in that direction. A carefree smile graces her face making a smile tug at my lips in response. She's laughing at Kate who can't get the hang of paddling and keeps turning herself in circles while Logan yells instructions to her. All it does is make Willow laugh more. Her eyes look and scan the water as if looking for me. Our eyes lock and her smile widens at me as I return it.

We lose sense of time out on the water, enjoying the sun and serenity of being out there relaxing. It makes me aware I have few moments in my life where I relaxed and enjoyed the company of my friends. I was too consumed with how I was feeling to realise the damage I would do to all of us by taking off. I was so lost in the moment, I made the decision to save myself but it cost me more than I realised I was willing to lose. If I could turn back time I would have run to Willow again but when I was in the moment I couldn't bear dragging her deeper into my shitstorm. My only thought was to free her of the crap surrounding me.

With my mood turning sombre, I pick the oar up and paddle away from my group to regather myself. I put distance between us, taking a big deep breath with each stroke through the water, letting go of the past. I can't change it and I've been working on letting it go but there are always moments when it creeps up on me, trying to pull me back to the dark place I was stuck in. I won't go back there though and I have to remain in the present. I take a few minutes to myself, breathing and pulling myself together before I paddle myself back to them. Willow's brows have a small furrow between them as I return as if she can sense a change in me but she doesn't say anything.

We spend a few more hours out there until the wind grows stronger and a few more clouds appear in the sky.

"Let's head in and get dinner sorted since we skipped lunch," Logan yells out. We all agree so we paddle into shore. I get to the sand before Willow so turn to help her with her kayak when she hops out, dragging it over to the stand with the others.

We dry off and head back to camp. Logan says he's going to check out the kitchen and use the microwave and toaster in there so we can have baked beans and spaghetti on toast. Kate joins him and Willow and I both head to the bathrooms for showers. By the time I get back, Kate and Logan are walking back from the kitchen with a huge stack of toast on a plate and two large bowls. One with baked beans and one with spaghetti. Willow isn't too far behind and we all sit in our camping chairs, grabbing slices and putting what we want on it. All of us are starved so it doesn't take us long to finish all the food. I offer to clean since the others cooked. I take the dishes back to the kitchen and wash them in the sink, leaving them there to dry as they belong to the camp kitchen.

When I arrive back, Logan is carrying the esky out of his tent he stowed in there last night. He thought of grabbing ice this morning and filled it with beer and wine again so it's all cold and ready to drink. He throws me a beer as I approach my seat, catching it without fumbling this time. He pops the cork out of the wine and fills a glass each for

Willow and Kate. I take a long sip of the beer, savouring the refreshing cool liquid which is nice after a long day out in the sun. Kate throws back her wine quickly, before grabbing her things and heading to the showers. Logan leaves his half finished beer following behind her.

"You know I'm glad you came with us," Willow's voice breaks through my thoughts.

"You are?"

"Yeah. I would have felt like such a third wheel if it was just me and them here," she says, taking another sip of her wine.

I glance at the sky as more grey covers it now.

"Are you sunburnt?" I ask.

"No, I don't think I got it too bad," she says, as she inspects her body for any redness.

"Well if you wanted I could give you a shoulder massage now?" I suggest. Her eyes light up at my suggestion.

"Oh my gosh that would be amazing. Especially after sitting in the kayak for so long. My back is killing me," she rushes out her words, excitement bubbling around her.

"Have you got any body lotion?"

"Oh yeah I do," she says, disappearing into her tent and returning a few beats later holding a pink bottle. She's also changed into a spaghetti strapped singlet so I have access to her shoulders and neck. She walks over and hands it to me. "Where do you want me?"

Wild thoughts flash through my mind before I say, "Grab a towel and sit on the ground in front of me." She goes back to her tent and returns with a towel, folding it and placing it on the ground between my outstretched legs. She turns so her back is to me, before dropping to the ground. My big thick legs crowd her as her butt sits on the towel.

Squirting some of her strawberry smelling lotion into my hand, I pass the bottle over her shoulder and rub my hands together. She ties her hair out of the way and I slip my hands against her skin as I lightly smooth the lotion out. Rubbing my hands back and forth, I warm up her skin before my hands work in sync, applying pressure to the sides of her neck and I push in deeper.

"Oh my gosh, it feels so good," she moans, and I can't help the twitch my dick makes at the sound. I keep my pressure firm as I glide along her shoulders, moving one hand across and working the right side before moving to the left. Her head drops forward as she relaxes. I run my thumbs along the sides of her spine of her upper back, feeling a couple of knots and working on those. It accomplishes more small moans from her and I can't help but smile.

"It looks amazing," Kate's voice says, breaking the bubble we were in.

"It seriously is so good," Willow tells her.

"Babe, I'll give you one if you want?" Logan tells her, which has her smile appearing. Logan sits in the seat he had vacated and Kate copies Willow and sits on a towel between Logan's legs. Willow passes over her lotion and Logan follows my lead and begins massaging Kate. I stop to take a drink of my beer otherwise we carry on massaging the girls for a while.

Kate pours herself another wine and she fills Willow's cup as well. I knock back the beer I had and Kate passes me and Logan a new one. I pull the tab back with a pop and take a long drink before placing the can into the cup holder of the chair. I apply more lotion and resume working the tension out of her muscles.

Other groups of campers are sitting around laughing and chatting, the same as us. I happily keep massaging Willow and she doesn't ask me to stop. The girls finish off their first bottle of wine and open another. Logan and I finish a few of the beers before we are greeted by the camp manager who walks over after finishing chatting with one of the other groups.

"How's everyone this evening?" she asks.

"Good," we all reply.

"Well I'm going around because there's supposed to be a storm brewing tonight. I want everyone to be prepared so make sure your tents are secured and everything else is stowed away if possible," she informs us.

"Thanks for warning us Laurel," Logan says to her, which has her nodding before walking away to go and inform some of the other campers.

Kate and Logan whisper to each other before Logan says, "Sully you can sleep in the tent with me and Kate will share with Willow."

"No. We aren't splitting you guys up. If the storm hits, Sully can jump in my tent. It's fine," Willow says, causing my hands to stop their movements.

"Are you sure?" I ask. She turns her face over her shoulder.

"Yeah it's fine. Don't keep me up with your snoring," she jokes, making me smile.

"I remember when you used to snore really unladylike back in the day," I chuckle.

"I did not," she denies.

"Oh yes you did Willow. I remember that night. You were fast asleep in the car, snoring louder than anyone I've ever heard," Logan joins in, and we burst with laughter while Willow crosses her arms over her chest in a huff.

"Don't worry, it was cute," I tell her.

"Yeah if you're into that type of thing," Logan jokes, causing us all to howl with laughter.

"I'm gonna get you," Willow shrieks, jumping between my legs as Logan leaps from his seat running off with Willow hot on his tail. Kate and I sit there laughing as she chases him through the campground while Logan continues to tease her by making loud snoring noises at her. She continues chasing him until she tires and begins walking her way back to us.

"My snoring isn't that bad, is it?" she says, quietly as she gets closer to me, dropping in front of me again. I place my hands back on her shoulders as if it's the most natural thing in the world to be touching her like this.

Leaning forward I whisper, "I'd put up with your snoring forever if it meant waking up next to you every day." She involuntarily shivers before glancing over her shoulder. The red of her skin runs from her cheeks to her neck as she blushes.

"Sully," she whispers back, and I shrug my shoulders at her before letting my fingers work her muscles again.

Chapter Twenty-seven

Willow

His firm hands knead my muscles and I am literally putty in his hands. He could do anything he wanted to me right now and I wouldn't stand a chance. His hands are magic. Sitting between his solid legs makes me feel safe, like I'm in a cocoon and nothing could harm me. The wine I've had makes me tipsy but still aware of what I'm doing. It loosened my worries and let them drift away. What I would give to always feel this relaxed.

Sully's words filter through my head. Why can't I forgive him and give him another chance? The thought of the pain I went through stings my chest and I realise it's still as raw as it always was. He left me and I don't know if I could ever let myself be vulnerable again or have to worry about him leaving me again.

The breeze is cooler now and a lot stronger than it was earlier as the sky has darkened while we've been out here. I place my hands on Sully's thick thighs to hoist myself up and he helps steady me.

"You okay Low?" he asks, giving my sides a gentle squeeze.

"Yeah, gonna grab a jumper because it's a bit chilly," I tell him, and he nods before he releases my waist. I stumble into my tent, comb through my bag until I find my grey hoodie jumper. I pull it over my head and walk out, feeling better already. I stagger towards Sully and see Kate and Logan have disappeared again.

"Where'd they go?" I ask, looking around for them.

"Bathrooms. Not sure how long they'll be though," he says, wriggling his brows at me, making me giggle. I stagger towards him intent on sitting between his legs to finish my massage but I trip instead and fly into him. He grabs me, before I go face first into his crotch.

"Sorry, I tripped," I tell him. I step closer between his legs, ready to sit and resume my massage but he keeps a hold of my waist, looking at me.

"What are you doing Low?" his gentle voice asks.

My brows pull together as I say, "I wanna finish my massage," laughing lightly. His smile stretches across his face.

"I can't massage you now with your jumper on," he tells me. I whack the palm against my forehead.

"Damn it. I was enjoying that," I tell him. A gust of wind blows past us, making me shiver again.

"Come here," he says, pulling me closer and turning me around as he pulls me into his lap. "I'll keep you warm." His warm breath caresses my cheek causing me to snuggle further. His hands wriggle their way into the pockets of my hood, wrapping around me, keeping me close. I sink into his arms more, my heart pounding. I know I should probably move off him as I'm giving him the wrong impression but the wine I've had is telling me it's okay.

"Stop moving Low." His deep voice sounds in my ear and I realise what he's referring to as he thickens underneath me.

"I can move," I tell him.

"No, it's fine. He'll behave," he tells me, chuckling. I relax against him, warming up quickly as he's like a built-in heater.

"It's not just me, right? They are taking a long time to pee," I say, and his body vibrates with laughter.

"Yeah they aren't peeing I'd say," he replies, making us both laugh. I close my eyes. The wine is making me sleepy. My head rests back against his shoulder but I turn it snuggling into his neck, eliciting a moan from him. He squeezes me tighter and again I wonder why him wanting a second chance is such a bad idea.

Rushing feet coming our way has me peeling my eyes open to see Logan and Kate racing towards us holding hands, wide smiles on their faces.

"You two took your time," Sully jokes, which makes their smiles grow. They both glance at me with a raised brow each but don't say anything about where I currently sit.

"You know," Logan says to Sully, shrugs his shoulders and Sully shakes his head at him.

"Kate, can you come with me to pee?" I ask, feeling nature call.

"Yeah sure." Sully removes his hands from my pockets and places his hands on my waist, lifting me to my feet. Kate grabs my hand and we stumble on the dark trail to the bathrooms. "I'm gone for five minutes and you end up in the man's lap," she teases. I laugh.

"I was cold and just kind of fell into it," I tell her.

"Sure you did." We laugh together as we enter the bathroom. I quickly pee. My bladder thanking me before I stumble to the sink to wash my hands.

"I'm ready for bed," I tell her, looking at her through the mirror.

"Alone or...," her voice trails off.

"Alone. Only yesterday I was telling him we couldn't be together. Oh my gosh how come it feels like we've been here for ages already?" I tell her, pulling my hair tie out and redoing it.

"You know even though it's only been a short while, I can see he's changed. It's as if he's shed the ghosts from his past which haunted him," she tells me.

"Yeah I don't think I've ever seen him smile as much as he has in the last two days," I admit, which makes me both happy and sad. Happy he was able to get to a point in his life where he's managed to heal and deal with the trauma they caused but sad I missed out on parts of his life.

"You know it's alright to let him back in your life if it's what you want to do," she says, pulling me in for a hug.

"For now I need sleep," I say, releasing her and letting out a burp. We crack up laughing and manage to make it back to our campsite without falling over.

"We're gonna crash," Kate tells the guys, and they both nod. They stand from their chairs and everyone says goodnight. Kate crosses over to Logan and they disappear into their tent, giggling as they do.

"Goodnight Low," Sully says, a small smile on his lips.

"Night Sully," I say, turning to my tent and entering. I zip my sleeping bag closed and wriggle my way into it and lay back on my pillow. I close my eyes, and drift off as the wind rattles my tent around me. The rustling lulls me to sleep.

Cracking thunder shakes me awake and my eyes pop open. Bright flashing lightning shines across the tent before another crack sounds through the night. Pitter patter of rain hits the tent and I snuggle into the sleeping bag, wanting to hide from the storm. I close my eyes again until a thought niggles at my fuzzy brain.

"Sully!" I scream as I scramble out of my bag, crawl to the tent door and unzip it. Holding it closed I release a corner to yell out.

"Sully?" I can't make out his body on the back of his truck so I call again. "Sully?" I scream, but the howling wind drowns my voice out. "Shit," I curse, knowing I'm going to have to venture out to find him. I release the tent and make a mad dash as the wind and stinging rain whips against me. I chuck the hood over my head, rush to the back of the truck but he's not there. I round the truck to the driver's side and bang on the window. His sleeping form shakes awake at my intrusion. He pushes his door open.

"Willow what are you doing? Get in here," he says, pulling me into his lap as he pushes the seat right back so I don't hit the steering wheel. I straddle his lap as he closes the door.

"I thought you were sleeping on the back of the truck in the rain. I came to save you," I tell him, which makes him laugh. His hand pushes my hood and smoothes my wet hair.

"Thank you for the thought but you look like a drowned rat," he tells me, chuckling to himself. I hit his chest.

"I do not," I huff.

"A cute rat but a wet one," he says, his smile remaining on his face. I lift my hand to hit him again but he anticipates it and grabs my wrist to stop my motion. His eyes flicker back and forth between mine and it reminds me of the boy I used to know. "Low?" he asks, and I lick my lips before I pull his bottom lip with my thumb.

"Sully?"

"Yeah?"

"Do you wanna be stupid for a night?" I ask, as the storm rages around us. His chest heaves as he contemplates the old words we would say to each other.

A minute passes while I wait for his response.

"Are you drunk?" he asks.

"No, I'm tipsy but most of it has worn off," I tell him, being truthful.

"And you want this?" I nod, staring straight into his eyes. "You want me?" his voice asks, quieter this time. I nod again. "No, I wanna hear you say it," he states.

Holding his gaze I say, "I want you," making his chest heave harder.

"Fuck it," he says. His hand cups the back of my head and pulls my lips to his. Our tongues lash against each other as all our emotions fight their way out of our systems. I wrap my arms around his neck, pulling myself flush against him. With one hand in my hair, the other slides to cup my butt and drags me closer still. We suck and bite and nip at each other, letting our pent up feelings release. His hand cups my face, taking control and manoeuvring me how he wants me.

The storm lashes against the windows as they fog up from our body heat. He breaks apart from me, his swollen, wet lips visible in the dark.

"Are you sure about this?" he asks again.

"For tonight," I tell him quietly, letting him know it's a one time thing. I don't want him hoping for more than I can offer. His hands grab the hem of the hoodie, lifting it over my head as I raise my arms. He does the same with my singlet, leaving me in my bra.

"You're so damn beautiful," he tells me, his eyes holding mine, not even looking at my body. I unclip my bra, pull my arms through and release my breasts. He caresses both of them, swiping my nipples. I fling my head behind me, closing my eyes and losing myself in the sensations. He grabs my butt again, pulling me against him. I can feel him easily through his basketball shorts so I rock against him, causing him to moan. He lifts me by the waist, bringing my nipple straight to his mouth, where he wants it. He sucks and bites. I push my shorts and underwear off needing more. Needing him.

He catches my movement so helps me stand on the floor board to manoeuvre my clothes off. He lifts his butt, yanks his shorts and briefs down, releasing himself. He looks thicker than I remember. All the time Sully and I were together, we did everything but we never took the final step and had sex. I never understood why and I know now is not the time to ask but the thought niggles in my brain nonetheless.

His thumb finds the spot, calling for his attention. He rubs it exactly how he used to. He remembers what I like.

"That's it sweetheart," he whispers, as his other hand fiddles with the centre console. He flicks his wallet open and grabs a condom out. I grab it from his fingers, and rip it open. I moan loudly as he keeps rubbing between my legs. I grasp him and slide the condom onto his silky skin. He picks me up, kneading my butt as he pulls me forward. Dragging my bottom lip between his, he devours my mouth again holding me in the air. I can feel myself getting wetter the longer he kisses me. I need him inside me but he holds me inches away from where I want to be.

"Sully," I beg, feeling his smile against my lips.

"Yes?" he asks, playfully.

"Please?" I beg. He releases my lips to stare into my eyes. He slowly lowers me and I close my eyes and he stops holding me in place.

"Eyes open and on me," he tells me. I do as he says, forcing them to remain on him. I moan as he fills me and even though my eyes want to shut, I keep them on him like he asked. His eyes crinkle as his lips form a firm line. His eyes flutter as if they want to shut too but he keeps them on me as I open my mouth as he lowers me all the way. His thumb rubs back against my spot and I have to fight not to throw my head back in ecstasy. Watching him while he's inside me is the most erotic experience I've ever had and I find the pressure building until I explode all over him.

"Fuck Willow," he moans, as he continues working me until the wave finishes. My relaxed body sags but he takes my lips in his, kissing me gently. I begin rocking on him and he grabs my waist, helping me move in the small space. Wrapping my arms around his neck, he uses one hand to keep me moving in rhythm while his thumb heads back to my sensitive spot. His lips lavish my neck before he bites my shoulder, sending a burst of an unexpected orgasm through me. He takes control of my hips as I become languid in his lap. He moves me as he pumps into me, chasing his own release. His face and his movements turn uncontrolled. His eyes squeeze shut as his deep moan fills the cab as he finds his release.

Our laboured breaths surround us as he opens his eyes. A lazy smile shines my way as he pulls me forward, taking my lips in a slow kiss. He pulls back and I rest my cheek on his neck, noticing he still has his shirt on.

"You didn't even get fully undressed," I tease.

"Guess I was too excited," he says, running his fingers through my hair. We stay like that for a minute longer before I lean back. Although he smiles at me, there's a sadness in his eyes as he lifts me off him, breaking the connection between our bodies. He unrolls the condom and ties it, before pulling his shorts and briefs back on. He helps me wriggle my own shorts back on before I clip my bra back in place and put my singlet and wet hoodie back on.

The storm continues raging around us as we stare at each other, a tension that wasn't there before now evident.

"Come back to the tent with me," I tell him.

"I shouldn't," he tells me, pushing his lips to the side.

"Come on. You'll get a better sleep in there than in here," I argue, as I stroke his cheek with my thumb. He closes his eyes at my touch before he grabs my wrist. He turns, kisses my palm and opens his eyes.

"Let's go," he softly says, and a smile springs to my face. He grabs the keys to the truck and puts it in his pocket, along with the used condom and wrapper.

"On three. One, two, three," I squeal, flinging the door open and making a run for the tent through the pelting rain. I turn around expecting him right behind me but he's not there. He arrives a few minutes later, crawling in beside me, with his sleeping bag tucked under his arm.

"Had to throw the rubbish away," he says, explaining why he took so long. He pulls the cord open on his bag, pulling his sleeping bag out. He unzips the whole thing, grabs hold of mine and does the same before he attaches them together by the zip, making one big blanket.

"Get your wet clothes off," he instructs me. I pull the hoodie over my head as it caught the brunt of the storm. It still rages outside, whipping and lashing at the tent. My shorts are wet too so I wriggle out of those as well. He lays the sleeping bag out.

"What about your wet clothes?" I ask, ogling him in the dark. He holds my gaze in the moonlight, his face covered by shadows but I see it. His wall flies up. I don't know what causes it but I was so used to seeing the same expression on his face for so long, it's etched in my memories. He's pulling away. My hand grasps his and squeezes tight. He releases it and eases his shorts off, staying in his briefs. He closes his eyes, taking a deep breath before he opens them. He grasps the hem of his shirt pulling it over his head, before closing the distance not letting me inspect his body like I wanted. He turns me so my back is to him. He lays us down, stealing the pillow for himself and slides his arm under my head so I can use him as a pillow. Pulling the blanket over us, warmth envelopes me from his body. I sink into him as he pulls me in tighter, snuggling his face into my hair as he breathes out a sigh.

"Sleep sweetheart," he tells me, and it's exactly what I do.

Chapter Twenty-eight

Sully

Staring at her, while her snores fill the air I can't help but feel like I'm losing her all over again. Last night was more than I ever imagined it could be. To say I'd dreamt about having her in that way is an understatement. I'd wanted her from the moment I met her in the dark room all those moons ago. I still wanted her. Frankly I'd never stopped wanting her but I didn't know what else I could do to prove my love to her.

With my body wrapped around her, an ease settles in myself I haven't felt before. If only I could convince her to take another chance on me.

I loosen my grip on her to find my t-shirt. Feeling along the ground, I find it but it's still soaked. The rain still rages outside so it doesn't matter if I put it on wet as it's gonna get wet regardless. Coming to my decision, I slip my arm out from under her and move away from her to put it on.

"Sully?" she gently calls, causing me to forget my discarded t-shirt as I turn back to her. She's lying there with her eyes closed. Sighing I slide in behind her and wrap my arms back around her. "Mmm that's better," she mumbles, before her snores fill the tent again. Breathing in the scent of her hair, the only thought I have is to hell with the consequences as my eyes close and I drift back to sleep.

A soft melody plays and drags me from my deep sleep.

"Shit," Willow says. I still have my arms wrapped around her as she pushes out of my grip. I peek an eye open and catch her sweet butt right in my face as she's crouched over, feeling around the ground for the sound. As she wriggles in front of me, I can't help the feeling of wanting to bite her skin bubbling inside of me. Before I give in to temptation, the sound stops for a couple seconds before sounding again. She locates it and pulls the phone to her ear.

"Hey Stephen," she greets, and my ears perk up. I'm guessing it's her stepdad unless she knows more than one Stephen these days. She's silent for a beat before she adds, "What? When?" She glances at me before listening to the person on the other end of the phone. "Okay. Yeah, I can do that. It's not a problem. Yep. I'll be there as soon as I can. Bye," she says, before she ends the call.

"What's wrong?" I ask.

"My mum had a fall and broke her leg. My stepdad's got a conference he's gotta go to for a few days so he asked if I can go and stay with her until he gets back," she explains.

"So you gotta cut this trip short?" I ask, pain stabbing at my heart, realising she might be slipping out of my grip faster than I anticipated.

"Yeah. He's gotta fly out to his conference tomorrow so I gotta leave as soon as possible. I'll have to break it to the other two that I've gotta go. I was enjoying it here too," she tells me, as she looks at me. We smile at each other but her gaze wanders and I realise the sleeping bag has slipped to my waist, leaving my chest bare and exposed. Her breath catches as mine picks up. This is not how I wanted her to see this. I catch her pupils widening as her gaze flickers back to the tattoo covering one side of my chest and along my side to cover my scars. "What? What is that?" she stutters, before she pulls away and puts some distance between us. I focus on my breaths, keeping them under control. I haven't had a panic attack in so long but the thought of her running from me now is enough to cause one. "Why do you have huge sunflowers with dirt at the bottom tattooed on you, Sully?" her voice shakes as she asks.

Pulling deep breaths in, I force air into my lungs.

"You know why," I tell her. She scrunches her eyes shut before they flash open.

"You don't get to do this. You don't get to walk right back into my life with this sunflower field and a tattoo. I don't even know what it means and amazing sex and what, I'm supposed to accept you left me?" she rants.

"Amazing sex?" I focus on the wrong thing, as her eyes burn at me. I hold my hands up in defence. "Okay, okay, ask me what the tattoo means," I tell her. She huffs out her breaths, gaining composure before talking.

"Fine, what does it mean?"

"It means unwavering faith and unconditional love," I tell her, which makes her eyes widen more.

"Shit Sully. What? You're so frustrating," she cusses, standing and pulling her wet shorts on.

"What? Why?" I ask, grabbing my own shorts and pulling them on. She flings the zip of the tent open and steps out into the gusty wind. The rain has stopped for now but the chill hits my bare chest.

"You left me. Do you get how much it hurt me? How much it still hurts you walked away from me like it was the easiest thing in the world," she yells.

"You've got no idea how much it pained me to do it."

"Well you've got a funny way of showing you care."

"I never once doubted how I felt about you. I only ever doubted how I was never enough for you," I yell back. She swipes at the tears that trickle over her lash line like they've betrayed her.

"Don't worry, I know you're not worth my tears," she says. It breaks my heart how the words I used to say to her hold so much weight. It reflects everything I used to feel about myself. The hatred and self loathing I unknowingly directed at myself when it wasn't my fault at all. Those feelings come rushing back and I'm so worried about

Willow I don't notice Logan and Kate have emerged from their tent until Logan's voice pierces through my thoughts.

"Sully?" I glance at him, my vision blurry but I quickly flick my eyes back to Willow, who is my main focus. Her shocked face stares at me but her image blurs. Raindrops splatter on my cheeks. I wipe it away but it keeps coming. I glance at the sky and realise it's not raining. The water is coming from me. I'm crying. I swipe at my face, not knowing how to make it stop. I catch Logan out of my peripheral, he takes a step closer but I take a step back. My hands shake, my breaths spike again and I have no other choice but to run.

Minutes later Logan finds me sitting by the grassy bank in front of the water. He must think he's given me enough time to calm down.

"You alright man?" he asks, as he sits beside me.

"Yeah," I sigh, hanging my head forward.

"You want to talk about it?"

"All the emotions I held in when I was younger came rushing back to me. It overwhelmed me because I didn't even realise I was crying," I confess. He pats me on the back.

"You're safe now man. The bastard will never hurt you again," he grunts.

"I know. I'll make an appointment with my therapist when I get back and talk it through with him," I tell him.

"Sounds like a good plan."

"Did Willow tell you guys about her mum?" I ask, remembering she needs to leave.

"Yeah. We are gonna head off if that's cool with you? Could we call your mechanic friend on the way and see if the car is ready?" he asks.

"Yeah, let's get going. If it's not done, you can take my truck and I'll get it off you when your car is done," I tell him.

"Thanks man," he says, patting my back again before standing. I join him and we walk back to the campsite together. The girls aren't around but all the bags sit in the back of the truck bed and the mattress is deflated and packed away. I help Logan as we get one tent dismantled in record speed. The girls appear from the bathroom, looking freshly showered. I avoid their gazes, working with Logan to get the other tent put away quickly so we can get going.

"I can finish up here if you want to quickly shower before we go?" Logan whispers to me, and I nod, leaving him to it. I grab my bag and head to the bathroom taking a minute to get my emotions in check. I wash quickly not wanting to hold up Willow any longer than I already have. When I'm done, I chuck everything back into my bag, zip it closed and carry it back to the truck. Everything is loaded and the girls jump in the back.

"Logan?" I call, and he turns to me. I pull out the keys and throw them to him. He offers me a sad smile. It's better he drives as my mind is all over the place.

He pulls out of our camping spot and I can't help feeling bittersweet about how our trip ended. The place where I had Willow is now the place where I'm losing her again. He pulls into the spot near the manager's office and goes in to inform Laurel we have to leave early so our spot is free for someone else. As he hits the road and we drive further away from the place I want to be, I can't help the pull it causes in my heart. I lean my head against the window and feign sleep, losing myself in my thoughts. I'm not great company right now anyway.

Willow

Half way through the drive back to the sunflower field, Logan asks Sully if he can call Chewy the mechanic to see if the car is fixed. I listen to the one sided conversation as Sully talks on the phone. When he hangs up, he turns to Logan and tells him it's not finished but it's fine to take his truck and they can swap over the cars when his is fixed.

It isn't long before the road leading to the sunflower field comes into view. I still can't get over how he planted all these flowers in the hopes I would randomly come across it one day. We are making great progress on time and it's still early in the day as we were awake at the crack of dawn when my stepdad rang as he wanted to give me enough time to get back before he left.

Logan pulls into an empty parking spot Sully guides him to which says reserved. Logan and Sully both exit and walk around to the back of the truck bed.

"You gonna say bye?" Kate whispers.

"I don't know if I can," I tell her.

"You know what?"

"What?"

"You'll regret it if you don't," she says.

"Bye ladies. I hope your mum is okay Willow," Sully's voice says, from the open window.

"Thanks," I reply.

"Bye Sully," Kate says. His gaze lingers on me before he taps the side of the door twice and moves out of the way for Logan to get in.

"Ring me," Logan says, turning the car on.

"I will," Sully tells him. He steps back, throws the strap of his bag over his shoulder while his sleeping bag dangles from his fingers. He stands and watches us as we reverse out of the car park. Logan pulls away and I turn to watch Sully. He still stands there as we drive off and my heart clenches.

"You sure you don't want to try to work things out?" Logan asks, as we travel away from Sully.

"I don't know if I can ever get over the hurt of him leaving," I sigh, as a single tear runs down my cheek.

"You know I used to have my reservations about Sully but I think he's changed," Kate adds.

"Sometimes it's too little too late," I mumble, before leaning my head against the window.

"Hey, how about I come to your mum's house with you? It's probably about time I popped in and paid my family a visit too," Kate tells me.

"You saw them the other weekend," I tell her, smiling.

"Yeah well you know them. They'll be missing me already," she laughs.

"Okay. That would be great."

"Well I guess it'll be me and Milo having guy time," Logan jokes from the driver's seat.

"He's probably feeling neglected anyway so spending some quality time with your cat won't hurt you," Kate tells him. They chat the rest of the car ride, distracting me from any thoughts of Sully trying to take root.

It feels like the drive to our apartment doesn't take long at all. Once there, we all drag our bags inside. Kate and Logan show Milo love with lots of pats and kisses which he graciously accepts. I carry my things into my room and remove all the dirty clothes and repack my bag, grabbing a few extra clothes in case they are needed. Going through the bag of things I got from the sunflower field gift shop, I decide to wear the new top. I pull my old top off, replace it, and already feel lighter wearing it. I pack my new book with the sunflowers on it and the goals I had listed. Hopefully inspiration will hit me while I'm in my hometown.

I walk back out with my repacked bag in hand. Logan is making sandwiches while Kate cuddles Milo on the couch.

"I never thanked you guys properly for paying for all the stuff at the gift shop for me," I tell them.

"What stuff did we pay for?" Kate asks.

"The bags of things I got from the sunflower field. Remember?" I tell her, my brows scrunching. Her gaze passes me as she looks at Logan. I turn to face him as he keeps his eyes on the bread in front of him. He keeps buttering it even though there's plenty on it.

"Logan?" I ask, walking towards him.

"Fine, it was Sully okay? He didn't want me to tell you but he saw you in the shop on his security cameras and rang his cashier to let her know to give you everything for free as a birthday present," he explains. The phone call. That was him when I stood there waiting at the counter. My mouth hangs open as I stare at Logan. "What? He does own the place you know," he tells me, before dropping some ham onto his bread and placing another piece of bread on top.

"I thought you guys got me all of it," I confess.

"Nope," Logan says, before taking a huge bite of his sandwich. "Here. Eat before you guys hit the road again." Kate drops Milo to the couch before she washes her hands and grabs her own sandwich. I do the same but I don't even taste the food as my thoughts wander. Sully did that for me?

"I'll go to the bathroom and we can hit the road," Kate tells me, while I sit in a daze. Logan comes to sit beside me.

"He's always loved you Willow. Loving you was never the problem," he tells me, as he squeezes my shoulder. Kate comes up behind Logan, wrapping her arms around his neck from behind.

"I'll miss you babe but I'll be back in a few days," she says, kissing his cheek.

"Hurry back," he tells her, swinging her around the couch so she's lying across his lap. I take my plate to the kitchen to give them a minute to themselves.

"Let's get this show on the road," Kate calls, a few minutes later. I grab my car keys from the hook by the front door and give Logan a hug goodbye before grabbing my bag and leaving with Kate. Once our bags are in the boot and I'm pulling out of the parking garage, Kate turns to me.

"So now we are alone. Tell me, tell me, tell me," she giggles.

"What?" I ask, confused as I take the turn off for the highway.

"Don't play dumb girl."

"Seriously, what are you talking about?" I ask, confused.

"You and Sully and sex," she squeals, and my eyes widen as I keep focused on the road. "We heard you guys fighting this morning and I specifically heard the term amazing sex," she says. I glance at her, catching her wide smile as she waits for me to fill her in. "Soooo?"

"Well it was amazing okay," I huff. She throws her head back sighing.

"I liked you guys as a couple. You were happy with him," she tells me.

"I thought you hated him?"

"Hate is such a strong word. It was probably more I was mad at what he did to you. After what I've seen the past few days, I've decided to give him another chance. Logan is so much happier with Sully around. I feel bad about keeping him from his best friend," she tells me.

"That's my fault as well."

"No it's not. I chose to be on your side and I don't regret it. I wish Logan hadn't been caught in the middle."

"Yeah I know what you mean," I sigh.

"Things will be okay but Sully will probably be around a lot more now. Will you be alright if he is?" she asks.

"Yeah. I told him I'd try to be friends so we can do that but we need to keep our clothes on," I tell her, which has her laughing loudly so I join in.

We chat and laugh the rest of the ride home and my thoughts keep coming back to Sully. Can we still be friends with all our history?

Chapter Twenty-nine

Willow

It's the third day being back at my mum's house and I already feel claustrophobic. I hardly ever come back home because our relationship never recovered after she left Dad. I come and see her and Stephen for the holidays but I much prefer seeing my dad over coming here. Even when I stayed here in high school, it never felt like my home.

I'm staying in my old room and memories of Sully keep flooding past my gates I have erected. All the time we spent here during the last year of school haunts me. Sully was a passing thought recently and it made my heart ache. Over the years the ache has lessened to more of a dull pain but I'm so accustomed to it accompanying thoughts of Sully, they went hand in hand. I'd think of Sully and my heart would hurt but I'd manage to push the thoughts away and the pain would go with it. Now he's taken over my head and heart. Thoughts of him are consuming me again and this time my head and heart are at war, tugging and tearing me in opposite directions.

My head, which was the sensible organ in this scenario, didn't want me to get hurt again but my heart was hurting and told me I'd never feel whole again without the missing piece from my life. Sully.

"Hey babe," Kate says. Her voice drags me from my thoughts as she bounds into my room.

"Hey when did you get here?" I ask, as she's been staying at her parents' place.

"Just now. I let myself in with the key you gave me," she tells me, as she takes a seat next to me and leans back against the headboard. "How's your mum today?"

"Feeling sorry for herself. She told me to get out of the house because she feels bad Stephen called me," I tell her.

"Why don't we go out and have a drink tonight? I could use a break from my crazy lot. I forget how loud they are when I haven't been around them for a while."

"Yeah, I can't imagine the noise of six kids growing up. It was always me by myself and it was so damn quiet," I tell her.

"Trust me. You'd need ear plugs if you lived with my family," she tells me, laughing to herself but the love she has for her family is apparent on her face.

"A few hours out of here might be nice," I agree.

"Cool. Wanna watch a movie or something?"

"Sure. Put something on. I'll check on Mum to see if she needs anything," I say, throwing her the television remote and hopping from the bed. I walk and knock on my mum's door before pushing it open and peeking inside.

"Hey dear," Mum greets me, from her bed as she sits and watches her television. Her leg in the cast is elevated on pillows in front of her.

"Hey Mum, do you need anything?" I ask, walking further into her room.

"No, I'm good for now. Stephen called and said he doesn't need to stay tomorrow like he originally planned so he's gonna fly back tonight. You'll be free from your babysitting duties soon enough," she laughs.

"It hasn't been that bad," I tell her.

"Honey, I know you. You may not think I do but I know my daughter. You've been here physically the last few days but your mind has been a million miles away," she says, as one side of her face pulls into a knowing smile.

"Sorry. I've had a lot on my mind lately."

"Anything you want to talk about? I can't run off so I'm a good listener at the moment," she jokes, making me laugh as she pats the bed beside her. I sit and face her before I let out a sigh. Getting an outsider's perspective might help.

"I've felt a bit lost lately. I told you I quit my job," I remind her.

"Yeah. Is that what's bugging you?"

"No, I hated my job so I'm glad I quit."

"What's wrong then?"

"Someone I thought was gone from my life has recently come back into it," I confess, dropping my face into my hands.

"Ahh I see," she says. I take a deep breath to tell her about my conflicted feelings when she adds, "Please tell me it's the Sullivan boy."

"What?" I ask, my brows pull together in confusion.

"The Sullivan boy you were with in your last year of high school. Gosh the way he looked at you even had me melting," she swoons, and I stare at her in shock.

"What are you talking about? You were hardly around."

"Well yeah, that's my fault. I thought you weren't entirely happy to be here with me and I avoided you as I didn't know how to fix it. I'm sorry," she confesses, as tears appear on her lash line. "I'm really sorry honey."

"Why did you want me here that year?" I ask, as my own tears spring to my eyes.

She releases her own sigh before saying, "Honestly I was being selfish. I was worried when you went off to college you'd never come and see me again. You were already distant with me since the divorce with your dad and I felt like you were slipping away. I should have never uprooted you from your life," she admits.

"It worked out in the end," I tell her, because if I didn't come here, I wouldn't have met Logan, Kate or Sully. I hardly kept in touch with anyone from back where my dad lived so it shows moving to live with Mum was the better choice. She holds out her hand so I wriggle forward and give her a hug which has been a long time coming.

Pulling apart, she wipes at her eyes before she says, "So is it the Sullivan boy?" making me laugh.

"You never told me when you saw him looking at me?"

220

"Oh honey we are rich but we are not dumb. I know we left you alone a lot over the weekends. I usually spent my time away watching the security feed of the cameras we have around the house because I was worried about you," she says, wincing. "I saw you having your friends around more so I stopped," she explains.

"Okay. I'm not sure how I feel about that but okay," I tell her, scrunching my face. What is it with people watching me on their security cameras?

"Don't worry dear, the cameras aren't in your room or anything," she tells me.

"Mum!" I cry, making her laugh.

"What? We are both adults and I told you, I saw the way he looked at you so I don't blame you," she says, smiling at me as my face reddens.

"You saw this on the cameras?" I clarify.

"Oh yeah. Every time I saw him on the cameras, I was entranced watching him. You'd turn away from him and his eyes would be on you. He looked at you like you hung the moon for him. I remember telling Stephen if you ended up with him, I would know you were in good hands. Stephen being Stephen told me to stop spying on you. I was always sad he left how he did but I knew there had to be a good reason for him to leave you, especially after I'd seen the way he looked at you."

"Well you're right, it is him who's returned. I don't know if I can get past the hurt of him leaving, you know?" I admit.

"Have a think about it honey. If he's half as in love with you as he was back then, I'd say he's crazy about you. What does he do now?" I roll my eyes.

"Well it's kind of a funny story. You know how I love sunflowers?" She nods. "He grew a whole sunflower field in the hopes I would find it and fall back in love with him," I tell her. Her eyes widen in shock. "I know, it's crazy right?" She continues to stare at me, as her mouth drops open. "Mum?" She shakes her head and focuses her eyes on me.

"Go over to the top drawer of my dresser honey," she tells me. I walk across the room. "The left one," she directs me. I open it and find a stack of opened envelopes. I turn to her and she says, "Yeah bring me the stack." With my brows pulled together, I pull them all out and carry them to her. I pass them to her and she pulls out the contents. "I thought it was weird we kept receiving these letters. They have been arriving for a few years now, once every couple of months. It increased to once a month and this last year they've been coming once a week," she tells me, as she hands over one of the envelopes. "I couldn't keep all of them but I thought it was a sign or something, especially with the name and your love of sunflowers. I was planning to ask you if you wanted to go there one day," she says, as I pull out the leaflet in the envelope. There staring back at me is the sign of Willow's sunflower fields. It even has a photo of the sign explaining the story of how the owner lost his one true love. A tear drops on the leaflet and I wipe my eyes, brushing the remaining tears away. "That's his field?" she asks.

"Yeah," I croak.

"I'd say the boy hasn't stopped thinking about you all this time honey. You deserve a great love in your life and I don't know many people who would do all this for someone they love," she says. I look at her through my teary eyes. "It's okay to be scared but sometimes we gotta risk it all and believe in unwavering faith and unconditional love," she says.

"What did you say?" I ask, staring at her.

"Unwavering faith and unconditional love. It's on the back of the leaflet. See?" she says, as she turns the one over in her hands and shows me. My shaking hands grab the one from her. He did all this for me? To make me see it so I'd find my way back to him.

"Mum, will you be okay if Kate and I go out for a drink tonight?"

"Of course. Are you still planning to head off tomorrow when Stephen is back?"

"Yeah, Kate is due back at work soon."

"Okay honey. Could you help me to the bathroom before you head out later?"

"Will do. I'll come back later with your dinner too," I say, hopping from the bed and walking to the door.

"Willow?" she calls.

"Yeah?"

"I love you."

"I love you too," I say, smiling before making my way to my room. Kate is still in the same position watching a movie.

"Everything okay?" she asks, as I sit beside her.

"Yeah, I had a long overdue conversation," I tell her, handing over the leaflet.

"What's this?" she says, taking it and her mouth drops open.

"He's been sending them to my mum for years in the hopes I'd see them and go have a look."

"Oh gosh Willow. The man is truly crazy about you," she whispers, still in shock.

"I need a drink."

"Me too," she says, and we laugh as I rest my head on her shoulder.

With my nicest pair of jeans and a silver halter top, I take Mum her dinner, placing it on the tray over her bed.

"Thanks. You look nice honey," she tells me, as she begins to eat her food.

"Are you sure you'll be alright?"

"Yes. Stephen is due to land shortly anyway."

"Okay, well if you're good we are gonna head out," I tell her.

"Have fun," she says, as I walk out the door.

Since we are both going to have a drink, we uber the short drive into the main stretch of town. Jimmy's, the old diner I worked at, is at one end along with one of the bars we decide to check out.

We walk into O'Connell's, ready to let loose. My brain is a pile of mush at the moment with all the information I've found out about Sully this past week and it's overloaded. For tonight, I want to push it all away and try to live in the moment and not in the what if. It's quite quiet as it's only eight o'clock so there isn't much of a crowd in here yet but it doesn't bother us.

"What can I get you ladies?" the bartender asks us.

"Two chardonnays please," Kate tells him, and he nods, turning to grab two white wine glasses and a bottle from the fridge. He pours a serving in each before placing them on the bar. Kate taps her card on the eftpos machine. "You get the next round," she tells me.

"Sounds good," I say, as we grab a glass each and head over to a round table with two tall stools.

I take a big sip out of my glass, as my eyes survey the room. A few patrons sit at tables while a couple are at one end of the bar. There's another room connected to the bar with slot machines where you can hear the ringing and bells of people winning.

"Have you ever been here?" I ask Kate.

"Logan and I came here for a drink the last time we were at my parents' house. He needed space from the house too," she laughs. Not everyone can handle the amount of noise her siblings can produce.

"How's Logan doing without you home?" I ask, taking another sip of my drink.

"He's whining, asking when I'm coming back. I haven't told him we are coming back tomorrow. I thought I would surprise him," she tells me, and I roll my eyes at how happy they are.

"I'm glad you guys got together."

"Yeah I'm glad you friend zoned him," she says, making me laugh.

"Gosh it feels like so long ago, I had completely forgotten about it."

"Nah as soon as your heart set its eyes on Sully, Logan never stood a chance. Good for me though."

"Yeah," I add, as I close my eyes and move my neck side to side.

"Your neck hurting?" she asks, noticing my movements.

"Think it's the tension from overthinking everything," I tell her.

"Well you know you could always get Sully to work the tension out," she says, winking at me.

"You're awfully keen on me giving him another chance."

"I honestly think he's trying so hard to win you back, it's gotta be worth something. If Logan vouches for him, it's gotta count for something right?"

"Yeah I guess," I say, tipping the glass to my lips and draining it. "Another?" I ask, turning in my seat before dropping my feet to the ground.

"Sure," Kate says, passing me her glass. I carry them back to the bar. The bartender is at the other end of the bar where some patrons are sitting and drinking so I move closer to him to place my order.

"Come on George, you've had enough," the bartender says, grabbing an empty glass in front of a dishevelled looking older man.

"All the same. Useless. Serve me my damn drink," the disgruntled man says.

"Last one then you're out of here," the bartender tells him. He turns his back on him, pouring in mostly coke and adding a small amount of bourbon to the glass before pushing it in front of the guy. "Hey. Sorry about that. Another round?" the bartender asks me.

"Yes please," I tell him. He turns his back to me but the drunk patron notices me.

"Hey pretty lady," he says. I wrinkle my nose and pretend I don't hear him. "Hey, I'm talking to you," he calls.

"Leave her alone George or you are out on your arse," the bartender says, coming to my rescue.

"I'm being friendly," George says. I can't help it so look at him and his eyes squint at me, as if he's seeing me properly for the first time. "It's you." His accusing tone has me raising my brows.

"Do I know you?" I ask.

"You know my pathetic excuse for a son. He's a worthless piece of shit," he states, as his voice gets louder. He slams his glass and his drink spills over the bar. I take a step back in retreat.

"I don't know who you're talking about," I tell him. Someone brushes against me from behind and I whip around to find Kate.

"Willow he's...," Kate says, but George cuts her off.

"Reed. My sack of shit son is Reed," he scoffs. His admission has my whole body vibrating with anger at this man. I never knew who he

225

was. Sully never took me around to his house for obvious reasons and he kept me as far away from him as possible.

"Your son is ten times the man you'll ever be," I shout, causing him to stand.

"You think you know him. He's a fucken coward. The best thing he ever did was run away from me. Couldn't even fight me like a man," he says, and his words swirl through my head. Run away from me. He ran away from him. Him. It was him he ran from. Not me. Sully ran away from his dad. Not me. Never me. "He's not worth your tears," he says, causing me to step back as if he stabbed me.

"What?" I stammer.

"Your tears girl. He's not worth them," he spits at me. I lift my hand, touch my cheek and feel the wetness. I didn't even realise I was crying. A blinding rage comes over me and my body takes over. I step forward slapping him hard across the cheek, causing his head to whip to the side. My palm stings but I ignore it.

"He's worth every fucken tear I've ever shed for him. It's you who isn't worth shit and I pity you old man because you'll never understand how wonderful he is in spite of you. You know what? Fuck you," I scream at him, not holding back. I let it out for the boy this man hurt, who never fought back and for the man he's become who's fought so hard to overcome his demons this man created.

"You little....," he screams, as he steps toward me. Strong arms wrap around him, halting his movements at the moment he lifted his hand like he was going to strike me.

"You're done George. Go the fuck home. I don't want to see you back in my bar again," the bartender says, as he wrestles him out the door. Another patron kindly joins him in hauling him out the door. They let him go and he falls to the footpath.

"You okay?" Kate asks, as she wraps me in a hug. I wrap my arms around her, bury my face into her neck as I release all my emotions. She rubs my back. "Shh it's okay," she comforts me, until another voice breaks through.

"You ladies alright? Sorry about that. I won't be letting him back in here ever again," the bartender tells us.

"Could you call us a taxi?" Kate asks him, holding me still as I shake in her embrace.

"Yeah sure," he says. We continue to stand there while I cry into her arms. I'm not ready to let go. A few minutes later the bartender returns and says, "Taxi is here. I'll walk you out." Safely walking us to the taxi and telling the driver he's familiar with, he will pay for our fare home. There's no sign of George anywhere and I'm thankful.

Kate holds my hand the short drive home and we thank the driver. We walk in the door and are greeted by Stephen.

"You okay?" he asks.

"Yeah a drunken patron got on our nerves, so we cut the night short," Kate tells him.

"Okay. Good idea. Your mother is sleeping. Thank you so much for coming and taking care of her. She has enjoyed you being here," he tells me, and I let out a genuine smile.

"Anytime Stephen. I've enjoyed spending time with her too," I tell him.

"Good. Well I'm off to bed. Night," he says, before he walks up the stairs.

"Night," we both call, as we follow behind and head to my room.

"Are you sure you're okay?" Kate asks again, as she flops on my bed.

"Yeah, a bit emotional. That was a lot, you know?" She nods in agreement.

"So what are you gonna do now?" she asks, as a small smile tugs at her lips.

I close my eyes, and release a deep breath before saying, "For tonight I'm going to go to sleep. I'll figure the rest out tomorrow."

"Okay," she says, kicking her shoes off and hopping under the covers. I grab some pyjamas and throw another set at her. We get changed in silence and both crawl back under the covers and close our eyes. I let out another deep breath, calming myself, and hope sleep comes fast.

Chapter Thirty

Sully

It's been ten days since she left me. I got the call from Chewy saying he finished fixing Logan's car this morning. He dropped it off a while ago so I'm currently in my office ringing Logan. He answers after the fourth ring.

"Hello?" he calls. I can hear the static, it sounds like he's driving.

"Hey man, you driving?"

"Yeah."

"Is now a good time?" I ask, spinning in my chair to look out the window overlooking the sunflower field. My office sits above the gift shop and has the perfect view looking out on the miles of yellow flowers.

"Yeah man. What's up?"

"Your car is ready. I was thinking of driving out to you so we can swap vehicles."

"Oh I can come out to you if you want?" he suggests, causing me to rub my forehead.

"I wanna see her man, even if she doesn't want me. I still want to see her," I confess. He's silent for a beat.

"Hold on man," he says, and the static of the car stops before his voice comes back on. The car door shuts before he speaks again. "You there?"

"Yeah I'm here man. Can I come to you?" I ask.

"Willow's not here," he says, and my heart sinks. Well there goes my plan. The call waiting beep comes through on my line.

"Logan, I'll ring you back. I got someone ringing through on the other line."

"Yeah man. Talk soon," he says. I connect to the other call.

"Sully," I answer.

"Sir, could you come to ticket admissions please? We have a bit of a situation," Stanley tells me.

"What kind of situation?" I ask, standing and making my way out of the office.

"You might want to see this for yourself," he says. I release a huff.

"I'm on my way," I tell him, stomping down the steps and out of the gift shop. I rub my forehead to ease the tension building. I round the corner, walk to the front gate where the ticket office is situated and the sight has me halting my steps. Logan waves at me and Kate wears a huge smile on her face but it's the woman in front of them who stops my feet. Her black hair whips around as her bright smile shines at me, causing my heart to race. At the sight of me, she pushes off racing to me as if I am the air she needs to survive. Her dress with the sunflowers on it, swishes with her strides and as soon as she's next to me, she leaps into my arms and presses her lips to mine as she wraps her arms tightly around my neck. With her legs wrapped firmly around my waist, I hold her dress around her butt as my other hand goes into her hair so I more easily devour her mouth. Her lips smile against mine as she pulls back, her beautiful face looking at me.

"I'm sorry," she says.

"For what?"

"For taking so long to realise I can't live without you," she states, and my heart hammers in my chest.

"Really?" I ask, my chest heaving.

"Really. I'm yours if you still want me," she says, shrugging her shoulders.

229

"Are you crazy? I'll always want you sweetheart."

"I'm crazy about you. I love you."

"I never stopped loving you," I confess, taking her lips with mine again. Hooting and hollering comes from Logan and Kate but I ignore them as I've got the girl who I let slip away firmly in my hands and I'm not letting go. She breaks away looking at me again.

"Does your job offer still stand?" she asks, making me chuckle.

"What do you think about Spain?"

"Spain?"

"And Italy?"

"Italy?"

"And New Zealand?"

"New Zealand?

"And some states in America?" I ask, smiling.

"What are you on about?"

"Our sunflower fields. There's nine of them. I thought the more I had, the more likely it was you may come across them wherever you ended up in the world," I confess, causing her eyes to widen.

"You're crazy," she laughs.

"Crazy about you Low. Only you," I say, tucking a piece of hair behind her ear before pulling her to me again. My heart pounds in my chest but this time it's from feeling at ease. For the first time in my whole life, I feel free and I can't wait to see what all of my tomorrows bring with the girl of my dreams beside me.

Epilogue

TWO YEARS LATER

Sully

I stand in front of Logan and adjust his black bow tie for him.

"You ready man?" I ask.

"Yeah," he says, his huge smile shines back at me. We turn back to look at the small aisle as the music plays. I stand beside my best friend as we wait for our girls to make their way to us. As the piano music plays around us, the most beautiful girl comes into view. Her black hair is cut shorter like it was when I first met her. She has her contacts in today, and her bright eyes lock on me as she walks down the aisle in her pale pink dress. She holds a bouquet of white roses and as she sees me looking at her, her eyes drop to the bouquet before glancing back at me with a scrunched nose. I smile widely at her, giving her a small shake of my head. Yes sweetheart, I know they aren't sunflowers. Her obsession with the bright yellow flowers has gotten worse since she began working for our business.

She reaches the end of the aisle giving Logan a smile before taking her place on the opposite side. The wedding march plays and the family and friends of Logan and Kate stand as she makes her entrance. Her white princess dress drags behind her as her dad walks her down the aisle and I look at Logan to gauge his reaction. Happy tears swim to the surface as a huge smile shines at his bride. I pat him on the back before he wipes the tears with his index finger.

Kate's dad hands her off to Logan, shaking his hand before they turn to the officiant who stands under the marquee adorned with more white roses.

I catch the eye of my beautiful goddess who stands beside Kate and I can't wait until the day I get to see her walking towards me in a white dress.

"Ladies and gentlemen we are gathered here today to witness the union of Logan and Kate," the officiant begins, and I force my eyes off Willow which is a hard feat these days. Since she came back to me, I've been thanking my lucky stars that my crazy sunflower field plan worked. I do wonder at times if I had done what she'd said and tried to come back to her sooner if she would have accepted me. I still hold on to the guilt of having hurt her like I did because it was necessary. I wasn't happy with myself and how could I love her fully if I didn't love myself? I needed time to work on myself and be the best possible version to give her all of me because she deserved nothing less.

"You may kiss the bride," the officiant says, breaking through my thoughts and my best friend kisses his new wife. Taking her hand and walking down the aisle, the guests throw red and white rose petals at them as they pass.

Willow places her soft fingers in mine, making me sigh. Her touch calms me in a way no one else ever could. I link our fingers as we make our way following Kate and Logan.

"When we get married, I want sunflowers. You know that right?" she says, glancing at me, a cheeky grin tugging at her lips.

"I'm thinking roses may not be too bad," I tease, and her hand twitches in mine like she wants to gently hit my chest which she usually does when I tease her. "I'm kidding," I laugh. "I was thinking we could get married in the middle of one of our sunflower fields."

"Sounds perfect," she says.

"You're perfect."

"I love you," she says, as she kisses my lips at the end of the aisle.

"I love you more," I say, pulling her into my arms and closing the distance.

Sully's Note

What did you think of my advice? I told you it would work. I know a bouquet of sunflowers covered in dirt, scratch that, a dozen bouquets would have sufficed in worming my way back into Willow's good graces but I decided to go big. I know nine sunflower fields scattered over multiple continents might have been overkill, or what others might call insane, but it did the job, didn't it? Remember, it's never too late to grovel especially if it's for the girl of your dreams. Go big or go home. With great risk, comes great reward. You get the gist.

As for Willow's Sunflower Fields, we wanted to keep the hope and magic alive for people all over the world who knew the story behind our business. Our story was edited and added to over the years so people knew I found my happily ever after and my lost love found her way back to me. Remember, it's never too late.

Thanks for reading.

THE END

Feedback

Did you enjoy this book? Would you like to give feedback? Did you know word of mouth is what makes the publishing world go round? It's especially true for an indie author like me. If you enjoyed reading this book, please feel free to share your opinions or post a review online. We would love to hear from you. Or even better, let your friends know and encourage them to read the book.

Check out my Facebook and Instagram. I love hearing from my readers.

www.facebook/sarahdelanywrites
www.instagram/sarahdelanywrites

If you enjoyed this book, you may enjoy my other books. I have written a series called the TNT Trilogy and a book about friendship set in the nineties called Chance and Lacey. They are available on KU (Kindle Unlimited) in ebook form. They are available for purchase on Amazon in ebook and paperback form. You can also purchase them in paperback form from many online bookstores. If money is a problem, you can also borrow them from your local library. Did you know if it's not available in your local library, you can recommend it to the librarian. They are always looking for new books for their patrons. It's a great way to help and support indie authors like me.

About the Author

------Sarah Delany------

'Not Worth Your Tears is   Sarah Delany's fifth novel, her second standalone book and her first attempt at new adult fiction. She is one of eight siblings, has a loving partner and is a stay at home mother to four boys and one girl. Sarah is a New Zealander who currently resides in Brisbane, Australia.